A Third Is Darkness

Also by Murray Bailey

Cyprus Kiss
The Killing Crew
The Troodos Secret

Singapore 52
Singapore Girl
Singapore Ghost
Singapore Killer
Singapore Fire

Once A Killer
Second To Sin

Map of the Dead
Sign of the Dead

The Lost Pharaoh

Black Creek White Lies

A Third Is Darkness

Murray Bailey

First published in Great Britain in 2023 by

12342347

copyright © Murray Bailey 2023

The moral right of Murray Bailey to be identified as the author of this work has been asserted in accordance with the copyright, Designs and Patents Act of 1988.

All rights reserved. No part of this publication may be reproduced, stored in a retrieval system, or transmitted in any form or by any means, electronic, mechanical, photocopying, recording, or otherwise, without the prior permission of the copyright owner.

All the characters in this book are fictitious and any resemblance to actual persons, living or dead, is purely coincidental.

Cover design by Blue Dog

Three Daggers
An imprint of
Heritage Books, Cornwall

Chapter One

Cold. The first waking sensation was an ache that felt like death crawling through his bones. His muscles and tendons were tight, his skin goose flesh. The cold was all around, soaking through his skin.

Water. I'm lying in water.

He felt its movement. Small, regular waves that rocked his body.

Opening his eyes, he saw darkness. Details gradually appeared. He was on his back, looking up at layered clouds, pewter gray and oppressive. Night with no stars or moon, just an ambient glow and distant pinpricks of light.

His leaden arms moved until his hands felt rough wood beneath his body. A platform. He was lying on a platform.

Part of his mind told him to stay there. He could get used to the cold. The sensation was already fading, becoming less important. He was so tired, so achy. The water and darkness could take him.

But then another part of his brain kicked in.

Move!

Without debate between the two, he flipped onto his front and pushed up. Muscles in his chest and arms screamed, but he kept pushing and then brought up his legs. He knelt and paused and breathed. Calming breaths sucked warmth into his chest.

He was looking straight across the water now. He could see the island.

Hong Kong, he told himself. *Of course, Hong Kong. I'm opposite the island... Stonecutters.* Then to the right: *Kowloon. The peninsula.*

He blinked as the thoughts rapid-fired in his head. The scattered lights in windows highlighted an imposing structure. *Williamson Building.* Behind, rising to the Peak, were odd spots and shapes, the mansions of the elite.

Who am I?

The sudden, alarming question shattered the less important thoughts that were crowding in. He'd been distracted, avoiding the big ones. Who the hell was he and why was he here?

He sucked in air and strength and forced himself to his feet. He swayed and went down on one knee. The wooden platform was an unstable, submerged jetty.

With clenched teeth and hands, he pushed up again and held his ground. Two breaths later, he was turning carefully, forcing his legs to move, focusing on his balance.

A dark wharf was only five paces away. That was his guess, but he shuffled and staggered, losing any sense of the time and distance.

Two stone steps at the end took him up to the quay. On dry land, he sat on the edge, his shoes lapped by the water. His clothes clung to his body, heavy with their wetness. He was wearing a jacket and took it off.

His back brain screamed panic that he couldn't remember anything. Despite being wet, he sensed the jacket was too heavy. Would he find ID? A search of the inside pockets yielded nothing.

The left-hand pocket was also empty, but the weight lay in the right.

And there he found a knife.

Images flashed in his mind. Chaos. Blood. Lots of blood. A feeling of desperation and lack of control washed over him, and his head lurched. He jerked forward and back, fighting darkness, fighting unconsciousness.

Acid burned in his throat. He tasted bile.

Breathe.

He could hear a voice telling him to inhale to the count of three, exhale to the count of five. A woman's voice. It was in his head. A memory. He liked her. She was smart and attractive. Who was she? Her name escaped him, but he remembered she'd told him to breathe and focus.

Gain the control.

Doctor Swift. Georgina. Yes, that's her name.

He remembered what else she'd said.

Find focus.

She had a statuette in her office. It was a funny thing made of silver, six inches tall and ugly. An elf or goblin or something. It was hard to know. That was part of it, she'd said.

"Look at it and study the detail. Use your senses. Let that bring back the reality."

Bring back the reality.

That's what he needed. He was lost in his mind. Confused. He needed to come back to reality. And then he'd remember.

He stood and gripped his sodden jacket. The water squeezed through his fingers, dripping. The water was cold. His fingers tingled, electricity warming them. He clenched and unclenched. He felt the stitches in the cotton.

Breathing in, he focused. There was the tang of the sea but there was also a faint whiff of rotten fish and smoke.

He listened and heard the lapping water, but now he could also hear distant sounds, creaking timbers on boats. The rumble of an engine. No, three engines, one to the east and two inland. Cars.

Car. There's a car.

He looked up and down the quay. The wharves loomed large and dark. He closed his eyes and pictured where he was.

There's a car. I came in a car. Where is it?

Instinct took him west and then between two *godowns*. There was a road on the far side that fed the docks. The smell of rotten fish was stronger here. It felt wrong. He got onto the road and turned right, back on himself.

Smoke wafted along the dark road, twisting and turning in the breeze, like lost ghosts.

He kept going, looking left and right, trying to remember, trying to picture the car. And then he found it. A black Austin was tucked between the buildings, hidden away.

The car was empty but unlocked.

When the door opened, a tiny light came on.

He climbed in but left the door ajar, imagining the light's faint heat. He smelled leather and stale cigarettes.

Is this my car? He didn't think so.

There were no keys in the ignition. There were no keys hidden where he might have secreted them.

He reached over and popped the glove-box. There was a wallet inside made of expensive leather.

He opened it and found a card alongside a wodge of cash.

Charles Balcombe.

He said the name out loud. It wasn't his name, but it was.

It's the name I use now. I'm a different person. I'm rich. I'm a playboy.

He smiled and then glanced in the rear-view mirror. He was dishevelled but good-looking. Like that film star, Errol Flynn, people said.

Then the smile froze. He touched his eyebrow and felt a stickiness that wasn't sea water.

Blood.

The knife.

This wasn't his blood. It was in his hair and smeared on his cheek. He looked at his hands and even the faint light told the truth. They'd been bloody. There was blood under his nails too.

He knew who he was, knew where he was, knew about the car, but this wasn't his car.

He looked in the back. There was a satchel behind the driver's seat. It had papers inside. Police paperwork.

And the name on the top sheet froze his heart.

Detective Inspector Munro.

What have I done?

Balcombe looked back in the mirror. He didn't see the film star this time. He saw something much darker in those eyes.

He saw BlackJack.

Chapter Two

Two weeks earlier

It was a perfect day. The skies were clear and the air fresh. Charles Balcombe had spent two hours climbing the Peak's crags. Now he strolled across Statue Square with his friend Roy Faulls.

There had once been an impressive statue of Queen Victoria inside a canopy the size of a house. The statue was now in storage on the island, although it had spent time in Japan intended for the furnace. The canopy had gone too, dismantled to allow for the tram and temporary buildings—which were becoming less temporary with each passing year.

On the island, the number of motor vehicles was increasing at a rapid rate. The rest of the square had become a parking space. This was definitely temporary because the government had announced plans. Work on reclaiming a vast area of land was progressing fast. There would be a new County Hall and car park. So far, Queen's Pier remained, but within a year it would be gone, reassembled beyond the new block of land.

July 1954 and Hong Kong was changing, which in Balcombe's opinion was a shame. At least the cenotaph and its garden remained. And the neo-classical buildings around the square, except for the temporary offices and towering banks, harked back a hundred years.

Balcombe and Faulls approached the much-vaunted Hong Kong Club. Faulls had become a member. Finally. Now he could hob-nob with the great and mighty whenever he chose. He was still a junior partner at Butterfield & Swire but saw this as a major steppingstone to promotion.

"Enjoy your lunch," Balcombe said, patting his friend on the shoulder.

"I will."

"There's music and billiards at Cheero..." Balcombe grinned. "But if all you're after is a boring conversation with old men..."

"There are waitresses," Faulls said with a wink.

"Out of bounds, I'm sure."

"Well..." Faulls was smirking.

"Well, what, Roy?"

"I hear that fifty dollars in the right place can get a gentleman"—he waggled his eyebrows suggestively—"a friend for the night."

It was an open secret. Balcombe knew his girlfriends' husbands didn't need to stay over at the club. But they did. Regularly. There were other attractions, other arrangements.

He watched Faulls nod to the uniformed man on the door and disappear into the dark interior.

Good luck, he thought.

As he turned to continue along the front. He spotted a bottle-green Mercedes pull into a parking space. A smartly dressed man exited, followed by his wife. They were both in their thirties. He had money, she had good looks. And she had an interest in Balcombe.

He'd seen her six times before recently ending it. Each time, there had been no risk of *in flagrante delicto*. And she treated him like a paid gigolo. Is that what he was?

No. He'd decided. Julia Wendsley wasn't for him. Little fun. No danger.

Two days ago, after their roll in the hay—or more precisely, their tryst in a hotel room—he'd told her it was over.

She'd laughed lightly, poured herself more champagne, and kissed him goodbye.

He was now down to four girlfriends, having finished with four and gained two over the past two months. Was the shine going off his affairs? When he'd arrived on the island eight months ago, he was amazed at how his new persona, and free time, worked wonders on the bored housewives of Hong Kong society. It had been fun, but he was now thinking that at least one of the others had to go. They got in the way of his social life and main hobby of free climbing.

"Charles, are you hiding from me?" He recognized Julia Wendsley's voice immediately. Her husband was Polish—he'd changed his name from Wolenski—but Julia hailed from the West County as most evidenced by her occasional long *r* after a vowel. She tried hard to sound posh although regularly let it slip. In bed, her reference to Balcombe as her *lover* was both endearing and amusing at the same time.

After spotting her exit the Mercedes, he'd been staring absent-mindedly across the bay. There were Marine Police boats out there. One was coming to shore.

"Oh hello, Julia. With your husband?" he enquired, noting she was now alone.

"Gone into the club," she said. "I'm alone for a few hours, Charles."

He deliberately didn't respond to the implied suggestion.

"Have you had lunch?" she said, standing very close. He could smell her scent. Not the one she'd worn for their rendezvous but alluring nonetheless.

"I've a meeting at the Cheero Club," he lied.

"That downmarket place? Throw it off," she said. "We could eat first or get a room and eat afterward. You choose."

"Julia."

"Yes?"

"Do you not remember our conversation? Two days ago? It's over, I'm afraid."

She pulled a half-grimace, half-smile and shook her head. "No, no. You weren't serious."

He took a step away. "I'm sorry, Julia. I was."

Her eyes were wide, her face frozen.

"I must go," he said and left her standing like a statue in the titular square.

He didn't look back and focused on the water again. The police had been more active than usual over the past few days. They were moving the boat-people and cleaning up the bay. An American movie production company was in Hong Kong. Rumour was that they'd taken over half of the Peninsula Hotel with their actors and senior crew. The lowly crew were billeted at a boarding house on Cameron Road.

Balcombe recognized the tall figure standing at the prow of the approaching boat. Inspector Garrett. It tied up, and he was first off.

Previously, Balcombe had only seen him in plain clothes. He'd been the senior detective investigating the BlackJack murders. Although, he knew them as the Squeezed-heart cases. Today Garrett was wearing a tan-coloured uniform, shorts and short-sleeved shirt. Despite his unkept beard, he looked reasonably presentable.

Balcombe kept walking, but Garrett must have spotted him.

"Balcombe!" There was no friendliness in the hail.

Balcombe stopped and nodded politely.

"I see you've found your calling, Garrett."

"It's temporary."

Balcombe shook his head. He hoped not. The inspector had failed monumentally in his hunt for the killer. He'd hounded Balcombe and subsequently blundered by arresting two upstanding members of the community. In the eyes of the chief of police, Garrett was a fool. At least that was Balcombe's interpretation.

The inspector closed in; his mouth set in a snarl. "I'm on to you, Balcombe."

"I beg your pardon?" Balcombe feigned innocence. "You'll die young if you let prejudice eat at your heart. A Chinese doctor told me that once."

"Prejudice?"

"An opinion without basis in reason or experience."

Garrett leaned close. "I know what prejudice means!"

Balcombe could smell the man's musty clothes and sour breath.

"Have you been eating rotten fish, Garrett? Tell me the name of the restaurant so I can avoid it."

"You're a funny man."

"At least one of us has a sense of humour."

He could imagine a miniature DI Munro on his shoulder, whispering, telling him not to bait Garrett, but Balcombe couldn't help it.

Garrett stiffened and subconsciously swayed back an inch.

"I'm still watching you, Balcombe."

"And trying to ruin your career even further." Balcombe smiled politely. He knew the police commissioner didn't like old cases. Anything not solved within three months was dropped in favour of the new. Too many crimes, too few detectives. The Squeezed-heart cases were now too old.

Garrett said nothing.

Balcombe shook his head and stepped away. "Good day to you, Inspector." Then before he could stop himself, he added: "Keep up the cleaning work. We don't want the Americans filming anything they shouldn't."

Garrett spun on his heel and marched away.

Julia Wendsley had been watching and sashayed beside him as Balcombe continued along Connaught Road.

"That was interesting," she said with a tease in her voice.

Balcombe didn't look at her.

She continued: "I've been thinking."

"It's over, Julia."

"But I don't think it is, Charles." Pause. "You see, I know things. I know lots of things."

He stopped and faced her.

She smiled. "I know your paramours, but more importantly, I know their husbands."

"You're suggesting you'd tell them about me?"

She kept smiling.

He said, "What about your husband? He'll find out and—"

She laughed lightly. "He doesn't care."

"Maybe none of them care," he said, although he doubted its veracity.

"It only takes one," she said. "And I see you have an enemy. In the police, no less." She paused and licked her painted lips. "Things could get very uncomfortable for you, my darling."

He started walking. "I've got to go," he said. "Meeting at Cheero."

He glanced back and she finger-waved. "Think about it, Charles. Then let's make plans."

Damn. Was nothing straightforward?

It was not a perfect day after all.

Chapter Three

The run-down building was at the end of the wharf near the P&O Pier. The upper floors had been unused from before the Japanese invasion. No one knew who owned them and no one seemed to care. Except for Munro, the half-Korean, half-Scottish detective who'd found the place two days before Christmas 1941. Criminals had used it to stash their booty. They'd never returned. It had become Munro's refuge and source of goods that he'd traded on the black-market during the occupation.

Still unclaimed, it was his chosen meeting place. Grimy windows meant no one could see in. The rotten staircase warned him of approaching visitors. The quiet of the night-time wharf meant there was rarely anyone who saw him come and go.

They didn't see his clandestine meetings with Charles Balcombe.

Tonight, he was sitting at the table with his best friend, Fai Yeung. They were both in their forties, but while Munro was boyish and slim, Yeung looked older, with heavy eyes and build. In the light of the weak bulb overhead, Munro thought his friend looked even more tired than usual.

Yeung had brought a bottle of baijiu and poured two glasses.

"You're nervous," Yeung said without his usual joviality.

Munro knocked back his shot. "I'm always nervous about these meetings." He patted the gun by his side. "And I always come armed."

"I don't like it."

Munro nodded. "I know, I know. I'm grateful, Fai, but what other choice do I have?"

The other man raised an eyebrow. "Seriously? You shoot or, at least, arrest him."

"You know it's more complicated than that."

Munro didn't get into conversations about the penal and justice system of Hong Kong. He kept his politics to himself because the authorities wouldn't understand. His job was to get the criminals off the streets. The only problem with that was the system. The prisons were overflowing to bursting with people charged with the most ridiculous petty crimes. The British demanded things their way, but the law was too restrictive and that had implications for the serious criminals. And to make matters worse, the pressure of *statistics* meant it was better to get a serious criminal for a petty crime than get true justice.

And so Munro had made a deal with the devil.

The door moved, making Yeung jump. Neither of them had heard anyone on the stairs.

Balcombe came into the room but stayed in the doorway.

"What the hell?" he said, staring at Yeung.

Yeung stood up and tried to sound confident. "I know all about you."

Balcombe put a hand in his jacket pocket, probably reaching for a knife. Munro put his finger on the gun's trigger.

"Calm down," he said.

Balcombe shot him a glare. "You'd better explain, and fast."

"This is my friend, Fai Yeung. He's the assistant pathologist on the island."

"And?"

"And," Yeung said sharply, "I've been covering up your mess. If it wasn't for me—"

Munro cut him off; his tone measured. "Yeung spotted the link between what we were calling the Squeezed-heart murders and your others."

"But he didn't know it was me."

"I had to explain. It was that or Garrett would have had his evidence." Inspector Garrett had been working the case until his failures, orchestrated by Balcombe, had removed him from the case.

"Garrett didn't know it was me either!"

"He was close. More evidence would have got him more support, and he'd have taken my job."

Munro had expected that outcome. Garrett had been the man brought in to improve the results and almost did.

Yeung said, "I worked out what happened. You killed that priest."

"Not a priest," Balcombe said.

"You were there. It was BlackJack's trademark slice, not a kitchen knife. I had to lie in my report."

It had been the first time that Balcombe's alter ego had been mentioned.

"And," Yeung said, gaining in confidence, "I've been covering up your murders ever since." He reached for his glass and took a slug of his clear alcohol. Then he topped up his glass and poured a third. He held it out.

Balcombe breathed and stepped up to the table. He took the glass. "What is this?"

"Baijiu. I suppose it's somewhere between whisky and vodka."

Balcombe knocked it back and Munro noted that the man didn't flinch. Unlike Munro, he was a whisky drinker and enjoyed the burn in his gullet.

"Nothing like whisky," Balcombe said. "It's rough but I'll have another anyway."

All three men took a drink and Balcombe sat.

Yeung said, "I should go. Wife and kids..." He gripped the bottleneck. "Should I leave this?"

"Good idea," Balcombe said.

Yeung poured the man another glass, then gripped Munro's shoulder. "See you tomorrow."

I hope so, Munro thought.

Once the door shut and the pathologist's weight was making the stairs groan, Munro said, "I thought it was the best way to tell you. Now the three of us are involved."

"Do you trust him?"

"With my life. And I've trusted him so far. We wouldn't be here now if we couldn't rely on his discretion and help."

"So why *are* we here now? Was it just so I could meet your friend?"

"I have a job. An unusual job. One that requires Charles Balcombe rather than BlackJack."

Balcombe's eyebrows knitted together.

Munro explained. "A young woman is missing."

"Sounds like a job for the police," Balcombe said.

"It's a job for me, but off the books. This morning, the Chief called me into his office and told him to find the girl."

"Who is she?"

"Patricia Albright, the daughter of an important person." Munro took a sip of the fire-liquid and watched as Balcombe tossed back another measure and refilled his glass. "It's sensitive."

"Why?"

"Her father is aide-de-camp, the personal assistant to the governor."

"Morris," Balcombe said, referring to the governor. "Know him, but never met him."

Munro nodded. Sir Edmond Morris was known for extravagant parties, although Munro wasn't the right colour or class to receive an invite.

Balcombe continued: "But that doesn't explain why it's sensitive."

"Agreed, but you know how some people in the highest echelons can hold... unusual opinions, shall we say?" He took another sip and decided it would be his last. Munro was a beer drinker and would stick to beer. "She's seventeen—almost an adult, plus she's done nothing wrong—"

"As far as you know," interrupted Balcombe.

"I think that's what we need to find out. There's bound to be more to this."

"You're assuming I'll help."

"Will you?" Munro paused. "I'm asking for your help as an investigator. I know you're good at it. And I know you like the distraction."

"You're asking because it will distract me from being BlackJack. That's what you're hoping. Be honest."

"Yes."

Balcombe finished his drink and set down the glass. Then he gave the answer Munro had hoped for.

"I'll do it."

Chapter Four

The room lacked focus. It rushed and swirled.

He wasn't dreaming. He knew he was awake. It had happened before. There would be a hand. It reached for his face. He swatted it at, made no contact. The hand went and was suddenly back.

The monster was trying to smother him!

He writhed and pulled back to escape the hand. He couldn't see it clearly. It blurred and moved psychedelically like he'd taken drugs.

There was no strength in his muscles. They were bags of sand. His arms flopped. He couldn't stop the monster.

"No!" He found his voice. It seemed weak, far off.

But the hand didn't stop.

He was in his front room, on a sofa.

It was dark except for an orange glow from the street outside. He was in his clothes and soaked with sweat. And he had to stop the hand—the monster—smothering him. Despite knowing it wasn't really there.

Time had no meaning, but he figured it was over an hour. He'd timed it a few nights ago. It started as a dream and as he woke, it didn't stop. It was in the room. In his head. He knew it, but all logic was gone. He just had to wait for the thing to subside.

When it did, Balcombe gulped for air. There was vomit on his jacket. That was usual, although the smell of alcohol was also strong.

He gripped the sofa's material until his hands hurt. Then he pushed himself into a seating position and confirmed he was in his front room.

How did he get here last night?

He'd lunched at the Cheero Club, spending longer than intended. Most of the afternoon, in fact.

He'd drunk a lot. Then someone told him of a poker game at the Stag Hotel.

Under normal circumstances, Balcombe wouldn't patronize the Stag. It was bawdy and served bourbon rather than whisky.

The proprietor was a big man called Ellis. He'd been a champion boxer in Montana—nicknamed "Powerhouse"—and a barkeeper in Shanghai before buying the hotel in Hong Kong. There were photographs of him on the walls in various fighting poses. Balcombe figured it was to remind the customers of his background, should they get too unruly. Despite this, there were regular fights in and around the hotel.

Outside, on peeling plaster, Chinese writing proclaimed the hotel rooms to be comfortable. In reality, they were small and cheap, and people could rent them by the hour.

Aside from the rowdy bar area with its off-key piano, there was a billiards room and poker room.

Balcombe remembered being in there last night. He remembered the girls with excessive makeup and full dresses. He remembered the harshness of rough bourbon.

He remembered being down to his last few chips and retiring to the bar.

He'd had more drinks there. There was a vague memory of singing and having a girl on his knee.

And then he'd woken up at home.

"What happened last night, Albert?" he said to his paid-for rickshaw girl after he'd asked her to take him to Mackintosh's. He intended to buy a new suit.

"After the Stag, master?"

"Yes."

"Do you remember being thrown out?"

"No."

"Well, sort of. Two men brought you out and dumped you on the street. You were drunk."

"And you brought me home?" He knew there must be more to the story. Albert wouldn't have been allowed to bring him inside the apartment block.

"You got into the rickshaw and demanded I take you to the ferry. You wanted to go to Kowloon."

"Ah." They both knew what that meant. He was out for blood. BlackJack was taking over.

"But I tricked you," she said. "You thought I was going to the pier, but I went to Mr. Faulls's house."

Thank God!

"And Mr. Faulls took me home?"

"Yes, master. I hope you don't—"

"I'm grateful, Albert. You did the right thing."

★ ★ ★

"Yes, he did," Faulls said, although he knew nothing of Balcombe's alter ego, BlackJack. Nor did he know Albert was a girl. "You were blind drunk again."

"It looks that way." He waved a hand over his outfit. "Hence the new clothes."

"Nice. You've been shopping, now you need to apologize at the Stag Hotel."

Albert said she could take them both because it wasn't far, but Faulls insisted on a separate rickshaw.

On the way there, while they were side by side, Faulls leaned across.

"Bad dream as well?"

"Yes."

Faulls shook his head. "Charles, you should get help. This is getting worse."

"We'll see," Balcombe said without commitment. Then: "What's going on here?"

There was a crowd outside the Stag.

They expected trouble, but when Balcombe and Faulls got off their rides, they saw activity inside and mere interest from the onlookers.

Balcombe went in first and immediately noticed the smell of the place. It didn't stink of booze, it smelled clean. Of cleaning fluids, anyway.

A man was directing others. There were sweepers, dusters and polishers. Three people were painting walls, turning amber stains to brilliant white.

Lights were being fitted, some on stands. The piano had been moved and so had the tables and chairs. In fact, Balcombe thought the furniture looked newer than last night.

"You can't be in here!" an American voice said. A little man, wired with energy bustled up and flapped.

"I'm looking for the proprietor, Phil Ellis."

The man's head twitched like a bird's before he said, "Powerhouse? He's in the rear."

Balcombe and Faulls followed the directions and found the ex-boxer lounging in a kitchen, wearing nothing on top and smoking a fat cigar.

"Oh, oh! Trouble!" Ellis said when he saw them. He stood and had four inches on Balcombe. He had plate-sized hands too, but his best years were probably at least twenty behind him. Muscle had turned to flab. But he was still intimidating.

"You threatened to kill me last night," Ellis said with a grunt. His accent had only a hint of stateside in it. "I don't take kindly to threats."

"I'm sorry," Balcombe said. "That's why I'm here—to apologize."

Ellis chuckled, and his enormous chest wobbled. "It's been a long time since anyone had the balls to challenge me to a fight. But you were drunk as a skunk. Even if you hadn't been, I'd have pulverized you."

Balcombe doubted it. Despite having no knife, he reckoned he could beat the big guy. Bulk didn't equate to strength after all.

"You spent over two hundred last night—in the bar and gambling, so no hard feelings. Although you might want to apologize to my girl, Gabby."

"What did he do?" Faulls asked.

"Turned down her advances!" Ellis chuckled again. "And you might apologize to my barman."

Balcombe shook his head, vaguely remembering an argument. "I criticized the bourbon?"

"You said it was Chinese gnats' piss." Ellis waggled a scolding finger. "Which is a cheek because it's high-quality Shanghai gnats' piss."

Ellis cast a quick eye over Faulls, then held out a mitt. Balcombe's hand was swallowed as he accepted the shake.

Powerhouse Ellis squeezed and his jovial demeanour abruptly shifted. "You owe me for your last bottle, pal—or for the girl. Take your pick. Twenty dollars."

Twenty dollars for a two-dollar bottle of hooch or a three-dollar prostitute? Balcombe took a breath. He hardened his hand against Ellis's pressure, not returning the gesture of dominance, but deadening its impact.

"Charles!" Faulls said, fearing a fight would ensue.

Balcombe laughed. "You're strong, Phil, I'll give you that. I'll also give you the twenty dollars. I'm embarrassed about my behaviour, and it won't happen again."

Ellis's eyes sparkled as he released his grip. "You're damn right it won't. Mainly because I think I'm selling up. Should make enough from this movie."

After receiving his cash, Ellis pulled out a bottle of bourbon and poured three shots. The label read Glen Grant.

"The good stuff," he said, then toasted the others. "This isn't gnats' piss."

Balcombe knocked it back and appreciated the burn if not the depth of flavour.

"Soldier of Fortune," Ellis said. "That's what they say the movie will be called. My hotel's having a facelift and name change. It'll be called Tweedie's." He laughed and poured another three shots. "Can you imagine a bar in Hong Kong called that? Ridiculous! But they're paying, so Hollywood can call the place whatever they damn well like. Hey, have you thought of applying?"

"Applying?"

"You're a good-looking guy. They're looking for extras. The bar scenes, for example. I'm too damn ugly and most of my regulars are too damn rough. But you're a gent. You should be what they're looking for. Hey, I'll introduce you to Marty."

Before Balcombe could stop him, Ellis was in the bar area and speaking with a man with a clipboard. Marty had wild hair and equally wild gray eyes behind round glasses.

"Woah!" he said, staring at Balcombe. "Mr. Gable won't stand for being upstaged by an Errol Flynn lookalike!" He was distracted for a moment, then looked up again from his clipboard. "David Niven… Hmm…"

"What about David Niven?" Faulls asked. Balcombe thought his friend was taking far too much interest in the prospect of him being in the film.

"Dropped out. Niven… Flynn… similar looking. Can you act?" This was directed at Balcombe.

"No. I socialize, and I climb."

"You climb?" He shook his head, bemused. "What? Stairs? Ladders?"

"Rocks. He's a free climber," Faulls chimed in enthusiastically.

"We're going," Balcombe said. "No hard feelings and good luck." He shook Ellis's hand again and this time there was no attempted crushing.

"You could seriously be in the pictures," Faulls said as he emerged into the sunlight a few seconds behind Balcombe.

"No," Balcombe said firmly. "It'll never happen." He checked his watch. "Thanks for your help, Roy. I've an appointment with DI Munro."

He climbed on the rickshaw bench.

"Think about what I said… about getting help. I know a psychoanalyst. Doctor Swift."

"I will," Balcombe lied. Then to his rickshaw 'boy' he said, "Government House please, Albert."

Chapter Five

"DI Munro," the detective said, introducing himself to the medium height, portly man who'd just entered the meeting room. Balcombe let Munro lead, despite expecting the white official to regard him as the boss.

"Charles Balcombe. Here to support the inspector."

They were inside Government House, and this was the father of Patricia, the missing girl.

The room was warm and bare except for four chairs, a side table and two paintings. One was of the new queen. The second was of sailors meeting Chinese officials. Balcombe hadn't seen it before but recognized Hong Kong Island and Royal Navy battleships in the harbour.

Albright looked them over for a couple of beats before speaking. "Please sit, gentlemen. Thank you for coming."

He was mid-forties with tired skin but intelligent blue eyes. His voice betrayed public school, probably Eton. He had the air of the upper-class and a look to match. Without saying much, he portrayed an impression of superiority. Munro was of mixed race and Balcombe probably appeared to have no status.

Albright met Balcombe's eyes. "I know DI Munro has an exemplary reputation. Tell me about yourself, Mr. Balcombe."

"I've been on the island for nine months and, unofficially, I support the police and perform the odd private investigation. I can't match the inspector's exemplary reputation—but that's because I don't advertise my services."

Munro said, "He's good."

Albright inclined his head slightly.

"I have a formal background in detective work," Balcombe added. "British, obviously. I'm not at liberty to say more."

Albright's eyes narrowed. He said nothing for a moment, and Balcombe expected the government man to conclude he was part of British Intelligence.

Albright nodded again and took a breath. "All right, gentlemen. What do you know?"

He'd said this, still looking at Balcombe, although Munro answered.

"Your daughter, Patricia, is missing. She's seventeen and hasn't been seen for two days."

"Approximately. I last saw her on Monday evening."

After a beat, Munro continued: "It's highly unusual behaviour. I understand she's never stayed away from home before, and she told no one where she was going."

"That's correct."

Balcombe said, "We've been told to be discreet."

"I hope I can count on it."

"You can, sir," Munro said.

Balcombe leaned forward. "Excuse the impertinence, but we need to know why."

"Why?"

"Why the secrecy? Why aren't you demanding that the entire police force search for her?"

Albright clenched his teeth at Balcombe's direct questions. His eyes narrowed again.

Balcombe shook his head. "Sir, we need to know. It could help us find her."

Albright looked away and then back. When his eyes found Balcombe again, they looked softer.

"Yes, yes, of course. It's because of my position, my status. You can understand that, Balcombe, I'm sure?" He paused and breathed. "I can't afford any scandal. *We* can't afford any scandal. As you are undoubtedly aware, I'm His Excellency's aide-de-camp. If my daughter has…"

When Albright stopped, Munro said, "Sir?"

"Well, I don't know what she might have got herself involved with." He looked from one to the other as though expecting them to understand. "Do either of you have children?"

"No, sir," Munro said.

"But we've both searched for missing children before," Balcombe said, then added: "And been successful."

"Of course," Albright said.

Munro said, "Could we see a photograph?"

Albright pulled one from his breast pocket. Unusually, it was in colour. A pretty girl in a school uniform. The blue blazer had a green and white trim and a pocket crest with the letters KGV.

Patricia Albright had shoulder-length brown hair. It was curly with a centre parting. She had her father's bright eyes, but apart from those, her features differed from his.

Albright said, "This was at the start of the school year. Patricia is in the first year of her A-levels—she came second top in her School Certificate. We're very proud of that."

Balcombe said, "Very impressive. Which subjects did she choose?"

"French, History and Politics."

Munro said, "The schools have broken up for the summer."

"Last week."

"So a few days. The weekend. And then you haven't seen her since Monday." Munro paused. "It would be useful to hear about Monday. Tell us about the last time you saw Patricia."

"I arrived home from work at eight. The three of us, that's me, my wife Elizabeth and Patricia, sat down for supper together. Roast pork—is that relevant? Afterward, I had a brandy in the study before retiring to bed."

"The last time you saw her?" Munro prompted.

"After that—after dinner. I believe she went straight up. And in the morning, she was gone."

"Where do you think she went?" Balcombe asked.

Albright frowned. "That's your job."

"It would help, sir, if you could speculate."

"A friend's house. And before, you ask, I don't know which. If I did know, I would have fetched her back and grounded her for a week." He pulled a piece of neatly folded paper from his inside jacket pocket. "Here."

Balcombe took the paper, which had the governor's letterhead.

Albright said, "I expected you to ask for a list. These are all the friends my wife and I can think of."

There were twenty names written on separate lines in perfect copperplate writing.

"Anyone we should focus on in particular?" Munro asked.

"No. What will you say to them?"

Balcombe said, "We'll start by asking whether they know where Patricia is."

Albright flared his fingers on both hands as though warding something off. "What I mean is: you won't mention me."

"Absolutely not!" Munro said.

"Good." Albright pointed to the painting of the sailors. "I saw you glance a few times, Balcombe. That's Commodore Sir James John Gordon Bremer in 1841, shaking hands on the agreement to transfer Hong Kong to the British. We have a fine history in this country. Very fine indeed."

★ ★ ★

"What do you think?" Munro asked as they stood outside on Kennedy Road.

"I think two things," Balcombe said, looking back at the grand white building partially hidden behind trees. He'd noted that Albright had been more comfortable dealing with him than Munro but put that down to racial prejudice. Although this hadn't been a formal police interview, a white officer would be expected when interviewing a white gentleman. He continued: "The first is: why here? Why not meet us at his private residence?"

"Ah, I can answer that. I queried that with the Chief, and he said Albright didn't want us going to the house. Police visiting his home would not be discreet. What's your second thought?"

"That in cases like this, I would expect concern. I would expect fear of foul play. Patricia might be hurt. She might have been kidnapped. Who knows? But Albright was too placid. He appeared more uncomfortable about the directness of our questions than the fate of his daughter. And what was that nonsense about grounding her for a week?"

"You're curious?"

"I'm more than curious, Munro. I'm downright suspicious."

Chapter Six

Four days gone

"That's how he copes," Elizabeth Albright said to Balcombe in the drawing room of the sprawling Victorian property on the high levels. "Ernest is worried, of course he's worried, but it would be inappropriate to show it."

To me or the police? Balcombe thought.

He hadn't told Munro he was coming here because the detective wouldn't have approved. However it was the logical step. Albright hadn't provided a complete picture as far as Balcombe was concerned. The man was conflicted. On the one hand, he wanted to find his daughter, but on the other, he was afraid to disclose information. He'd given them little to go on and Balcombe hoped Mrs. Albright would be more open.

It had taken him two days to get the introduction. He'd asked a girlfriend because he knew she moved in the same circles. She hadn't had direct contact with Elizabeth Albright but knew someone who did.

In the meantime, Munro had visited the friends on Mr. Albright's list. Balcombe had been to all the shipping offices and checked passenger manifests, just in case. He'd found no trace.

Two more days with no sign of Patricia. The worry showed on her mother's face.

Patricia got her good features from her mother. Elizabeth Albright was a handsome woman a few years her husband's junior. Her clipped speech was like his, although her reserved expression had a soft edge. Her black dress had gold trim and short sleeves and she wore matching heels and a simple gold locket. She looked like she was about to go to a ball, and Balcombe hoped this wasn't her normal attire. Perhaps she'd dressed up especially for his visit.

"Thank you for making contact," she said. "I have been concerned about Ernest's approach. I couldn't go against his wishes, of course, so you can understand how relieved I was to hear about you." She paused. "And you're not a police officer?"

"No." He opened his hands, showing his palms in a gesture of trust. "Anything you tell me remains between us."

"My husband?"

"He won't hear of my visit. Not from me anyway."

He nodded.

She breathed out and straightened. "I'm afraid I can't offer you tea. Would you like a glass of water?"

Despite being in her house, he'd seen no staff. And the Albrights would have staff. Which meant she'd gotten them out of the way. She hadn't wanted anyone to witness their meeting. No one to make tea, but she had had water prepared in advance.

When she poured the drink and handed it to him, he noticed the ripples in the water as her hand trembled.

"Let's start," he said after a sip and deciding it tasted too strongly of cucumber for his liking. "Tell me about the day she disappeared."

"She'd been to a tea dance at the Hong Kong Hotel Roof Garden. That was Sunday. I think something happened on Sunday.

"Normally, she comes back in a good mood, but by Monday she was… I should have guessed something wasn't right. She was out for most of the day—It's the school holidays, of course. When she returned, she didn't skip through the door like she would, normally. And at dinner she was particularly quiet. In fact, I don't remember her saying a single word. Sullen. Yes, that's how I would describe her. Which wasn't like Patricia. Not like her at all."

"So, she's a happy girl, generally?"

Mrs. Albright smiled at a thought. "Very. I wouldn't say carefree. No teenager is, but relatively she's a happy girl."

"After dinner?"

"She and Ernest had words."

Balcombe raised his eyebrows. "Had *words*?"

"Would you assure me once more, Mr. Balcombe? You won't disclose this information. My husband mustn't—"

"I just want to help find your daughter, Mrs. Albright." He opened his hands again and nodded reassuringly. "Trust me. I have no interest in besmirching your husband's or anyone else's name, for that matter."

She took a deep breath, which appeared restricted by her fitted dress. "They argued about something. I don't know what because he wouldn't tell me, but I heard him raise his voice to her."

"Was that unusual?"

Mrs. Albright pursed her lips before speaking. "Well, Ernest can be a little stressed at times. The Governor can be demanding. It's a difficult job. My husband does it well, though."

"And after you heard him shouting?" Balcombe thought she might say the raised voice wasn't shouting, but she didn't correct him.

"It was just before bed. I didn't see her afterward. Ernest said Patricia had gone up. He didn't retire for an hour or so afterward. He had a few drinks. He does that sometimes after a stressful day."

"Did Patricia go to bed?"

"Well, no, she can't have. In the morning, I noticed her bed hadn't been slept in. The maid said she hadn't done it. There was also a bag missing and a few of her clothes, I think."

That was new information and vital, as far as Balcombe was concerned. It appeared she'd had an argument with her father, packed some things and left.

"How often did Patricia argue with your husband?"

Mrs. Albright thought. "Not often. Usual moans and complaints. At me too."

"Your husband or Patricia?"

"Patricia," she said, although her tight smile suggested the statement applied to her husband as well.

"But this time it was different?"

"Possibly." She shook her head. "As I told you, I heard Ernest's voice. He was the angry one. That's what I thought at the time, anyway. Perhaps—"

Balcombe took another sip of water, buying time. When she didn't continue, he prompted: "You had a theory?"

"Work. He was stressed by work. Hence the drinking."

"And Patricia?"

"She... I think there's a boy. I think Ernest knew and wasn't happy. He probably told her she wasn't to see him again."

"You knew about the boy."

She nodded. "He was the one she'd gone to the dance with."

"You know his name?"

"Geoff Tanner."

Balcombe nodded. It was one of the names on the list of friends.

"My husband didn't approve."

"Of any boys?"

Mrs. Albright forced a smile. "Particularly Geoff. He's older. Not at the school. Not just older, but not the right sort, according to Ernest. There are plenty of eligible young men in Hong Kong—in my opinion anyway. Ernest..."

Balcombe waited and took another sip.

She said, "We'd talked about her going away to Europe for a while."

"What did Patricia think about that?"

"She didn't know. At least we never discussed it openly with her. Ernest's plan was to find a suitable opportunity and... and, well, just pack her off."

"Could she have found out?"

"It's possible... although I don't know why Ernest wouldn't have told me."

Balcombe nodded. He figured the couple didn't talk much. From meeting him at Government House, Balcombe suspected Ernest Albright didn't find it easy to talk about anything other than work.

"Your best guess is that Patricia is staying with a friend. Possibly as an act of rebellion?"

"I expect so."

"All right," he said. "I think I've something to go on. If I need anything else…?"

"Of course. And you will be diplomatic? Ernest mustn't—"

"Don't worry, Mrs. Albright. Your husband won't find out that we talked. I promise."

As he stepped out onto the driveway, Balcombe glanced towards the Peak, thinking about his next climbing session.

"That's the governor's place?" he asked.

"There's a back way up there." Mrs. Albright's brief expression implied disapproval before she hid it. "Ever the servant, Ernest likes to be available whenever Sir Edmond needs him."

"And that's too often?"

Mrs. Albright gave him a weary smile. "Goodbye, Mr. Balcombe. Bring Patricia back home."

Chapter Seven

"You did what?" Munro snapped. Balcombe hadn't seen him this angry before. The harsh voice didn't seem appropriate for the normally placid, cherub-faced detective.

"I spoke to Mrs. Albright," Balcombe said again.

Munro shook his head. "I knew this was a mistake, involving you. This is sensitive, Balcombe! I've been trusted with the job and now you've threatened it—threatened my career for Christ's sake—all for what?"

"For useful information."

Munro didn't seem to be listening. He shook his head, huffing.

"So what have *you* learned?" Balcombe asked. "You spoke to all the friends."

"I've a few leads."

From his tone, Balcombe doubted it. "You have leads for the night she disappeared?"

Munro looked away, in the direction of the giant bank buildings. Or maybe the courts that were hidden beyond. Or even Kowloon. He turned his attention back and shook his head. "Nothing."

"Don't worry about Mrs. Albright. She won't tell anyone."

"Why?"

Balcombe repeated what Patricia's mother had told him about the girl's last movements.

"Oh goodness," Munro sighed. "Albright might have argued with her. He was the last to see his daughter!"

"Yes."

"Does Mrs. Albright think... think her husband did something?"

It had crossed Balcombe's mind. She'd been reluctant to say much, but she'd said enough. "It would explain his behaviour. The way he spoke. The lack of information," Balcombe said. "He could have disposed of her body and taken a bag of clothes to make it look like she'd run away." He paused. "What's just struck me is that Mrs. Albright was wearing black."

"Mourning?"

"At the time, I thought she was overdressed. It's a possibility."

Munro started pacing.

Balcombe continued: "You need to interview him. You need—"

"I can't do anything!" Munro interrupted. He stopped pacing and sat, head in hands. "I can't treat Albright as a suspect, not unless I'm absolutely sure. And I can't use what you've learned from his wife—that's just as damning."

"Sometimes the truth—"

"Stop lecturing me, Balcombe! This isn't just about my boss. Albright has connections. The ultimate connections. This goes all the way up to the police commissioner and the governor. I'm on a damn suicide mission."

"Then you turn a blind eye. You investigate and write it up. You give Albright what he wants."

"A whitewash."

"He gets away with it," Balcombe said.

Munro closed his eyes, tilted his head up and stayed like that for a minute.

"Can you get Mrs. Albright to accuse him?"

"I didn't get the sense that she thinks he's guilty. And she didn't know exactly what happened after she'd gone upstairs."

"Not yet," Munro said with hope in his eyes. He was right. People could remember things they'd forgotten. Or they changed their minds about an interpretation. There was also the possibility that she was protecting her husband. That could change too. Guilt, even by association, could be a rodent gnawing at your guts. Eventually, most people couldn't take the anxiety any longer.

"I'll try."

"Sensitively, Balcombe."

"I'll also talk to the staff"—he raised his hands—"Sensitively, don't worry. I'll find out whether there was any history, any suggestion of Albright being capable of killing his daughter."

"Was there anyone else there at their dinner on Monday, or afterward?"

"Mrs. Albright said not, but again, she may have been lying."

Munro removed his glasses and rubbed his face. "God."

Balcombe waited for the detective to replace his glasses and refocus. Then he asked what the friends had said.

"Lots of personal stuff," Munro said. He provided Balcombe with a general summary that painted a picture of a happy, fun-loving girl. She was doing well at school.

"Relationship with her father?" Balcombe asked hopefully.

"No one mentioned any problem with her parents."

"Mrs. Albright said he was thinking of sending her to Europe."

Munro frowned. "None of the friends mentioned that. Not *sending*, anyway. She planned a holiday to France with four of them. They'd expected to go last year, but it got cancelled."

"Interesting. Did anyone say why?"

"Patricia cancelled it. They didn't know why."

"What about Geoff Tanner? Was he one of the four going on holiday?"

"No." Munro checked his notes and provided four girl's names.

Balcombe nodded. He hadn't expected a boy to be allowed along on a girl's holiday even though he had no doubt they would be closely chaperoned. "What did Geoff say about Sunday afternoon, before she disappeared?"

"Sunday afternoon? Nothing. He hadn't seen Patricia for a week. What?" Munro frowned. "Why are you—?"

"Tanner saw her on Sunday!" Balcombe exclaimed. "He lied to you, Munro."

Chapter Eight

"There's another possibility," Munro said as they met on the street close to Tanner's home on North Point Terrace. Munro had taken the tram. Balcombe had ridden in Albert's rickshaw. She was waiting a polite distance away, where the road crossed North View Street.

The air was clear, with a view across the bay. Although the panorama was partially spoiled by the bulky power station.

The wind was blowing in the right direction—which was out to sea. On a bad day, the black smoke from the power station could come this way. On a very bad day, there would be smog and a bitter, choking smell in the air. People living there called it the *Soot Wind*.

This wasn't a sought-after location. Most people lived here because of the work.

"Mrs. Albright could have been lying about the tea dance," Munro said. "Remember, she was wearing black. I've been thinking about why she agreed to meet with you. The whole thing could be a misdirection."

"You're right," Balcombe said. "I only have her word for it."

"We could check with the Hong Kong Hotel. They take reservations. If we're in luck, Patricia booked it in her name."

Balcombe thought it unlikely since the gentleman would normally book a table. But then Patricia had status, her father a VIP, so it was possible. This idea seemed more likely as they walked up to Tanner's home on North Point Terrace. The young man lived in a working-class area, a strip of connected, two-up, two-down houses. North Point Terrace was the last of four similar roads, the furthest from the industrial area.

Munro seemed to read his thoughts. He said, "I met Tanner senior as well last time. He described himself as an engineering manager, but—"

"Living here? He's unlikely to be a manager."

Munro nodded. "And he was here during the day."

"Night shift?"

"Possible," Munro said. "And Tanner junior works for a furniture shop in Kowloon. At least that's what he told me. Now I'm questioning whether anything anyone has told me is truth."

The detective rapped on the dark green door and waited. The curtains upstairs were closed. One twitched after Munro knocked again.

They heard footsteps on wooden stairs. The door handle turned, then stopped. The door didn't open. There was a click. A bolt on the other side, probably.

Nothing happened. A bolt locked, not unlocked.

Munro and Balcombe exchanged glances, then nodded.

The detective took hold of the handle and shouldered the door. It crashed open, wood splintered. The bolt clattering to the floor.

"Hey!" A burly man said. He was halfway down the stairs. "What the hell?"

Balcombe heard a click towards the back of the house. *Backdoor*, he guessed and took off down the hall.

"What?" The man descended the stairs.

"Where's your son?" Munro barked.

Balcombe kept going into a kitchen. He opened a back door. There was a small, brick-walled yard with an open gate. Balcombe burst through onto the track behind. The ground was open scrubland rising to a hill.

To his left, a figure was fleeing west. No doubt the young man. Balcombe started sprinting. The fugitive glanced back, almost tripped, then redoubled his speed. Tanner was fast, but Balcombe kept up, maybe even closed slightly. At the end of the terrace, the young man dodged right, out of sight. It was an alley before the next block of houses. Balcombe went through, got to the road and saw him again. Then, thirty yards later, Tanner was crossing into another alley.

Balcombe got there in time to see him disappear over a wall. Balcombe jacked himself up, ready to follow, but saw Tanner go over the next.

He's made a mistake. Easier to go round.

Balcombe darted to the alley and opened the second gate. No one there. He moved to the third. Empty again.

He paused as his brain caught up. The back door had a screen to keep out flies. It was moving. Balcombe went for it.

Inside, he saw the front door ahead swing shut. He raced through, heard a woman scream, presumably because of him, and charged out onto the street again.

Albert was there, pointing. "He's gone down Cheong Hong Street." That ran parallel to North View, with no housing on the left.

Geoff Tanner was on the road, heading in the direction of the power station.

Chapter Nine

Tanner crossed King's Road, continuing straight into the driveway of the power station. Balcombe followed some fifty yards behind.

To the left of the drive was an ornamental garden. To the right were building works. The foundations of the HEC power station B, Balcombe knew. No doubt the addition would look modern compared to the Victorian building front and left. An open gate led to a crammed car park.

Balcombe lost Tanner in the mass of cars. Ahead was a wide, low building with a pitched roof. A typical workshop, Balcombe guessed.

To his left was a three-storey block that looked like offices or maybe two floors of offices above an industrial unit. The ground-floor windows were almost double the height of the others.

Balcombe considered his options while scanning the spaces between cars. *Tanner could hide right here.*

There was a path between the office block and workshop. Balcombe jogged down it. The end led to the wharf. There was a narrow-gauge rail track with carts. There were low buildings and sheds.

Beyond the workshop, to the right, was a fence—the current boundary of the site. Balcombe went left.

He checked the buildings along the tracks.

Behind the office block was the main power station, all red-brick and imposing. You could see it from miles off—three stacks, the biggest of which was belching the smoke today.

Beyond the enormous building were more sheds and a coal yard with piles bigger than most houses. There were cranes and docks.

There were a hundred places to hide. And no sign of Tanner.

★ ★ ★

Balcombe returned to the house on North Point Terrace. He found Munro talking to Tanner senior in the living room. Now that he was no longer giving chase, Balcombe took more in. He noticed that the home was respectable and the furniture solid, maybe second hand and mismatched, but quality pieces.

Munro stepped into the hall for a quiet word.

"Any luck?"

"I lost him at the power station."

"Worth getting a squad out to search for him?"

"The kid will be long gone," said Balcombe, shaking his head. Then he nodded at the living room. "Learned anything?"

"He's not well, has trouble breathing." Munro took a breath himself. "And he's anxious."

"He's not a manager at the power station, is he?" Balcombe indicted their surroundings. A manager wouldn't live here.

"No. He's now told me he *used to be* a manager. Retired on sick pay, three years ago. Then his wife died, and they were struggling. HEC let him have the house for a nominal rent."

"And Geoff Tanner lives here?"

"Yes. I met him last time. He said he went to school with Patricia although, like I said, he denied seeing her for a few weeks. And the dad knows nothing."

Balcombe walked into the living room where Tanner senior was perching nervously on the edge of a chair. No doubt he'd been eavesdropping on their conversation.

"Why did Geoff run?" Balcombe asked.

The father shook his head. His skin looked pasty and clammy. Then he coughed and his lungs rattled.

"I need my medicine and some water."

He pushed himself up out of the armchair and shuffled to the kitchen. Balcombe watched as the man poured water and drank it with a handful of pills. He shuffled back to the chair and flopped into it.

"Why did Geoff run?" Balcombe asked again.

"I don't know."

Munro touched his arm and his eyes suggested Balcombe switch subject, which intrigued him. He took a mental note to make sure the detective explained himself later.

Balcombe said, "Tell me about Patricia Albright."

"A schoolfriend, I think."

Balcombe shook his head. "Your son's a few years older. And he's no longer at school."

"No, he's not. She *used to be* a schoolfriend, I think."

Balcombe doubted it but didn't think the man was lying. He just didn't know.

"Yesterday, Geoff told DI Munro a lie. He said he hadn't seen her recently. But he saw Patricia on the day before she disappeared."

Tanner senior's eyes flashed surprise. He didn't know Patricia was missing.

"They'd gone dancing."

Tanner senior shook his head. "I don't think so."

"They went to the tea dance at the Hong Kong Hotel."

The head shake continued. "If you say so."

Munro added: "The Roof Garden."

Tanner said, "Geoff wouldn't go there. He..." The man stopped to cough into a handkerchief. "He was too proud."

Munro waved a hand casually. "Because of this?"

"Yes, because of our status. I'm an embarrassment these days."

"But Patricia—"

Balcombe got it. "But they were friends from way back. Patricia didn't mind that you'd fallen on hard times."

Tanner nodded. "Not like the others. That girl has class and empathy. She's a good girl."

"And we need to find her," Munro said.

Balcombe said, "Your son would help her if she's in trouble, because of their friendship."

Tanner nodded.

"Is she in trouble?"

"I don't know anything. Geoff hasn't told me anything."

"Why did he run?" Balcombe asked, returning to the question he'd asked earlier. "He's not in trouble. We just want to find Patricia."

Tanner gave them nothing.

Munro asked, "Since you worked at the power station, you know it well?"

"Of course."

"What about Geoff?"

Balcombe said, "He knows the place, that's why he ran there."

Tanner was looking at him with rheumy eyes. He dabbed at them then coughed into his hanky again.

Balcombe said, "If you were hiding in the power station, where would you go?"

Tanner looked from Balcombe to Munro.

Munro said, "I promise he's not in trouble."

"And won't be? I want your word that you're not going to arrest him."

Balcombe glanced at the detective and was reminded that they needed to talk.

Munro said, "No promises if he's harmed the girl."

"He won't have hurt Patricia!"

"Then you have my word. I won't arrest him for anything else."

"My old shed," Tanner said suddenly. "That's where I would go, and Geoff has a key."

Chapter Ten

The shed was between the coal yard and main plant. Overgrown weeds outside suggested it wasn't in use, and the door was locked. But when Munro forced it open, they saw it had been in use. There were blankets on the floor and cooking things. A pan had recently been heated on a portable gas ring.

"What do you think?" Munro asked.

"That Geoff wasn't staying here. Patricia was. And she wasn't a prisoner. Like his father said, Geoff would protect her. He was hiding her here."

"Agreed."

Before they'd left the house on North Point Terrace, Munro had impressed upon Tanner senior the need for Geoff to come forward. "We can help Patricia," he'd said. "If I find out he's been back here and you don't report it, then you'll be in trouble. I won't arrest him, but I will arrest you. Understand?"

Balcombe wasn't convinced that the father would do anything of the sort.

"Don't worry," Munro said to him afterward. "I'll get an APB out for the kid. We have to be discreet about Patricia but there's nothing to stop me openly looking for

Geoff Tanner." He held up a photograph of the young man that he'd obtained from Tanner senior.

"You should also post someone and watch the house."

Munro said he'd ask, but suspected the chief wouldn't approve. Balcombe shook his head with disbelief, but he understood the constraints on CID resources. Too many crimes, too many criminals and not enough police to deal with them.

"Albert will do it," Balcombe said after a pause.

"Good, then we should split up. I'd like you to check with the Roof Garden about the dance. Meanwhile, I'll visit J.L. George."

"The furniture company in the Peninsula Hotel?"

"That's just a salesperson at a desk. There's a shop on Cameron Road. It's where Geoff works. Let's reconvene later."

Balcombe suggested they meet for dinner at the St. Nicholas Catholic Club restaurant in the King's Building.

Munro responded with a wry smile. Balcombe knew the detective wouldn't socialize with a killer, despite their close working relationship. He also had no religion and couldn't appreciate Balcombe's bond with Catholicism.

"Later then," Balcombe said.

As they parted, Munro said, "There's one good thing we know. Patricia is still alive. Her father didn't kill her."

★ ★ ★

So why was Ernest Albright relaxed about his missing daughter? Why wasn't he calling for a bigger search?

Balcombe was hopeful of progress, but by the evening and their rendezvous in the secret office at the end of the wharf, the news wasn't good.

Balcombe had checked on Albert and she reported seeing no one enter or leave the property. She was planning to stay all night in case Geoff tried to slip back under the cover of darkness.

Balcombe visited the shed at the power station and decided it hadn't been disturbed since they'd first seen it.

At the Hong Kong Hotel, he checked the records for Sunday and neither Tanner's nor Patricia's name was on the guest list. So, it looked like Tanner senior had been right and Mrs. Albright wrong. Patricia hadn't been to the tea dance with Geoff. Although this wasn't definitive. She may have been with another man who'd used his name for the reservation.

Munro reported that Geoff hadn't been to work at the furniture store.

The manager, a skinny man called Cooke, had said Tanner was a good, diligent young man and it wasn't like him not to turn up for work. Especially since he needed the money.

The manager had explained that he knew Geoff was supporting his father. The sick pension from HEC couldn't support them.

"And I'm surprised the pocket money he earns here is enough either," the man had said.

After Munro had provided his update, Balcombe said, "When we were at their house, you stopped me pursuing the reason why Geoff had run. And then later, his father was very concerned you wouldn't arrest him."

Munro nodded. "It wasn't just because of Patricia. In fact, the father thought it was another reason."

"He suspects Geoff is up to no good?"

"Only suspects. And it all tallies with the money question. They don't have enough income to live the way they do—and apparently Geoff tries to keep up with his peers. He doesn't make much as a shop assistant and can't be seen to be poor."

"So, he's making money elsewhere."

"Mr. Tanner doesn't know where he's getting the money. He's previously challenged Geoff but learned nothing. He hopes that the money's coming from Patricia or others. However he worries that it's from an illegal activity."

"Prostitution, gambling, money lending, drugs," Balcombe said. "Any idea which?"

"No."

Whatever Geoff Tanner was into, Balcombe suspected, wasn't big time. However he knew someone who might be able to help.

Chapter Eleven

Six days gone

Balcombe remembered flashes of his bad dreams, but in the morning, he felt energized and ready for a good climbing session. As he walked through the lobby, Bruce, the concierge, flagged him down.

"Mr. Balcombe, sir, I hope you don't mind."

"Mind what?"

"I've taken the liberty of letting them wait in the meeting room."

Balcombe's chest tightened. The last time he'd had unannounced visitors like this, it had been the police. Was Garrett making another move already?

"Americans," Bruce said. "To do with the film, I think they said. Although, of course, they called it a *movie*."

Balcombe sighed. "All right. Thank you."

He opened the meeting room door to find five people clustered and waiting expectantly. There appeared to be a main man with four young assistants, all holding notebooks with pens poised.

"Jeez, you do look like him!" the lead American said. He was wearing a garish checked jacket with mismatched trousers. "Charles Balcombe. I'm right, aren't I?"

"You are," said Balcombe, suspicious. "Who are you?"

One of the assistants stepped forward. "This is Mr. Thelwell, the casting director."

Thelwell inclined his head. He had a stiff military bearing and Balcombe wouldn't have been surprised if the man had clicked his heels.

"What's this about?"

Thelwell smiled. "You gave your name to the set manager at the Stag Hotel."

"I—" Balcombe began, about to explain that it had been his friend who'd provided his details, before Thelwell enthusiastically spoke over him.

"It's sure to be big, Mr. Balcombe. A Twentieth Century Fox movie featuring Clark Gable. It's sure to be huge. If you can be involved—well, you'll be dining out on it for years."

"I'm pleased for you," Balcombe said, having no need to dine out on his reputation.

"Do you have any acting experience?"

"I do not. And I'm—" He was about to explain that he had plans.

Thelwell waved him down. "Please don't leave. Just a minute of your time, sir."

Balcombe sighed and checked his watch. "Providing it really is quick. You have exactly five minutes. No more. After that, I'm gone."

The assistants were excitable youngsters providing a constant background of chatter.

Thelwell said, "Right, in brief, the story is that a wife is looking for her photographer husband who has been arrested by the Chinese as a spy.

"Mr. Gable plays a modern-day pirate operating out of Hong Kong. After a few mistakes and errors, Mr. Gable agrees to help her."

"He's fallen in love with Grace Kelly," one of the assistants said.

Another corrected him: "It's Susan Heyward now. Grace Kelly—"

Thelwell waved his hand to hush them. "The stars aren't coming yet. The script is still being finalized and we'll be filming other scenes. Where was I?"

An assistant said, "Mr. Gable has fallen for the leading lady but she's not available."

"Right. Not romantically available yet. The hero— Mr. Gable—has a series of adventures culminating in the rescue of the lady's husband from the Chinese. There's a boat chase—Can you sail, Mr. Balcombe?"

"I'm afraid not. I haven't got sea-legs."

"There are scenes at the bar and harbour—possibly the police station."

Balcombe shook his head. He wasn't getting involved in anything at the police station, acting or otherwise.

"The Peak tram. I'm not sure whether it's romance or action or—knowing the writer—probably a bit of both."

"Your time's up," Balcombe said after a glance at his watch.

"I'm sure we'd like to use you, Mr. Balcombe. I just need to find the right role. Nothing major, you'll understand. I can't have you upstaging Mr. Clark Gable!"

The assistants laughed appreciatively.

"Good day, Mr. Thelwell."

Balcombe left the room and crossed the lobby. Bruce looked up expectantly, probably hoping to find out what they'd been discussing. Balcombe ignored him and left the building.

"One more thing, Mr. Balcombe," Thelwell said, hurrying into the passage behind him. "May I ask why you're dressed like that?"

"I'm off for a climbing session."

"A climbing—?" Thelwell frowned, confused.

"Up there." Balcombe pointed in the direction of the Peak. "I climb rocks."

"You're a… climb… er," the director said slowly, as though processing the information. "Interesting."

Balcombe saw Albert standing on Queen's Road, threw Thelwell another "Good day," and jogged to the rickshaw.

"Quick, get me away."

Albert immediately started pulling, and they were soon moving at speed. However, Balcombe made her stop once they'd reached Statue Square.

"You look exhausted," he said.

"I *am* exhausted." He detected grumpiness in her voice. "That's what a night's vigil can do to a girl."

"I pay you," he said.

"I'm not complaining about the pay."

"Any news? Did Geoff Tanner return home?"

"Nothing. I had a good view of the road to the front and rear. It's possible that he found another way, but I doubt it. He didn't return."

Balcombe got off the seat. "I'm going climbing."

"There's another thing, master."

He felt a tingle of apprehension. When she called him master, he guessed something was up.

"Last night. I couldn't watch out for you."

Balcombe looked at her, suspicious of her next words.

She said, "So I had a friend keep an eye on you."

He said nothing.

"You left your building just after midnight."

He shook his head. He hadn't been out last night. The last thing he remembered was reading a book on Mesopotamian history accompanied by a few glasses of whisky. Although now that he thought about it, he couldn't remember going to bed or how he ended up on his sofa.

She said, "You don't remember, do you? My friend took you to a rough area over in Sai Ying Pun." She added a street name. He knew the area, under two miles west.

"I'm going climbing," he said, walking away.

She left the rickshaw and hurried a pace behind him. "My friend lost you, but said he saw you re-enter your building an hour later."

Balcombe stopped and turned to face her. A couple walking past glanced at them, probably assuming she was begging or trying to extort money.

"Go home, Albert. Get some sleep. You can pick me up after lunch." He gave a time and place, turned to walk up to the lower Peak tram station, then swung back to her. "And just so you can stop worrying, nothing happened last night. I do remember. I couldn't sleep and I went for a walk. That's all."

But it wasn't all, and Balcombe knew it. He couldn't remember a thing. And it explained why he felt energized this morning. BlackJack had struck again.

★ ★ ★

He pushed himself to his limit. Sweat made his fingers slip, but he found new handholds and routes, maintaining the challenge and thrill.

The excitement from his liaisons was waning but climbing, risking death, was still the ultimate adrenaline rush. At least that's what he kept telling himself as he took more and more risk.

BlackJack was out of control. He knew it, but there had to be a way to restrain his alter ego. He'd thought the drink could suppress the urges, but there was a growing battle between BlackJack's actions and the night terrors.

"Hey, excuse me!" An American voice broke into his thoughts just as Balcombe was about to attempt another ascent. "You don't use ropes?"

"Only for descents if there's no other way down."

"I noticed… pardon me if I've got this wrong… you dangling up there. May I ask what that was about?"

"Danger."

The young man wrote in a book.

Balcombe said, "You're from the film crew, aren't you?"

"Yes siree. Supporting Mr. Gann on the movie script. I was told… you must be Mr. Balcombe. I can tell because…"

"I know, I look a little like Errol Flynn."

He grinned. "You do. Yes siree. You do!"

"I can't act."

The young American shook his head. "Well, sir, I think Mr. Gann won't care about that—or Mr. Thelwell, for that matter. Or even Mr. Gable."

Balcombe eyed the young man, intrigued.

The American said, "Stunt double, you see. We could have a scene up here. I can see it now." He scribbled something in his notebook. "Oh, yes siree! Mr. Gable—which would be you playing him—can be chased up. You struggle, almost fall, but manage to reach the top and escape." His eyes were wide and a little crazy. "I can see it. It'll be exciting. Will you do it?"

Balcombe pondered. It could be a distraction. It could be fun. So he eventually said, "Fine, I'll do it. Providing no one tells me I can dine out on my fame."

The young man grinned. "We'll be in touch. You can count on it. We'll be in touch."

Chapter Twelve

Fai Yeung, the assistant pathologist, said quietly, "Did you authorize one last night?"

"One?" Munro said, unsure what his friend meant.

Yeung's eyes flicked from side to side, nervously. "You know! Your friend's nocturnal activities."

Ah, Balcombe/BlackJack.

"We've another one of his, I'm sure. I've written up the stabbing as a street fight, but the knife cuts are too clinical. It may have been a fight, but I suspect it was more one-sided."

Munro knew the case. One of his sergeants had taken it. A Chinese thug stabbed in a rough area near West Point. So it had been BlackJack again.

An orderly walked along the corridor, and they waited until he had passed.

Munro pointed to his heart. *Did he squeeze it?*

"No."

"Small mercies," Munro said with a sigh.

"So not authorized?"

Munro shook his head.

"You've a real problem, Babyface."

"I know."

"Let's talk outside. I don't mind the stink down here, but I'm sure you prefer fresh air."

They left the morgue and stood on the hospital steps. Yeung leaned against a wall. "How's your search going?"

Yeung was referring to Patricia Albright. He was the only one Munro had confided in about the case, other than Balcombe.

He'd just come from Government House after updating the father. Albright had liked that she'd been with someone recently. Although less keen that it had been a young man—and he claimed to know nothing about him except the name. Which troubled Munro. According to Balcombe, Mrs. Albright said her husband didn't approve of Geoff Tanner.

When Munro asked why the name had been on the list of friends, Albright said it had 'just come up'. He said, he didn't keep a track of the friends from school and elsewhere. He and his wife just knew the close ones and some other names. He listed the closest and Munro recognized them: the ones who'd mentioned the holiday.

Munro said, "She'd planned to visit France last summer?"

"Yes. Côte d'Azur. A friend has a villa—" Albright's eyes narrowed. "Why'd you ask?"

"It was cancelled. Anything might be relevant, sir."

"It's not, and I cancelled it because I could no longer accompany them. *We* could no longer accompany them."

Munro told Yeung about the meeting. "He's very cold... under the circumstances. Five days... and it was good news that we'd found a trace of her. She's alive. Surely that should have got a more positive reaction?"

"Come on, Babyface! He's British establishment. What do you expect? He's not exactly going to breakdown in front of you." He put on a British accent: "Still upper lip and all that, hey what?"

"I suppose."

Two orderlies stretchered a body past them. It possibly reminded the pathologist of BlackJack because he said, "What are you going to do about your problem?"

"He's getting help," Munro said. Although he didn't know if it had started yet, he was hopeful it would.

"Can he be helped?" Yeung looked at him with eyes full of doubt. "How does this end?"

They'd previously discussed it in the Wellington Inn over a drink. How did it end? Munro didn't know. He'd hoped the solution would be clear. If BlackJack could be restrained, then their arrangement could go on for years. But the killer wasn't under control.

Munro didn't answer straight away and eventually Yeung said he had to get back to work.

Munro gripped Yeung's arm. "Thanks again for your support. I don't know what I'd do—"

The pathologist rolled his eyes. "For you, anything old friend, but I'm not a miracle worker. A bird does not sing because it has an answer—"

"—It sings because it has a song." Munro nodded. His beautiful wife, Yan would have said the same. BlackJack was BlackJack. He would keep on killing.

Chapter Thirteen

Balcombe attended the eleven o'clock mass with Faulls before going for a late lunch at the Jazzles Club. They sat outside despite the noise from the reclamation work along the front. His friend wanted to know all about the film and Balcombe's role.

"I'll just be what they call a stunt double, although I don't look like Clark Gable."

Faulls laughed. "They don't care about that. I see it all the time. You take a big star like Randolph Scott—as soon as the action starts, the double takes over. Last film I saw, the so-called double had dark hair whereas Randolph Scott is blond!"

"I'll be climbing anyway, so all you'll see is my back."

They finished their meal in silence. Afterward, Balcombe said, "Tell me about that head-doctor you mentioned before."

"Doctor Swift."

Balcombe frowned. He knew the name, although he thought he was the senior pathologist at the hospital.

Faulls jotted down an address on Gage Street. "You won't regret it," he added with a mischievous grin.

"I already do, Roy, I already do."

* * *

Albert was leaning against her rickshaw outside Jazzles. She looked better than when Balcombe had seen her earlier.

"Where to?" she asked after he said farewell to his friend and sat on the bench.

"Remember Captain Van Ness?"

She looked at him as though he had two heads. "Of course!"

Van Ness was the head of Jardines, a private militia and the only organisation authorised to bear arms outside the military and the police.

They originated as a private naval force for one of the original trading houses on the island: Jardine Matheson. And their presence was still felt despite their modern irrelevance. Each day, they fired the noonday gun from their building at East Point, and Jardine's Lookout on the hill had taken the company's name.

They appeared to be nothing more than a tourist attraction, but Balcombe knew otherwise. Jardines was still a militia and they had links with the underworld. In crude terms, Van Ness was a gangland boss.

His headquarters were on Caroline Hill and that's where Balcombe told Albert to take him.

It was the far side of Happy Valley on the way to North Point. The house stood proudly at the end of a sweeping drive with uninterrupted views across the bay. Wrought-iron gates barred the way and were guarded by two men in Jardines' blue uniforms.

"Do you have an appointment?" one sentry asked. He didn't have a hand on his holstered gun, but looked like he could fast-draw it at any second.

Balcombe introduced himself. "Captain Van Ness will see me."

And he was right. It took fifteen minutes of waiting at the gates while one guard went down the drive to the house. However the captain wasn't at the house and the man soon returned to direct Balcombe to the racetrack.

The air smelled of fresh-cut grass as Balcombe walked past the stands and found Van Ness with another Jardines man standing at the rails. There was one horse charging around the track.

As Balcombe approached, the other man spoke into the captain's ear before being waved away. He took three backward paces and watched.

"Mr. Balcombe! Always a pleasure!" Van Ness spoke softly with a Dutch or South African accent.

Balcombe took the other man's hand.

"What do you think of her?" he said referring to the racehorse.

"She moves well."

"I agree. I've just bought her."

"Good investment."

"She's called Scarlet Pimpernel," Van Ness said. "Let's take a stroll."

They walked with the railing on their right. The third man followed a few paces behind.

Van Ness made polite conversation until he stopped walking and said, "You didn't come just to check on my health and my latest purchase."

"No, I'm looking for someone. He's called Geoff Tanner."

The horse thundered past, close enough to smell of sweat and turf.

Van Ness pursed his lips and frowned. "It's not a familiar name."

"He's a young chap. Lives over by the power station."

"And you thought I'd know him because…?"

"I wondered if he'd borrowed money."

Van Ness shook his head. "Not from us. Has he borrowed much?"

Balcombe cleared his throat. "It might not be money. You see, he's on the run. We wanted to question him and—"

"We?"

"The police."

"You're working with the police now? Interesting. Perhaps I need to regard you differently, Mr. Balcombe."

"I'm assisting, unofficially."

Van Ness said nothing.

"We're suspicious he's into something illegal. That's why he ran when questioned," Balcombe continued, avoiding any mention of Patricia Albright, the missing girl.

Van Ness lit a cigar and puffed on it as his horse galloped past again.

Balcombe said, "Money lending, drugs, gambling, prostitution. Probably small-time. Any ideas, Captain?"

Van Ness took a long drag and blew out a stream of smoke. "No. Big-time and I'd know. Small-time and"— he gave a shrug with his hands—"probably too small, but I will keep an eye out."

They turned and walked back towards the stands. The third man tucked in behind again.

Van Ness said, "Has this anything to do with Patricia Albright?"

Balcombe stopped. "What do you know about her?"

"Nothing except the word on the street is you're looking for her."

Balcombe tried to read the other man's eyes. Did he know anything? He had connections and sources of information. However Balcombe knew the Jardines' captain wouldn't betray any confidences.

"It might be," he said after a pause.

Van Ness kept his eyes on Balcombe's, presumably also trying to read his thoughts. Finally, he nodded to the third man who took a pace forward.

"Thanks for your visit, Mr. Balcombe. I'll let you know if I hear anything." He signalled to the third man and then spoke into his ear. Then Van Ness turned back to Balcombe, offered his hand before he strode away.

The other Jardines man followed Balcombe to the racecourse gates, like a shadow. Balcombe signalled to Albert and glanced at the other man.

"Is there a problem?"

The man shook his head and whispered.

Balcombe said, "Pardon?"

The man stepped closer and whispered again. "Bai long."

"By long? What does that mean?" Balcombe asked, but the third man was already walking away.

"Worthwhile visit?" Albert asked as he mounted the rickshaw.

"We'll see." He paused. "Does *by long* mean anything to you, apart from the obvious?"

She thought, played with the words and then said, "*Bai long*." She spelled it out. "It's Chinese for white dragon."

"Is that a reference to drugs?"

Albert shook her head as she pulled.

Balcombe leaned back and thought. Whether *bai long* was relevant or a red herring, he didn't know. What he was sure of was that Van Ness knew something about Patricia Albright. Whether he would help was another matter.

★ ★ ★

On Sunday evening, Balcombe met Munro. There was still no sign of Patricia Albright. Her father was still far too relaxed despite a week having passed.

Munro had been to the furniture store in Kowloon where Tanner worked and been told the young man hadn't turned up for work all week.

Balcombe told Munro about the meeting with Van Ness. "Have you heard of *bai long*?"

"A myth."

"So you *have* heard of it?"

"Not for a while, but in the past... From around the end of the war... It's a name linked to unsolved crimes. Never anything concrete, but Bai Long is possibly the name of a gang." Munro said he'd pull the files of anything linked to the name. "But I suspect the Jardines man was just playing games with you."

"Possibly."

Munro was studying him. Something on his mind.

"What is it?" asked Balcombe.

"I know about last night. Fai Yeung has covered up for you again." He paused. "Was the man you killed bad?"

"Yes," Balcombe said, although he didn't know. He'd tried to remember what had happened, but nothing came. He'd hoped Albert's friend had been mistaken. He'd hoped BlackJack hadn't killed. But here was more evidence.

Munro still looked awkward. "You need help."

"I'm getting help." Balcombe then said he'd called a psychoanalyst on Friday. The name, Roy Faulls had given him. A receptionist had booked Balcombe in for 2 pm on Monday.

"That's good," Munro said.

"I'll tell you what would be better. We need a breakthrough on the case."

It didn't take long. The following day, while Balcombe was seeing the psychoanalyst, the police were receiving an anonymous tipoff. About Geoff Tanner's whereabouts.

Chapter Fourteen

Seven days gone

The address on Gage Street was a broad glass-fronted store called Robinson Piano Co. Balcombe opened the door which rang a small brass bell fixed to the frame.

Unsurprisingly, the shop floor had an array of pianos, grand and upright. There was a counter at the back with cabinets containing other instruments. Many more were attached to wall boards.

This was not the office of a psychoanalyst.

A man stood up at the rear with an optimistic expression on his face.

"I'm looking for Doctor Swift," Balcombe said, and watched the shopkeeper's face fall.

"Above," the man said, then pointed to the left of the shopfront. "It's the black door on the side. That'll take you up."

Balcombe nodded and found the narrow door. An engraved plaque, little bigger than a postage stamp, read: *Dr G Swift, Psychoanalyst.*

There was no knocker or bell, just a large central knob. Balcombe pushed the door open and entered a dusty, bare wooden staircase. A dim light at the top provided illumination as he mounted the stairs, which doubled back on itself before arriving at a landing. There were four doors leading to rooms; over the piano store, he figured.

One door was at the end of the landing and three to his right. These were marked *Bathroom* and *Office*. Between them, the middle door had the same plaque as downstairs. A further handwritten sign said: *Please Knock*.

Balcombe complied and received, "Come!" as a response.

A woman's voice. The receptionist.

He opened the door.

The room felt like a cosy study. The woman was sitting at ease in a chair. She wore a simple silk blouse and slacks. Her shoes were flat. She managed to look relaxed and professional at the same time.

Her legs were crossed but her arms were open with one hand on her knee and one on the chair. She had good legs. That was Balcombe's initial thought. His second was that this was no receptionist.

Behind her was a desk with a blotter, pen holder, notebook and larger book, probably a diary. There was also an odd-looking silver statue. A thick rug covered most of the bare floorboards. There was a bookcase with objects and textbooks. Balcombe registered a painted wooden clog, a brass model of the Eiffel Tower, a London bus, and other memorabilia.

There were two sideboards, each with a lamp. The final item of furniture was a couch. Every psychoanalyst's office needed a couch.

There were no paintings on the walls, nor were there any windows.

"I was expecting Doctor Swift, he said."

Her hair was mid-length and auburn. Her eyes were pale olive and, when she smiled at him, the room seemed to fill with light. "My father?"

"I believe he's the senior pathologist at the hospital."

She nodded. "I'm the other Doctor Swift. Georgina Swift. I know it's confusing. Two doctors in the same family."

"At least you don't look alike." He wanted to add that she was considerably more attractive, but resisted the urge.

"You must be Charles. May I call you Charles?" She waved at a chair set at right angles to hers. "Please come and sit."

Balcombe took the small armchair. Despite the size, its brown leather was soft and comfortable. Swift's chair had no leather and looked firmer.

"So G stands for Georgina?"

She smiled again. Of course it did. She'd just told him so.

"You've been Roy Faulls's best kept secret," Balcombe said. "Keeping you to himself, I suspect."

"Hmm," she said, waited as though expecting him to say more.

She hadn't stood or offered her hand, or even introduced herself. Not really. But then again, there was no one else there, and she'd expected him. He was no analyst, but the small sign outside, the unostentatious surroundings and the lack of physical contact meant something. Maybe.

He said, "So you think you can help me?"

"That depends... mostly on you."

"All right. Let's start."

"Firstly,"—she pointed to the couch—"would you prefer to sit or lounge?"

"Sitting here is fine."

She spoke slowly, with a pause before speaking each time. He guessed it was deliberate. Probably to put her clients at ease.

Before she spoke again, he continued. "So, how does this work?"

"I ask questions and you talk."

"Judge a man by his answers not his questions."

"You're deliberately misquoting Voltaire," she said.

He nodded. "Do I call you Doctor Swift or Georgina?"

"Whichever you feel most comfortable with." Pause. "I won't judge you. I'll merely direct the conversation."

"And solve my problem?"

"Help you solve it." Breath. "If I can."

"Where do we start?"

"With you describing the problem as you see it."

"Nightmares," he said, which was true, although he wasn't willing to discuss BlackJack. "Trouble falling asleep and staying asleep."

She picked up a pencil and notepad and wrote rapidly.

He added: "Which leads to drinking."

She looked up. "You drink to help you sleep?"

"To avoid the nightmares."

"Does it work?"

He inclined his head. "My friend Roy mentioned my drinking, didn't he?"

She turned smoothly to meet his gaze. Her pale olive eyes were really something special.

"Ah," he said. "It's about me, not other people's perceptions."

She looked back at her notes. "These nightmares... Are they recurring?"

He said nothing for a minute, reflecting. "I'm often being chased and I'm getting away but then something goes wrong. My legs stop working or I forget how to run. Sometimes I'm running in slow motion."

She didn't look at him. "What's chasing you, Charles?"

He cleared his throat. "A monster. Silly, hey? It's the sort of thing a child would dream about. Monsters chasing you." He chuckled unconvincingly.

"Any other dreams?"

"Water."

"Water?"

"I'm in water. No, more like under the water. I look up and can see things above, but not clearly. It's all blurred by the water. There are important things, and I can't do the right thing because of the distortion."

Doctor Swift was writing in her notebook.

He said, "Sometimes the water is also a heavy weight."

"What wakes you up?"

"The feeling that I'm drowning."

"And in the case of the monster?"

"Do you mean, does it get me?" He thought. "No, it's the panic of not escaping."

Neither of them said a word for a moment. He noticed a strand of her hair was out of place, then the curve of her chin and pale neck.

"You've been in Hong Kong for eight months?" she said breaking the spell.

"Closer to nine."

"And before that?"

Malaya with the British Army, he thought. *Military Police Special Investigations Branch.* But he didn't say that. He'd fled the army. He'd changed his identity. So he told her a simple lie. "Travelling. I see from the items on your bookcase, you've travelled through Europe."

"How's your life here?" she said.

"Very good."

She prompted, and he told her some details, although omitted telling her about the married ladies he rendezvoused with. It was a privileged life, filled with dining and dancing. He partied and played games. In describing it, he realized how hollow his existence sounded, so he added that he read a great deal, was interested in history and was a committed Catholic.

When he finished, she stopped jotting notes and pierced him with her green eyes.

"That's it for today, Charles. Your hour is up."

The time had passed quickly. "Am I cured?" he laughed.

"If only it was that easy. But I'd say we made a good start."

She stood and her fine legs came into play. She was a tall woman, and his eyes were level with her brows. This time she offered her hand.

"Same time tomorrow?" he said, holding her hand a moment longer than customary.

"That would be unusual. Once a week, would make more sense. It gives time to—"

"I'd like to do this faster."

She took a breath and repeated: "That would be unusual, Charles."

"I like to think I'm the exception."

She studied him with those gorgeous eyes for a moment then reached for the diary on her desk. Then she nodded and met his eyes again.

"Alright. I've got space for a two o'clock each day. How does that sound?"

He smiled. "Perfect. See you tomorrow at two, Georgina."

"You're an intelligent man," she said.

He waited for the *but*.

She added: "Next time it'll be better if you don't hold back."

"I'm sorry?"

"Total honesty, Charles. You need to be totally honest with your answers."

Chapter Fifteen

An anonymous phone call told the police that Geoff Tanner was in Kowloon. He'd been seen the previous night at the northwest docks known as the Cosmopolitan Dockyard. It was on the western edge of Sham Shui Po district.

"He'll be back tonight," the mysterious caller said. "And make sure there's only one of you."

"I don't like it," Munro said after discussing it with Balcombe.

"Do you have a better lead?"

He didn't. He'd made no progress since the boy had fled. Tanner hadn't returned home or to the power station's shed.

"I don't like the *one of you* instruction."

Balcombe thought it wasn't unreasonable. The yard was a known drug dealing spot and a police squad could cause a problem. One man going in to arrest a boy—especially one who wasn't a gang member—would be nice and simple. A raid could lead to a shootout.

"They may even hand him over on a plate," Balcombe suggested.

"*They* being the drug gang?"

Munro thought the tip off had come from the gang. But why? Was Tanner stepping on their toes? Or was this something else?

"It could be a trap. This could be an opportunity for them to kill a copper."

"It could be, but it's our only lead."

Munro said nothing. Balcombe was right, but it felt like a reckless move.

Then Balcombe said, "I'll go too. I'll keep out of the way but watch your back."

They debated it for a few minutes before settling on a plan. Thirty minutes later, they took the car ferry over to the peninsula. Balcombe got out before the docks. Munro drove closer and waited.

The criminal activity wouldn't start until after dark. As the sun bled into the night sky, the wharves closed and men made their way home.

It was nine o'clock before Munro spotted a small boat dock and men unload boxes. A small flaming torch was lit and provided just enough illumination to see the setup. It looked like a stall served by one man. Two others positioned themselves on either side. He guessed they were armed and, when one turned, he recognised the outline of a submachine gun. Balcombe had been right. More police and there would have been a bloodbath.

Within minutes of the boxes being unloaded, a new figure appeared. A man slunk from the shadows and then made his way to the guarded boat. Despite the poor light, Munro could see a transaction take place. Money for drugs, no doubt.

After the first man, the others gained confidence and came. Sometimes alone, sometimes in pairs. They made quick trades. There was never a queue. Once one transaction was complete, another person or pair scuttled forward.

An hour passed. The visits waxed and waned. Another hour and there were increasingly long gaps between trades. Munro had deactivated the interior light so that it didn't come on when he opened the car door. He got out, stretched, and rubbed his bad knee.

It's a waste of time, he decided. *The boy's not coming.*

And then he saw a figure by the boat. For the first time, in the flickering torchlight, he thought it was a white man—more specifically, a young white man.

Munro moved from the car to the wall of a building. He tracked along the side, closing in.

Is Balcombe watching too? Has he spotted the boy?

The young man had a satchel which he handed over. One of the armed guards checked it, removed something—presumably money—and then passed both bag and money to the man at the stall. Something went from box to bag and the trade was complete. The young man stepped away.

Munro spotted the route and predicted where the boy would come out on the far side of the building.

He hurried to meet him.

Before he reached the end of the alley, two men barred his way.

"Don't move!" one said in Cantonese.

"Police!" Munro said tersely. Ordinarily, he would have barked it, but knowing there were at least two heavily armed men close by, he played it safe.

"Don't move!" another voice said behind and to his right. "Don't turn around."

Munro had been reaching for his gun, but now his hand froze as he felt a blade press into his lower back.

The man in front said, "Remove the gun and drop it on the ground. Do it slowly."

Munro complied.

A figure appeared where Munro had predicted the boy with the satchel would come out. The boy glanced and ran.

"Balcombe!" Munro shouted, deciding that the situation was beyond worrying about armed guards on the quay.

"Right here!" a familiar voice said, also behind him.

The pressure from the knife stopped suddenly, followed by a figure collapsing to the ground. Then Balcombe was standing beside him.

Munro breathed with relief and pointed. "Tanner."

Balcombe stepped between the detective and the two Chinese men blocking their way. "Go after him."

Munro hesitated and then moved. His bad leg meant he couldn't go fast, but Balcombe was facing off the remaining two attackers.

He snatched up his weapon and went to the end of the alley. There he turned left, following the direction the boy had taken. He came to a crossroads—a space between four warehouses. Left. Right. Ahead. There was no sign of a fleeing boy.

He spotted a figure in a doorway. A man was slumped there, probably wrecked.

"Did you see anyone?"

No response.

Munro pressed on. He came to a Judas door, slightly ajar. Inside, he heard scuffling and then running feet. He nudged it open and entered.

Black bales towered over him, smelling of canvas and dust and hot rubber.

"Police!" His voice echoed in the cavernous room. "Come out with your hands up!"

The sound of footfall had stopped. Was there anyone still here?

He edged forward, conscious that he could see very little.

"I'm armed. Come out!"

A noise to his right. He swung around just in time to see a tower toppling over. Bales crashed around him. He thought he saw a fleeing figure, but by the time he'd avoided the bales, the movement was gone. Silence settled with the dust.

Munro waited a minute, then edged back to the door. It was open wider than before. The young man had escaped.

Munro peered out into the alley between warehouses and saw nothing. He patrolled left and right. No sign of anyone. Even the wrecked man in the doorway was no longer there.

Disaster. Their only lead had gone. He'd failed to catch Tanner.

Gunshots from the wharf.

With his gun at the ready, Munro headed toward the danger. He passed where he'd left Balcombe. A quick check told him that his companion wasn't either of the two bodies on the ground.

Another shot and he arrowed toward the water.

The once tied up boat was now away from the quay. The stall had gone. But a figure was bending over something where it had been.

Munro aimed his weapon. "Police!"

The figure glanced up but continued. Munro saw the flash of a knife.

He closed in. "Police! Drop it!"

And then the horror of the situation wrenched his gut. He saw the craziness in Balcombe's eyes. He saw a man sliced like a butchered animal at his feet. He saw the blood.

BlackJack was here.

Chapter Sixteen

Eight days gone

Munro had been about to shoot when BlackJack turned and sprinted away. Munro knew he'd hesitated and shouldn't have.

If I'd killed him, it would all be over, he thought. *Balcombe would be blamed for the murders, and I'd be free of the monster.*

The thoughts troubled him all night. He should have shot him. Next time, he wouldn't think, he'd just shoot. Balcombe was out of control. He was a blood-crazed assassin. He wasn't a killing machine that could be used. He was just a monster.

It had been too late to get the car ferry back to the island, so Munro found a hotel away from the trouble. He'd wanted to stay at the Peninsula, but it and nearby boarding houses were full because of the film production company and its entourage. The place he found was clean enough and maybe the anonymity would work in his favour.

After catching the first morning ferry, he got a message to Albert and waited for Balcombe at their secret office at the end of the wharf.

He sat at the table with his gun in his lap. Who would come through the door? Balcombe or BlackJack?

Ninety minutes later, the door opened. Balcombe came in and didn't look his usual cocky self.

"You look tired," Munro said.

"So do you."

"It's not surprising after… do you know what happened last night?"

For a moment he thought Balcombe would deny it, like he had before, but there was something in his eyes that Munro hadn't seen before. Was it remorse or fear?

Balcombe said, "Tell me what I did."

"You killed three men."

"I remember you being attacked. I sent you after Tanner." The implication was that he remembered nothing else.

"You sliced the two where you found me. Then you killed another—probably the third man—on the quay. You were shot at by drug dealers who escaped on their boat. And as far as I could tell, the man you killed didn't have a gun."

Balcombe's eyes showed he couldn't recall any of this. He probably couldn't recall how he was slicing up the third man before Munro had interrupted him. But Munro didn't bother going into detail.

"Then what?" Balcombe asked.

"I stopped you. You ran." Munro wondered again if he should have fired his gun. "How did you get back?"

"I caught a junk," Balcombe said, although Munro suspected he didn't know for certain. He'd probably woken up in his own bed with no clue how he'd got there.

Balcombe looked keen. "So, Munro, did you get Tanner? What's the news?"

"If it was Tanner, then he got away." Munro told Balcombe about the chase and cornering someone, who he assumed was Geoff Tanner, in the warehouse.

"We need to go back," Balcombe said.

Munro shook his head. "There's no *we* in this. Not after last night. You need help."

"I told you I'm seeing a psychoanalyst. I had my first session yesterday."

Balcombe had seen the psychoanalyst during the afternoon and become the murderous BlackJack in the evening. However, Munro said nothing. He was relieved that Balcombe had finally gone to see her. In fact, he'd been the one to tell Roy Faulls. An introduction from a friend was better than the police—especially since Georgina Swift also helped with criminal evaluations.

"How was it?" asked Munro.

"An initial session. I like her." He paused. "I've another session today."

"All right," Munro said. "Carry on seeing her. When you have BlackJack under control, then we can move forward."

And let's both pray that happens soon.

★ ★ ★

After Balcombe had left, Munro headed back to the police station via Peddler Street. Whether it had been the stressful events of the evening before, or the dealing with Balcombe, he didn't know, but he had an odd sensation. He turned around three times as though there was someone following. There were plenty of people about, but no one seemed to be paying him any attention.

"Where have you been?" Chief Carmichael snapped as Munro found his desk.

"Sir?"

"There's been an incident over on the mainland."

Munro's heart pounded so hard he worried the Chief would notice.

"Incident, sir?"

"Get over there immediately, Munro, Garrett is already there. And before you ask why he's involved, it's straightforward. It looks like that Squeezed-heart murderer is still around and that's Garrett's case."

Chapter Seventeen

Julia Wendsley came out of the Windsor Hotel as Balcombe stepped into the sunlight on Queen's Road.

Her facial expression suggested a surprise meeting, but he doubted it. She'd been waiting in the lobby and darted out as soon as he appeared.

"Oh, Charles, darling!"

"Julia." His tone was flat.

"Do you have a minute? Could we talk?"

She looked alluring in a modern blue dress with white trimmings. Her heels were white and her jewellery subtle. She also smelled good.

Balcombe glanced at Albert and considered his escape.

"Please, just a minute," she pleaded. "I'd just like to talk."

He held up a finger for Albert to wait and then walked with Julia back to the entrance of his apartment building. He took her inside and threw a glance at the concierge. Bruce nodded and disappeared, providing them with privacy.

"I made a mistake," she said earnestly.

"Go on."

"When I confronted you... accosted you in Statue Square..."

"Yes, you did."

"I didn't mean those threats." Her eyes were wide. "I wouldn't tell the husbands."

He nodded. Of course she wouldn't. She'd be betraying the other women. And probably embarrassing the husbands.

"I just miss our relationship, Charles."

"Julia," he said firmly. "I understand, but it's over. Your husband—"

"My husband? He doesn't care. I don't know what he gets up to, but he's not interested in me."

"You'll find someone else."

"I don't want anyone else! I love you, Charles."

He shook his head. "I'm sorry, I need to go."

"Can I see you later?"

"No, Julia."

She stood stock-still, her hands by her sides. Then her body started shaking and, at first, he thought she was having a fit, but then the tears flowed, and the sobs started. She placed her head on his chest before he could react.

Instinctively, his hand went to her head, comforting. She moved closer, fit her body to his. Her hair smelled of fresh apples.

She said, "Take me upstairs."

The spell broke. "No." Balcombe disengaged and eased her away. "Bruce!"

The concierge reappeared.

Balcombe said, "Please would you make sure Mrs. Wendsley gets home safely?"

"Yes, sir."

As Balcombe left, Julia said, "If something happens to me, it'll be your fault."

Chapter Eighteen

Garrett had a supercilious smile on his face. Munro hadn't seen his colleague in plain-clothes for a couple of months. In fact, the last time had been when Garrett had been taken off the Squeezed-heart murder cases. He'd been humiliated by ill-conceived arrests and then returned to civilian duties. But here he was, looking smug and ready to challenge Munro for his job again.

"What have we got here?" Munro asked, trying to sound like they had a reasonable working relationship. He noted the Kowloon police had closed off the area and also spotted the local pathologists' van. No chance of involving his friend Yeung in this to cover it up. However he'd already come to that conclusion. It was too big and too far away. He'd hoped Kowloon would deal with it rather than flag up the killings to CID on the island.

Garrett didn't answer immediately. He strode away from the two bodies in the passageway and walked towards the quay.

"Two men killed there and one here," he said as he closed in on where a body lay on the concrete. "Sliced up."

Munro took a breath. "The Chief mentioned the Squeezed-heart cases. Is there any sign—"

"Looks like our killer was interrupted," Garrett said. He pointed as they got close enough. "He'd sliced off the man's shirt and slashed him across the chest."

There were deep cuts to the cadaver's face and arms. "More slashes than I've seen before," Munro said.

"It's our butcher."

"Maybe."

"What, Munro?" Garrett turned on him, a snarl on his lips. "You think because this looks slightly different that our killer isn't the same? I've told you before, Munro, killers change their style, they adapt. This murder looks more frenzied. All this blood." He nodded at his own thoughts. "This one was a fight. Others, he took by surprise. He would prefer to incapacitate first, but he cornered this chap, and they had a knife fight." Garrett paused and looked back along the quay. "But…"

Munro obliged: "But what?"

"Why did he stop? What interrupted him?"

I did, thought Munro.

They walked around and studied the body, and then the pathologist took over.

"Back to the other two," Garrett said.

They returned to the passage.

Munro looked closely at the two bodies on the ground. One had a puncture wound in his neck, the other had slashes to the face and a lot of blood on his chest.

"This one stabbed in the heart?" asked Munro.

"Close, we think."

"Rushed?"

Garrett nodded.

Munro looked back at the first body. "They confronted our man. He despatched one quickly with a knife to the neck. The second put up a bit of a fight."

"One in front, one behind," suggested Garrett.

Munro pointed to weapons on the floor. "They both had knives."

"Sir!" A uniformed constable jogged towards them. "Sir, we've found a witness."

★ ★ ★

The witness was an elderly Chinese lady, stooped and half blind. The constable spoke to her in Cantonese, and although Munro understood, the young policeman had to translate for Garrett.

She said, "There were men running along the dock last night."

"Where was she?" Garrett asked.

The constable spoke to her and then communicated a summary of her long answer. "She was on the quay. She was looking for goods—sometimes the fishermen leave reasonable fish. Sometimes the workers drop things."

"Ask her what she saw."

"She heard it. Gunshots."

"She just heard gunshots?" Garrett turned to Munro with widened eyes. "Other people—farther away—reported gunshots in Kowloon last night."

The woman spoke again, and the constable translated. "Before the gunshots, there were men running. And police."

"Police?" Garrett spoke to the constable. "Were any of your men out here last night?"

"Not as far as I'm aware, sir."

The woman spoke again. "They were chasing a young white man."

"There was a white man here?" Munro asked before the constable translated for Garrett.

"A boy," she said.

Munro looked at Garrett. "Our killer isn't a boy."

Garrett said, "Ask her if she saw anyone being stabbed."

The woman said, "Yes."

Garrett brightened up. "She saw the killer?"

"Yes."

"What did he look like?"

"It was dark."

"Was the man with the knife a white man?"

"I think so."

Garrett leaned in, excited. "Was it the boy you saw running? Did he have the knife?"

"I don't know."

Garrett leaned away and sighed. Munro breathed with relief. The woman hadn't seen anything incriminating. She waited, expecting more questions. When none came, she held out a hand to Garrett for payment.

He shook his head and gave a derisive snort. Then the woman switched her attention to Munro and expected payment. She was close and seemed to focus hard on his face.

"You!"

"What did she say?" Garrett asked.

The constable translated.

Garrett asked what she'd meant, but before he'd finished, the woman was already gabbling.

Munro shook his head.

The constable said, "She's claiming that the DI was here last night."

Munro shook his head again. His heart was a hammer in his chest.

"Munro?"

"She's just trying—"

Garrett scrutinized him. "Where were you last night?"

"This is nonsense." Munro looked away and then back. He felt that he'd just signposted his guilt and needed to defend himself. "I was in Kowloon last night, but not here," he said.

"Doing what?"

"Something for the Chief. Something off the books. You want to ask him to confirm that, you go ahead." Munro smiled inwardly. He could see the response had worked. Garrett wouldn't want to risk the Chief's wrath so soon after being reassigned the role.

Garrett thought for a moment, then dismissed the woman after handing her a few dollars and telling her to report anything else she saw or heard. Once she'd gone, he turned his attention back to Munro.

"Where was Charles Balcombe last night?"

"I'm not his keeper, Garrett."

"No, but you've been seen together."

"He's helping on the Chief's case."

"Does the Chief know?"

"Of course," Munro lied, knowing that Garrett wasn't about to check.

"And he wasn't here either last night?"

In case they'd been seen in the car or on the ferry Munro said, "He was with me early evening. We came over. He went back."

Garrett started walking to his car. Munro let him walk away, but after five paces, Garrett stopped and turned.

"Something's fishy, Munro, and I'm going to find out what stinks around here."

Chapter Nineteen

The second time he visited Doctor Georgina Swift in her office above the piano shop, Balcombe took the couch.

"I hope you've thought about yesterday, Charles. Are you ready to be honest? Totally honest?"

No, he thought. *Not the absolute truth. Not my history in Malaya or BlackJack. But everything else...*

"Yes."

"Then let's start with relationships."

Ah. After his meeting with Julia Wendsley, it seemed appropriate to talk about his relationship issues. But he hadn't expected Swift to bring it up. Did she have inside information?

"Tell me about your parents."

"My parents?" he asked, relieved. Not about Julia then. "They're Catholics. My mother was a strong woman. She had to be. She raised five boys and a girl and ran the home. She also worked in a haberdashery, raising some extra cash. My father is a senior doctor—a surgeon, or at least was. Harley Street in London." He felt foolish for adding *London*. Of course, she'd know where the famous Harley Street was.

He turned his head to see her face. Swift's eyes showed she was processing. "And?"

"And?"

"You could be more descriptive."

"Talk more about your father. About feelings," Swift said.

"I'm not sure he has any," Balcombe laughed mirthlessly. Her eyes suggested she knew he'd used humour to cover awkwardness.

She said, "Face forward, Charles."

"Why?"

"It's better if you aren't looking at me."

He turned away.

She said, "You were talking about your father. Describe him for me."

"A big man. Imposing. Stoic."

"Did he show you love?"

Balcombe shook his head. "But it didn't matter. And I didn't expect it."

"Think before you answer," she said. "Is there anything about the monster in your dreams that is your father?"

"No," he said a little too quickly.

Swift said nothing for a couple of beats, then asked, "Tell me about more about your relationship with your mother."

He shrugged.

"How was your childhood? How do you feel about her? Is she still alive? When was the last time you were in touch with her?"

"My mother left home when I was a child. She walked out one day and never contacted us again. How do I feel about her? I cared."

Swift wrote and waited. Eventually, she spoke in her slow cadence.

"Were you upset that she didn't get in touch?"

"I don't know how she could do it. I know her relationship with my father was cold. Thinking about it, maybe he was the cold one. Maybe she couldn't express her feelings because of him."

"Could you express your feelings?"

"At home?" Pause. "No. They lost a baby. My two eldest brothers died in the war. I never saw either of my parents cry. They soldiered on, I suppose."

"How did you cope?"

"I had my climbing. I had my friends." He paused for reflection. "My mother was the *rock* of our religion."

"How did she show that?"

"Her belief didn't waiver when her baby was stillborn. She told us 'Katherine's been called home to God as part of His plan that cannot be changed.' She also said we'd all meet again."

"She believes in fate?"

"Yes. The same when they received the telegram to say my two older brothers were dead."

"Do you believe we'll all meet again?"

Balcombe stared at the ceiling. He knew there was more. He'd felt a man's life-force leave the body. He'd squeezed hearts until the beating stopped and the spirit fled.

"Charles?"

"I believe we each have a soul. What happens to it after we die? We go to find the Great Perhaps."

"Is that a quote?"

"François Rabelais. Amazing scholar from the fifteenth century. He was a physician, among other things, and wrote chivalric romantic plays."

She said nothing for a moment, and he imagined her writing in her book.

"Chivalry," she said quietly.

"Adventurous knights."

"A code of behaviour combining loyalty, honour, and courtly love."

He hadn't thought about it until she mentioned it, but she'd nailed him; right down the love part. Because the knights didn't really get the girl and the romance was in their quarries' heads.

"Tell me about your girlfriend."

"I have more than one."

"Oh?"

He'd thought about excluding his liaisons from the discussion but decided only his fake identity and his alter ego should be out of bounds. She didn't know about Julia but she'd told him to be honest.

"No names," he said and then told her he was seeing four women concurrently.

"That seems a lot."

"It was six until recently."

"All married?"

"Yes. How did you—?"

"When was the last time you had a girlfriend, by the usual definition?"

"I haven't." He took a breath, expecting a barrage of revealing questions, but they didn't come. Instead, she switched subjects by asking about his passion for climbing.

"Without ropes?" she asked after he'd talked for a few minutes.

"Yes." He realized his pulse had quickened. The thrill of the danger.

"Don't stop."

"I have another quote for you," he said. "There are two means of escape from the misery of life. Women and climbing."

"Albert Schweitzer," she said. "Again, manipulated for your own ends." He thought he heard a smile in her voice. "Music and cats were Schweitzer's great loves."

Balcombe tilted his head and cocked an eyebrow at the pretty doctor. She met his gaze but didn't comment.

"Cats?" he said derisively.

After a pause, she said, "Pick an animal."

"A crocodile."

"Why a crocodile?"

"I don't know, just a random selection."

"It's never random. Your brain selected that animal for a reason. Think about it."

"Maybe because its prehistoric. It's a survivor."

"It's a killer. A monster."

"That's good," he said, "but before you ask, the monster in my dreams isn't a crocodile."

"What is it?"

He ignored the question. "Crocodiles are fast and adaptable. They're clinical."

"Most people choose a dog or another kind of pet."

"I never had a pet."

She wrote in her book. "Interesting."

"Why is it interesting?"

"We'll talk about that next time."

He sat up, checked his watch. "We've five more minutes. Tell me now."

"Most people who have pets learn about care, responsibility and love."

"You're connecting this to my inability to form serious relationships."

"I didn't call them that."

"You didn't need to."

"You protect yourself. It's a defence mechanism. If you don't get emotionally involved, you can't be hurt."

"I don't fear being hurt. When I climb, I'm fearless."

She said nothing.

"When Charles died from a fall, I questioned my faith, but I've heard his voice since. I've learned that the only thing we have to fear is fear itself." Another quote, he realized. He sat and faced her.

She was looking at him piercingly.

"I didn't manipulate that quote, if that's what you're implying."

She shook her head. "Who was Charles?"

"Charles? Did I say Charles? I meant Eric. Eric was my best friend. I looked up to him. My hero, I suppose."

"Your role model." She said it as a statement of fact.

"Yes. We were both just teenagers."

"Think on that until tomorrow," she said.

He stood to go and held her hand again, but she withdrew it first this time.

"I thought you'd ask how I slept last night."

"How did you sleep?"

"No better."

"It was only the first session."

"How long will it take?"

"I don't know. As long as it takes."

He shook his head. "You've got to give me more than that, Doc."

She ran her tongue lightly over her front teeth.

"I wouldn't normally do this, but... but I think you can deal with it. Dreams help us process information. They take the conscious and subconscious thoughts and try to make sense of them in a story. You are anxious whether you admit it or not. For one man it could be an existential issue. Their subconscious might find their life meaningless."

"That doesn't sound like a monster chasing me."

"Stress takes all forms," she said. "Your challenge is to identify what is causing the stress and face it head on. We'll talk more tomorrow."

Chapter Twenty

Nine days gone

The following day, Munro was back at the Cosmopolitan Dockyard. Garrett was off somewhere else and not focusing on the location of the killing. Munro, on the other hand, was still looking for Geoff Tanner, his only lead to finding the missing girl.

Before travelling across to Kowloon, he'd called in at Government House and updated Ernest Albright. He knew it wouldn't go well. It was a week to the day since his first meeting with Albright.

"And that's all you have?" Albright said through clenched teeth. "You've seen where you think she stayed—in a shed for goodness sake! You think she's running with this Tanner kid. And he might have been seen last night at a drugs deal in Kowloon."

Munro said nothing. Albright was correct, but it was interesting that he was finally showing emotion.

Albright was shaking his head. "It's not good enough."

"With respect, sir, it would help—"

"What would help?" Albright snapped.

"If you could tell me more. For example, why do you think Patricia ran away?"

Albright didn't speak immediately, then said, "Well now, I think it's obvious. We had a disagreement about who she keeps company with."

"And that's it?"

"DI Munro, I would appreciate it if you pay that respect you mentioned just now and remember who you're talking to."

And that was it. So Munro was back at the docks hoping for divine inspiration. He walked the way Tanner had run, between the warehouses, to the crossroads, past the wrecked man in the doorway to the shed with a Judas door.

The larger doors were wide open and black bales were being hauled away on carts. He stood to one side and watched. He'd come so close, assuming it had been Tanner inside last night. Had the young man known the Judas door would be open or had it been opportunistic?

When there was a lull in activity through the doors, Munro went inside. The smells from last night immediately took his mind back. But it was light now, and the bales no longer loomed threateningly.

He asked for a foreman and found the man in a cramped office. In Cantonese, he asked whether the white boy had been seen. He hadn't.

Munro explained what had happened, and the foreman said that the Judas door was broken. Anyone could get in although there was nothing worth stealing that a man could carry alone or get it back through the little door. And then he said something that sounded interesting.

"We have a problem with opium addicts around here. They just use the place to sleep and recover."

"But no white boys?"

"Not that I've seen, although you could ask Liu."

Liu turned out to be a part-time street vendor, part-time nightwatchman. When Munro met him, he realized he'd seen him before. It was the man from the doorway, two nights ago. He hadn't been wasted; he'd been watching the warehouse for vagrants although Munro quickly established why he'd been hunched up in the doorway. Lui had been asleep on the job.

He hadn't seen the boy go in, but he'd heard the commotion.

"I was about to check what was going on," he said meekly in an accent that wasn't native, "when the boy barged into me and ran off."

Lui hadn't been outside when Munro had left the warehouse. Had he also scarpered?

"You followed him?" Munro said, hoping for some good news.

"Yes, sir!" Munro waited expectantly as Lui found the words. "But I lost him."

"Did you see him well?"

"A little."

Munro showed the man the photograph of Geoff Tanner. "Was it him?"

Lui pursed his lips and shook his head. "I want to say yes, but I'm not certain. If I saw him again, I'd recognize him."

Munro put the photograph back in his wallet. "Do you think he's from around here?"

Lui shook his head. "Of course not!"

"But you'd seen him before?"

"The night before. He was looking for the boat…" He stopped and appeared awkward.

"Where they sell the drugs?"

The excuse for a nightwatchman breathed. "Yes, sir! He was looking around. "At the time, I thought it was odd. He was probably looking for someone selling opium."

Munro gave the man some coins and thanked him for his information. Of course Geoff Tanner was here about the drugs, but the night-watchman's story told him something important. Tanner didn't know where to buy them. If he was a dealer himself, he hadn't bought at the Cosmopolitan Docks before.

As Munro turned to leave, the nightwatchman touched Munro's sleeve. "Another dollar?"

"Do you know something else?"

"I know you could talk to the men from the boat."

Munro shook his head. "They won't talk to me."

Lui grinned. A policeman asking questions of an armed drug dealer? Nothing good would come of it.

Lui held out his hand. "Not that."

Munro hesitated then handed over the note.

Lui stuffed it in his vest and grinned again. "I know where one of the men lives. He'll talk for ten, maybe twenty dollars... providing you have someone who doesn't look like a policeman."

Chapter Twenty-One

On Doctor Georgina Swift's couch, Balcombe said, "I remember my dream from last night. It was different but it's one I've had before."

"Did you think about your stresses and try to face them?"

"Yes, and I didn't drink too much. I let the dream come."

Her pencil was poised. "Tell me what you remember."

"I'm in a big house. I don't know the place and yet it seems familiar. I'm not a stranger if that makes sense?"

"What do you think?"

"I think it's because I know it, but don't know it. And that's not because I've had the dream before."

"What happens?"

"I walk down a corridor. It's nicely decorated." He paused. "It feels homely."

She nodded.

"Why did you nod?"

"Remember, it's better if you don't look at me, Charles." She paused as he looked away. "Now, is it your home—a home from the past?"

"No." He paused. "At least I didn't think so, but now you ask…"

"You recognize it?"

"I've a sense more than anything. It feels like my childhood home."

"You are walking down a corridor. What happens next?"

"There are doors on both sides. I'm compelled to open them."

"What's inside?"

"Most of the rooms are empty."

"Most?"

"I know the monster is lurking in one of them."

"It scares you?"

"Yes."

"But you're looking for him. It is a *him* isn't it?"

"Yes."

"Did you find him last night?"

"Yes."

"What happened?"

"We fought. I stabbed him over and over."

She waited for more.

After a pause, he said, "I couldn't win. I stabbed, and it broke up and became a thousand spiders—big black ones with hairy legs."

"They scared you too?"

"I suppose that's fair to say. They're repulsive. I wanted to kill them."

"And did you?"

"I stabbed at them, over and over, but they didn't die. They darted away. Their big, hairy legs scurried. I couldn't catch them. And that's when my knife turned into a hammer. I could hit them. I pounded down with the hammer, squashing their bulbous bodies. And blood spurted out. But not like you'd expect. Not a spray. It came out in clumps, like blood clots. But it didn't end. The more I hit, the more they came at me. And then I realized that the blood clots were spiders too, and I was creating more new ones each time I smashed an old one."

"And then?"

"And then I woke up."

"Was there anyone else in the house?"

He thought about it. "Maybe. It feels like there are other people, but I never see them."

She asked more questions about the dream, and he sensed she was probing to connect the monster of his recurring dream with the spiders. Or perhaps it was the house.

"I can't kill the spiders. I can't kill the monster in my head."

She said, "Let's not dwell on those specifics for the rest of the session. I want to talk about sex."

"Doc!" He swivelled to look at her and grinned. Her response was a look that could freeze a bay.

"Your relationships with your so-called girlfriends..."

"Yes." He turned his attention to the ceiling.

"Do you think it's normal and healthy?"

He chuckled. "I think many men would choose that in favour of a staid marriage." He shrugged. "The amount of trade prostitutes get attests to that, I think. The benefit I have is my women aren't prostitutes. I know they want it. It's not about money."

"Sex with no commitment."

"Yes. And excitement."

"Danger?"

"Yes."

"Why does that appeal to you?"

"It makes the heart race. It makes me feel alive."

"Have you ever been caught in the act?"

"No, but it's come close. The closer the better, I suppose. Otherwise it's too safe."

"Climbing without ropes is dangerous. Is that the same thing?"

"Yes."

"Yesterday, you told me your friend, Charles—I mean Eric—died from a fall. Have you almost died climbing? Have you fallen and been hurt?"

"Yes. It's the possibility that's the thrill, I suppose. Life affirming."

"Have you ever thought about letting it happen? Have you stood on a cliff edge and thought about throwing yourself off?"

"Yes."

She nodded. "It's perfectly normal. The way our minds work is to consider options. The thought process is lightning fast and most of the time we don't notice it. We consider crazy things and then dismiss them as crazy. Does that make sense?"

"I suppose."

"When you try to kill the spiders, how do you feel?"

"Repulsed by them."

"Let me ask you something. Are you repulsed by yourself?"

"I don't believe so."

"Imagine that the spiders die when you hit them. Think about that now. Imagine it. How does it feel?"

"I don't know. Nothing. I have a job to do. I need to kill them."

"Would you feel their pain?"

"No."

"Is there anything else about the dream?"

"No." He waited a beat. "Well, yes. After the dream. When I wake up, I feel like I'm still in the dream. It's a psychedelic experience, I suppose. Nothing has proper focus. Sometimes the monster is still there. I see a hand trying to throttle me or strike me—but I can't quite see it.

I can't ward it off. It feels like a long time before I can grasp reality."

Swift was writing frantically in her book. When she stopped, she looked at him expectantly.

"Have you thought about what might be causing you stress?"

BlackJack is taking over more often. That was his stress. He recognized it, recognized the loss of control, but couldn't tell the psychoanalyst.

"I have a comfortable life."

"That you put at risk."

"I enjoy the risk. It makes me feel alive."

She nodded thoughtfully. "Why do you need to feel alive?"

He had no answer to that except an obvious glib one: life is for living. What's the point of existing without feeling the thrill?

She said, "When did the hallucinations start?"

"I don't remember, but they're becoming more frequent. Maybe they're causing the stress."

She said nothing.

He added: "It's not linked to the drinking."

"Do you drink too much?"

Roy Faulls thought so, but she wasn't willing to discuss other people's opinions. Balcombe didn't think there was a direct correlation between the blackouts, hallucinations and alcoholic oblivion. Although the nightmares were worse.

He said, "It helps me sleep."

"Alcohol isn't the solution. You're an intelligent man. You know this."

He nodded, looked at her.

She pointed to her desk. "Before we end today, I'd like to try something."

She picked up the statuette he'd noticed when he'd first entered the room. The goblin from the desk, not the model Eiffel Tower on the shelf.

"Look at it. Feel the contours and describe what you see and feel."

"It's a silver statue about six inches tall. It's an elf... no, I'd say it's a goblin. Funny looking. Ugly."

"Tell me more. Close your eyes."

"It's weighty with a heavy base. The feel is smooth and cold metal. And it's knobbly."

"Squeeze it. Feel its solidity. Feel *the reality*."

He squeezed hard until his knuckles strained.

"It feels real."

She said, "Focus on it. It *is* real. It is the only thing in the room apart from my voice. Now inhale to the count of three." She waited. "Exhale to the count of five. Nice and slow." She waited. "Good, now repeat and think of the... goblin, think of how it feels—all the smoothness and lumps. The shape. The reality."

After five times, she told him to stop and open his eyes. "Next time you feel you can't grasp reality—coming out of a dream or maybe during or in a blackout—grasp something, focus on it and do the breathing."

He nodded. "Thank you."

"We made good progress today, Charles. You're opening up, being honest with me, but more importantly yourself. Let's get you through this."

Chapter Twenty-Two

Balcombe travelled with Albert to the east of Kowloon City. It was all the way around Kowloon Bay and had once been called Chinese Town. It was where Lui the nightwatchman had told Munro he could find one of the drug dealers. As a policeman, Munro knew the dealer wouldn't speak to him. When he'd told Balcombe, Balcombe knew he wouldn't stand a chance either. Albert was a different matter. She was Chinese and no threat.

However Balcombe wasn't about to let her go alone. He insisted on travelling to the remote region with her, but he'd keep his distance. He would only intervene if there was trouble.

They travelled after nightfall, but the skies were clear and the sliver of a moon highlighted a multitude of boats and a low level wharf.

"There won't be trouble, master," she said as they drew up to a quay.

"Famous last words, Albert."

"Really?"

He grinned. "I don't know, but they should have been."

Albert climbed ashore, and Balcombe was about to follow when their pilot said something.

Albert translated. "It's too dangerous for a white man."

Balcombe dressed all in black, but his face could give him away. He snatched up a sack from the boat and wrapped it over his head and shoulders. With a stoop, he hoped he would be mistaken for an old woman. Maybe an old fisherwoman, since the sack reeked of rotten fish. He hoped it was worth it.

The Chinese pilot spoke again.

"He wants payment," Albert said.

"Tell him we need the return journey. He's to wait."

Albert and the man exchanged quiet but heated words.

"He wants it now—in case you don't return."

Balcombe noted that it wasn't *we* don't return. While Balcombe had been worried about Albert, the pilot was concerned about his paymaster.

"Fine," Balcombe said. He handed over the notes and looked the man in the eye. "I want to return. You don't go anywhere."

The man nodded.

Albert spoke.

The man nodded again.

"I told him I know his face and his family," she said. "If he isn't here when we get back, he'll regret it."

Balcombe grinned.

The township was the last before the hills, with China beyond them. After the quay, the place consisted mainly of temporary buildings. The sewage system, if it existed, was clearly inadequate and Balcombe soon became oblivious to the smell of his head garb.

Albert walked ten yards ahead and clearly knew where she was going, despite the lack of distinctive streets.

No one questioned her until she reached the destination.

Balcombe shrank back as a man came through a door and confronted her. When the man moved, Balcombe saw a machete.

He slid closer, still judging he'd be too slow should the man suddenly strike her.

The exchange took three seconds before the man stepped aside and Albert passed through the door and into darkness.

Balcombe could hear his own breathing, loud in the night. Dogs barked, someone shouted, and something rat-like scratched around his feet.

Come on, Albert!

He'd given her two photographs just in case. Lui, the nightwatchman had mentioned a boy, so she had the picture of Geoff Tanner. Balcombe had also provided Albert with Patricia's picture since she was who they really wanted. Tanner was just the lead to finding her.

And each lead seems to take us further away, he thought.

Movement in the doorway. Albert appeared. She didn't walk towards him. Instead, she scuttled right. Balcombe was just debating how he could follow when he heard a sound behind.

"Master," Albert whispered. "Let's go."

They retraced their steps to the quay, Balcombe desperate for an update.

Their boat was where they'd left it, and Albert didn't speak until they were under-sail.

"I did a deal with the man," she said. "I gave him all the money and he told me a lie. He'll pay me half when I go back. An introduction fee, you'd call it."

Balcombe said nothing.

"All right, I confess, I was joking. I'm not very funny. They searched me and took all your money, but I don't think he told me a lie."

"You showed him the photographs? Did he see or deal with Geoff Tanner?"

"Firstly, he was one of the men on the quay at Cosmopolitan Dock. He confirmed that. He also confirmed that a white boy with a satchel had bought drugs. And…" she stopped. "You can remove the smelly sacking now, master."

Balcombe had forgotten his disguise and quickly cast it to the floor.

"And?" he prompted.

"It wasn't Tanner. He said the transaction was odd. He couldn't explain why. He was suspicious of it being a trap, but of course it wasn't."

"He didn't know about DI Munro?"

"He didn't mention police. Oh, and I asked him about *Bai Long* and he showed no recognition."

Clever girl! Balcombe hadn't asked her to check whether the drug dealers were linked to the gang mentioned by Van Ness's man. He'd thought it too dangerous.

She continued: "And he hadn't seen the girl." She paused. "I'm sorry. This lack of information has cost you thirty dollars."

Balcombe travelled the rest of the way in silence. Thinking. It had cost thirty-two dollars, including the taxi boat, but it hadn't been for nothing. As a military police trainer at Mytchett Hutments in Hampshire had explained. *Learning nothing is learning something.* That had made the men laugh, but the trainer had been deadly serious. He'd said that if you learn information is incorrect, then you can cross it off. Policing isn't just the identification of the facts, it's the elimination of the non-facts.

So, it hadn't been Tanner buying drugs at Cosmopolitan Dock. It had been someone else. The drug dealers thought it was odd. What was the boy up to?

Balcombe stared at the dancing, moonlit black water.

Munro had chased after the boy. The boy hadn't wanted to get caught. That was understandable.

But did the white boy want to be seen?

Chapter Twenty-Three

Ten days gone

Munro received a message from Balcombe about the visit to Chinese Town last night. Balcombe was a good investigator and thought the lack of information helped in some way. In Munro's experience, it was rarely like that. What a detective needed was luck. Although a good detective created his own luck.

BlackJack had killed four nights ago west of Victoria and three nights ago and at Cosmopolitan Dock. Last night, he'd taken a huge gamble by visiting the Chinese-only region. Had he killed again? Was this all coming to a head?

At the hospital, Fai Yeung reported no bodies for last night. He placed a call through to his counterpart in Kowloon and got the same message.

"You were worried he'd struck again, Babyface," said Yeung. It wasn't a question.

Munro shook his head. "Just checking."

"This can't go on."

"It won't."

Yeung raised his eyebrows.

Munro added: "Georgina Swift is seeing him."

Again the eyebrows. "She was here earlier, popped in to speak to her father."

"She's still around?"

Yeung didn't know, so Munro went in search of the psychoanalyst.

He found her on the second floor between wards.

"Doctor Swift," he called.

She turned and smiled.

He said, "You're seeing Charles Balcombe… He's helping me on a case."

"Ah," she said, and checked her watch.

Munro asked how it was going. He explained he knew Balcombe had issues and needed to know whether they would be a problem. "For me and the police," he said hopefully.

She nodded. "I wouldn't normally… but since he's working with you… Charles Balcombe has a strong moral compass. So much so, I would say that he has a formal policing background. What's interesting is that he plays the role of a detective and yet denies any training. He plays the role of a carefree playboy as well, but that's not him."

"It's not?"

"He has a lot of bottled-up secrets."

"Bottled up?"

"Secrets can either be deliberately withheld or unconscious." She raised her hand in a shrug although he suspected it was just a signal to offset a difficult subject.

"Tell me what you see," Munro said.

She checked her watch again. "I really need—"

"Just briefly."

"He is bold and charming. He's carefree and impulsive."

"And that means?"

"Well, he has narcissistic tendencies."

Munro nodded. "You, yourself described him as a playboy."

"Absolutely, but what I'm saying is he uses those to cover… no, *suppress* is a better word… to suppress his true self."

She checked her watch again. "If that's all, Detective Inspector…?"

"Briefly… can you help him?"

She took a breath. "The drinking… the nightmares… hallucinations. There's been some trauma in his past… We haven't got to it yet, but I should think so."

She hadn't mentioned blackouts or violence. Munro started to speak, but she waved him down.

"I'm sorry, I've got to go. Hopefully that's helpful. Another time?" And with that, she hurried away.

Chapter Twenty-Four

After the hospital, Munro spent the morning travelling around the island talking to his snitches.

The conversation with Georgina Swift kept playing in his head. Swift and Balcombe both believed the introduction had been through Faulls, but Munro had told Faulls. They both knew Balcombe needed help although Munro was sure Faulls didn't get the whole picture. He just thought Balcombe had a drink and nightmare problem. That's also what Swift seemed to think. No mention of blackouts or BlackJack killings. Just a nightmare.

It certainly is a nightmare—for me too, Munro mused.

He was on his fourth snitch when he got a positive response.

"I've heard something about the girl." The snitch whispered through the side of his mouth.

Munro pretended they weren't talking to one another.

"Patricia Albright?" he whispered back.

"Yes. And in connection with *Bai Long*." The man turned briefly to squint at the inspector.

Munro slid five dollars into the man's hand.

The snitch gave an address in west Victoria and said, "Ask for Lucky Tony."

* * *

Lucky Tony, it transpired, knew nothing. He wondered if *Bai Long* or White Dragon was referring to a brand of drugs. But he was just speculating and trying to earn some money. He said he knew Patricia but couldn't describe her. Rather than show her photograph, Munro said her eyes and hair colour were different. He said she was Eurasian and Tony agreed.

So, he hadn't even seen her. He knew nothing.

Tony was just a chancer.

Today, the detective hadn't made his own luck.

Munro stepped out onto the street. A rickshaw went past, the passenger complaining at a woman who had got in the way. The streets were busy with people preferring the shade and causing constrictions and chaos. Munro looked left and back to get his timing right. And that's when he spotted a man. He'd seen him before. He'd seen thousands before, but this one set the hairs on his neck tingling. Because on both occasions, the man had been looking at him and then away. Once could be explained as chance, but two consecutive days meant trouble.

Perhaps it was a lucky day after all.

Munro moved into the flow and headed away from the observer. He didn't hurry; he walked with purpose, looking straight ahead, concerned only with the traffic and collisions.

At the first junction, he went left and into the bright sunlight. There were fewer pedestrians here and doors instead of open shopfronts. A gap between buildings came up, and he took it, then stopped and turned. He drew his revolver and counted. He predicted five seconds and was out by one. On the count of six, a man hurried into the passageway.

He leapt backwards like a scolded cat as soon as Munro moved. The man held up his hands, his Japanese face full of fear as he regarded Munro's gun.

"I'm a police officer," Munro barked as a handful of other people darted away. "I could shoot you!"

The Japanese man stood rigid. "No! No, don't shoot... please!"

"Why were you following me?"

The man took a deep breath to calm himself. "You are Munro, no?"

"Who are you?"

"My name is Kaito Hashimoto." He took another calming breath. "Please, can I put down my hands?"

"Are you armed?"

"No!"

People filtered back into the street. A rough semicircle of onlookers gathered.

"Raise your coat and turn around slowly."

The man complied, and Munro assessed him as he did so. He was in his late twenties with the bearing of a soldier, but a softness to him. Unthreatening. There was no obvious weapon.

"I'm unarmed. You don't know me, but I know you," Hashimoto said.

Munro lowered his gun but didn't holster it. "What do you want?"

"I want to say sorry... for your wife."

Munro's world blurred. He sensed what was coming, but instead of anger and focus, his head spun. And suddenly he was on the street with his beautiful wife Yan. They'd survived under Japanese rule in what had been called New Hong Kong. Until that fateful day when Yan looked at a soldier in the wrong way. The occupiers expected deference and respect. They expected heads lowered and eyes averted, and before Munro realized what she'd done, a soldier was upon her. Then three others. Munro had tried to protect her from the blows. He saw her crumple; he saw her blood and then he saw her limp body lose its life-spark. He hadn't fought back and blamed himself every day for merely taking some blows from the soldier's sticks.

Nine years of pain.

Bile surged into his throat. His focus came back to the present. The Japanese soldier was standing in front of him, still holding out the edges of his jacket.

"You!" The words from Munro's mouth sounded far off, alien. He'd dreamed of this moment a thousand times, although in his imagination he'd hunted this man down. He'd tracked him and cornered him and made him beg for his life. It always ended the same way. Munro shot him once in the head and once through the heart.

The ex-soldier looked at him with sad eyes. He was speaking but the words didn't register. Munro raised the gun. At the same time, he heard a whistle and then the crowd started to move. It swelled and ebbed like a single organism. Munro's focus was on the man's breast pocket—his heart. End it. Blow away the monster who had shattered his life.

"Police! Police!"

The crowd was pulling away and replaced by three uniformed officers.

"Put the gun down!" one was yelling. Munro switched his attention to the man. "Put the gun down!"

The three policemen were closing in. They were coming for him!

"I'm going to shoot!" The lead policemen said.

Munro dropped his arm. "I'm a DI!"

The nearest man's expression changed. It went from aggression to horror faster than a strike of lightning.

"Sir... Sir, the sunlight. I couldn't see..."

Munro swung his attention back to the Japanese soldier. But he wasn't there.

"Idiots!" Munro pushed past the remorseful policemen, ignoring their further protestations of innocence. He drove through the remaining people on the side street, scanning left and right. He hit the main street fast, still scanning, still hoping to spot a Japanese man in a tan jacket, probably hurrying away. People everywhere.

He'd gotten away.

Munro tensed, hands balled, and raised his face to the burning sky. "No!" he screamed. "No!"

He'd had his one chance to avenge Yan's death. Life might give you one shot to put things right. It had to be taken. Then and there.

He'd failed nine years ago, and now he'd failed her again.

Chapter Twenty-Five

When Munro got back to the office, a young DC, called James Tattersall, flagged him down.

"Sir, we've had a phone call from Kowloon. One of your cases. They've a body matching your description—"

"Male or female?" Munro asked, feeling his chest tighten. Was Patricia dead?

"Male."

Thirty minutes later, Munro was in the morgue below the Kowloon police HQ. He'd inserted Vaseline up his nose to deaden the smell.

The assistant pathologist beamed. "Welcome, Inspector Munro."

"You have a body for me?"

"This way." He walked over to a trolley and pulled back the sheet that covered a body. "Is it him?"

The body was bloated and gray, but there was no doubt. It was Geoff Tanner.

Munro nodded.

"You'll take him?" The pathologist's eyebrows rose with expectation.

"Yes, you can get him shipped over to the island." He looked again at the body. "He's been in the water."

"For more than a day, but my preliminary assessment is that he didn't drown. Since you're taking him, Fai Yeung will be able to do the PM but my guess is that he was strangled with a rope." He indicted welts on Tanner's neck. "And was bound at some point." There were thinner marks on both wrists. "And there's this…" He rolled the body and showed a number of burn marks. Munro quickly counted eleven of them.

"Torture?" he asked.

"Looks that way. Fai will confirm. And when you see him, I've got a joke."

Munro waited. It seemed the pathologists lightened their dark lives with humour.

The man said, "Ask him how many fish it takes to eat a dead clown."

Munro nodded. "All right, and what's the answer?"

"None. They won't touch a clown because he'll taste funny." The pathologist laughed.

Munro shook his head. The corny joke didn't lighten his mood. Geoff Tanner had been murdered. And since he'd been running with Patricia Albright, the prospects for her were looking increasingly grim.

Chapter Twenty-Six

The CID team in the office that day saw Inspector Garrett in with Chief Carmichael. There was no shouting. They'd notice that. They'd notice the Chief was treating him like a detective again.

Garrett was the Commissioner's man, brought over from the Suez to get improved results. He knew the Chief hadn't been totally bought-in, but the latest murders had sharpened his mind.

Garrett nodded to the men as he left the office. Not long and he'd be running this team. They'd be his men.

He'd been reviewing the files again. Two months out, doing civil policing roles hadn't dulled his memory. When he read through the first Squeezed-heart murder, he was delighted with how much he remembered. The man who'd been holding and selling young women above a laundry had been stabbed in the neck. The victim hadn't put up a fight, so the blade probably paralysed him. His chest had been surgically sliced open before something—they assumed a hand—had been inserted and stopped the man's heart. What Garrett was most interested in was the witness statements that mentioned a tall white man with facial hair. There was no agreement as to whether he had a beard or just a moustache.

Charles Balcombe had a moustache. And he was tall and white. Granted, there were hundreds of Islanders who matched that simple description. But Balcombe's name kept cropping up.

Garrett flicked through the *Sham Shui Murders* file. Six men killed in a building. Interesting that they were also holding girls as prisoners. They were probably part of the same business. The man above the laundry being the middleman, perhaps.

Garrett didn't think that was the reason for the killings, however. Could one man kill all six on his own? The accepted wisdom was that the murders had been by a rival gang, but there were clues suggesting a single attacker. All the victims had been killed with a knife. Not just stabbed. Most of the cuts were clean and surgical. One of the men had been mutilated, again with surgical precision.

The logical conclusion was that the killer had medical training. Was he a doctor and rival gang member?

The killing of the man known as Pingping had been concluded as gang-related. Garrett opened his file while keeping the Sham Shui one open.

Pingping had been sliced open, and his guts spilled. He'd been brutalized pre-mortem. He'd woken up and crawled before the shock and loss of blood had killed him.

And that case had similarities with the murder of a pig butcher six months earlier. He'd also been sliced open, and his guts exposed.

He'd also been hung on a meat hook.

The butcher had no connection with a gang as far as anyone knew. But he did have a predilection for abusing young women. The police hadn't proved he'd killed the girl found in cold storage, but it was highly probable.

A surgeon and a strong man. It would have taken considerable strength to have lifted the butcher onto the meat hook.

Another case. A low-life in Kowloon. Not stabbed in the neck, but probably knocked unconscious first. Very similar to the first Squeezed-heart case. And there were the witness statements. Nothing for the butcher. Nothing for Pingping, but in the Kowloon Squeezed-heart case, two people reported a white man with a moustache seen in the area.

The three dead men at Cosmopolitan Dock were all slashed. One had a puncture wound in his neck. Was it the same killer? It looked like a fight, more frenzied than other killings. These men weren't drunk or drugged. The murderer hadn't taken them by surprise. The old woman, the only witness, had mentioned gunshots.

Was the killer fighting for his life? Was that the difference?

If only the old woman wasn't half-blind. She thought it had been a white man but couldn't be sure. Garrett was sure. He felt it in his gut.

One of those men had been stabbed in the heart, or close to it.

What did the cases show? What was the killer's profile? Tall and white. Probably moustachioed. He had medical training. He killed men. Bad men. A vigilante possibly? He might be obsessed with the heart. He was brutal. He was a skilled fighter.

The man knew how to fight with a knife, how to use a knife. Garrett couldn't rule out that he was more than just a knife-man. There were plenty of other murders, but nothing ticked the same boxes.

There had been five other murders in recent months, stabbings that could have been similar. One witness statement mentioned a tall white man dressed all in black.

The climber's rope hanging from the building where Pingping was slaughtered. The masseur had provided a statement before he'd been released. He'd attested that the rope had been his. But Garrett didn't believe him. However he could find no logical justification for the lie.

Tall, white with a moustache and a climber. Climbers would be fit and strong.

Charles Balcombe was a climber.

Balcombe had admitted being near the laundry earlier in the day before the first Squeezed-heart murder. He'd been in Sham Shui on the day of the six murders there.

He'd also visited a Japanese girl on the evening before she'd been stabbed to death. Admittedly, the stabbing hadn't been surgical and seemed an act of passion, but Balcombe had been there.

He'd been in Kowloon on the day of the Cosmopolitan Dock murders.

Could it be him? Again, the ache in Garrett's gut said Balcombe was a prime suspect.

What he didn't know was whether Balcombe could use a knife. Charles Balcombe was a socialite—or at least seemed to be. He had money, and he enjoyed it. He didn't work, but his backstory seemed fake. Balcombe claimed to be employed by the British Government. He implied that he worked in Intelligence. He seemed to have detective skills, but enquiries turned up nothing. The police commissioner knew nothing and said the governor hadn't been informed. Which meant Balcombe wasn't in Hong Kong on official business.

Garrett didn't believe Balcombe's story.

He sat and thought. How could he trap Balcombe? He scratched at his unkept gray bread. Could he expose Balcombe's skill with a knife? How could he achieve that? How?

He pondered, and gradually, a plan formed in his mind.

Chapter Twenty-Seven

Balcombe was back in Georgina Swift's office. Piano music sounded flat through the floorboards. Bach, he thought. Prelude in C Major, possibly, but he wasn't sure.

He took the chair. She watched him.

"Can we just chat today?" he asked.

"All right," she said uncertainly.

"I mean more two way. More of a conversation."

"Less analytical?" she said, nodding.

"That's fine."

"Thanks. I didn't have a nightmare last night, but I had the hallucination again. The focusing helped a little, although I struggled to find something."

"It doesn't need to be anything special. You can use the fabric you're lying on or grab a handful of earth. Let's try it again with the statue."

She handed him the silver goblin, and he went through the routine of describing what he felt and his breathing.

"Excellent," she said as he handed it back. "I'd like you to visualize your father. If that's all right, Charles? Just conversation." She waited. "What do you see?"

"A proud man. He's tall."

"You're looking up? Are you a child?"

"Yes, I suppose so."

"How does he feel about you?"

"I don't know... disappointment?"

"Why is he disappointed?"

"I had been doing well with my studies. He made me read medical books. He was pleased but I didn't enjoy it. I told him I didn't want to be doctor."

"He wanted you to follow in his footsteps?"

"Yes, but I wasn't interested. I wanted to read history."

"Apart from teaching, did he spend time with you—personal time?"

"I remember him reading to me when I was very young. I remember his deep voice more than the stories."

"Where were you when he read?"

"In bed, before I went to sleep."

"Ever anywhere else?"

"No, it was only my sister who sat on his knee."

"How did you feel about her being close to him—closer than you were?"

"I don't know. I suppose I just accepted it. He carried me once when I fell and gashed my shin."

Swift paused for a beat. "He wasn't your role model. Your friend Eric was who you looked up to."

Balcombe nodded. "My father was boring. Eric was exciting."

She wrote in her notebook. Balcombe became aware that the piano music was no longer playing.

"Did you see your parents show affection to one another?"

"I don't... No, in my memory, they're always separate... cold."

She asked more questions about his family and his feelings before changing tack.

"Yesterday you mentioned marriages being staid. Are all relationships between couples dull and boring?"

"Mine aren't."

"Sex with no commitment."

He detected something in her tone. "Are you analyzing or judging me, Georgina?"

"Sorry, you just wanted to talk."

"Yes."

"All right. I was thinking about the instinctive drive," she said. "The urge to have sex and reproduce."

"The ID," Balcombe said. "I read about Freudian Theory last night."

"Very good. My theory deviates from an ID, ego and super-ego model. I'm not debunking the theory, you understand? I just find in my line of work—"

Balcombe's eyes swept the room. "You mean you're not a psychoanalyst?"

"I have three jobs. This private one is in its infancy. My main is at the hospital."

"Of course," he said.

"And I do a bit of work for the police—trying to understand the criminal mind. From my studies, I've concluded that a third of the mind is darkness."

"Darkness?"

"A term I use for the crazy things. Thoughts of taking ridiculous risks. Thoughts of doing something that will kill us. The last component is the rational overlay. It's the part of the brain that says, 'Hey, jumping off this cliff will kill you. You don't want to do that!' So you don't."

"Some people do."

She breathed in and out. "Yes, they do. For those people, the darkness has gained the upper hand. It may only be for a moment, but the rational part is unable to stop the act."

He said nothing.

She said, "The same is true of evil acts." She paused, then: "The criminals I have analyzed may have committed heinous acts. Some of them are remorseful, others are not. It depends on whether the rational brain has been delayed and succumbed to a moment of craziness or whether the darkness has over-developed."

"Can you cure those people?"

"No. I'm afraid I can't cure anyone. However I can provide the tools to help the subject find their own cure. The first part of the journey is the recognition of the problem." She said nothing for a few minutes, letting him process her words. Then she said, "The room with the spiders…"

"My darkness? I want to destroy it."

"What do you think the familiar house is?"

"My mind?"

"Who is the monster?" she said, firing it quicker than her normal questioning.

"I don't know."

She waited, as though expecting him to reconsider his answer. After a few minutes of silence, she said, "Returning to sex."

"Doc! I'm starting to think you're obsessed."

"You use humour as a defence mechanism."

He shrugged and smiled coyly. "It's just sex."

"Is that how your lady-friends think of it?"

An image of Julia Wendsley popped into his head. He dismissed it. "I expect so."

In a matter-of-fact voice, she said, "Are you proud about your achievements—in bed, I mean?"

"Yes."

"Satisfaction in a job well done?"

"Yes."

"You're good at it?"

"I'd say so. My ladies are certainly satisfied."

"But are you, really? Being honest with yourself. You like the danger. Without the danger, as it becomes routine, does it become less satisfying?"

"I suppose I've noticed that on occasion."

"And how do you deal with it?"

"End the relationship. Boring, isn't fun."

"Sex can be an expression of love rather than the darkness," she said. "To make progress you need to understand yourself and address the anxieties. This was interesting, but to make progress we need to dig a little deeper. For our next session, I'd like you to think about your experience of relationships."

"Tomorrow, same time?"

"I can't tomorrow," she said. "Three days. Monday at two again."

He patted the goblin and flashed a smile. "In the meantime, I'll definitely think about relationships."

Chapter Twenty-Eight

Eleven days gone

Tanner senior looked even paler than when Munro had interviewed him last time.

"How? What happened?" the wretched man said. He had his head in his hands and his voice trembled with emotion.

"We can't say for sure."

"It's... it's definitely him?"

Munro had already explained that Mr. Tanner needed to visit the morgue to identify the body of his son. The man was desperate to hear that it might be a mistake, but from his face, Munro could see Tanner knew the truth. Maybe he'd expected it.

"I'm afraid so. I'm sorry."

Tanner looked up, his eyes wet and aged by a thousand years in a matter of minutes.

Munro needed answers. He needed a lead, and he felt bad about asking, but he had to do it.

"Tell me the truth."

"The truth?"

"Your son had been tortured." Tanner's face turned gray. He looked like he'd vomit. Munro pressed on.

"What did he know? Why was he running with Patricia Albright?"

"I don't know." Gasp. "I don't know."

Munro waited and long seconds ticked by.

"What am I going to do? Geoff supported me. My wife died and then I got ill. The company let us move here, but the cost of my medication... What am I going to do?"

Munro left the man fretting about his future and made him a cup of tea. He added three sugars, returned and watched as Tanner sipped. Eventually, the man calmed down enough for Munro to proceed.

Tanner's words had made him wonder. "How old was your son?"

Tanner blinked and thought. "Twenty-one."

Four years older than the girl. "How did he know Patricia?"

"I... I don't know."

"Through school?"

Tanner frowned and shook his head. "He had been to the same school—King George V—but, I don't think so. I hadn't seen the girl before, until a couple of weeks ago. He never mentioned her but... Not her anyway."

"But someone else?"

"Yes. A girl called Laura. Laura Quincy."

Quincy. The name rang a bell.

Tanner said, "You know, the girl who died last year? It was significant somehow. Geoff never said, but her death really affected him. He changed."

"Changed? How?"

Tanner blinked and thought, and Munro guessed the man's brain wasn't firing properly. Maybe he was wondering what he should or shouldn't say.

"Before, he... Well afterward, he changed his ways. That's when he started working at the furniture store. He stopped going to the parties, stopped wasting money. I told him he didn't need to pretend to be middle class. He didn't need to keep up with the others." Tanner huffed and shook his head vigorously. "Simon Morris in particular. Geoff couldn't keep up with the governor's son. I told him not to try."

"How could he afford it?" Munro asked, already suspicious. You said he changed. What did Geoff give up, Mr. Tanner?"

Tanner's eyes brimmed with tears again. "You've got to understand. He was a good boy, and I'd lost everything."

"What did he do?"

"He did some illegal things."

Munro nodded. "Including trading in drugs?"

Tanner's brow creased. "I suppose. He wouldn't talk about it. I just know he was getting cash and living well. But it had all changed, honestly!" Tanner seemed desperate for Munro to accept that Geoff Tanner had been a good boy despite a possible criminal past.

"A year ago?" Munro checked.

Tanner nodded.

"After Laura Quincy died?"

"Yes."

"Was he friends with Laura?"

"I don't know. No, I don't think so. He never mentioned her before she died."

"Was he involved in her death?"

Tanner shook his head emphatically. "No."

"But you can't know for sure?"

"I... No, I don't think so. He was a good boy." Tanner took a shuddering breath. "Geoff was troubled. He said he knew something."

Chapter Twenty-Nine

Garrett stared Zhan in the eye. He needed to let the young Chinese man know what he was up against if he didn't play along.

Zhan looked back, emotionless.

"Have you got it?" Garrett challenged.

"I understand what you want."

The junior civil police officer holding Zhan looked uncomfortable. Garrett wasn't worried about him. He wouldn't say anything to anyone. His role was to keep hold of the criminal and let him go when instructed.

Garrett said, "If you stab anyone, you'll regret it. There will be no place to hide. I will get you and put you away for a very long time."

"I understand," Zhan said coldly.

They were inside an old building, the quay just yards away in one direction. At the other end was Queen's Road. Between them was the entrance to the building where Charles Balcombe lived.

Garrett showed the man a photograph again. "This is what he looks like."

"You showed me before."

Garrett returned the photograph to his pocket and drew his weapon.

"Release the prisoner."

The police officer swallowed twice before he removed Zhan's handcuffs.

"Now we wait," Garrett said. He'd checked with the doorman that Balcombe was in the building. Now he prayed his prime suspect would appear soon.

* * *

Balcombe nodded to the concierge, who appeared preoccupied before stepping through the front door and out into the passage.

Queen's Road looked even busier than usual. He'd heard talk of the film people being in the Square at some point. Perhaps they were drawing crowds.

A girl's cry from the opposite direction made him swivel. A young Chinese girl was running towards him. Her arms pinwheeled, her eyes were full of panic, and her head swung from side to side.

And then Balcombe saw why. A man was chasing her. Fast. And in his right fist, the pursuer wielded a knife.

The girl raced past. Balcombe stepped out.

Something's not right, his back brain screamed.

The man with the knife was almost upon Balcombe. His eyes weren't crazy. They were cold and not focused on the girl. He was prepared for Balcombe.

He's coming for me.

The Chinese attacker didn't break his stride. As he ran, his knife-hand went back, ready to slash.

Balcombe caught a glimpse of someone at the end of the passage. Not coming. Watching.

The urge for Balcombe to draw his knife was strong, but he fought it. The attacker sidestepped and lashed out with the knife. Balcombe read it a fraction before it happened.

Don't draw your knife. Block.

Balcombe reacted. He struck the other man's wrist. The assailant's knife flew away. Now the man's face screamed alarm. He was no longer an attacker. He wanted to flee.

This is all wrong! Balcombe's front brain caught up with his instinctive one.

Balcombe let him go but swung out a leg as though to trip him, then twisted and tumbled and sprawled on the ground.

The assailant didn't break his stride.

A young, uniformed policeman sprinted to where Balcombe lay. The man collected the knife, then blew his whistle.

Balcombe levered himself up. "Shouldn't you be going after him?"

"I er…" the policeman stuttered, flustered, "Are you all right, sir?"

"I'm fine." Balcombe pointed to Queen's Road. "You need to go after him. He was chasing a girl, right?"

"Yes, of course." He blew his whistle again.

Another policeman appeared and, close behind, came Inspector Garrett.

* * *

Garrett rushed forward.

"My God! Balcombe are you all right?" He reached out to help Balcombe up, but the suspect ignored his hand. So, he snapped his attention to the first policeman. "What are you doing, man? Go after him!"

Balcombe brushed himself off.

"I saw what you did!" Garrett said, trying to sound impressed.

"I fell," Balcombe said.

"You disarmed that attacker!"

"Oh, you saw that?"

In Garrett's mind, there would have been a knife fight. Balcombe would have killed or at least maimed the Chinese man. He'd have demonstrated his skill with a knife.

He'd have condemned himself as the prime suspect of the Squeezed-heart murders.

But he hadn't. Balcombe had quickly disarmed Zhan. Was that evidence enough?

There were civilians in the street now.

"I saw it," a lady said. "Oh my, it was scary! That Chinese man just ran past, and poor Mr. Balcombe fell over."

Garrett looked at her. He hadn't counted on an innocent witness—and to cap it all, she knew Balcombe.

She said, "I live here," and pointed to the building that Balcombe had exited. "A few seconds earlier and it would be me on the floor and not poor Mr. Balcombe."

Balcombe was brushing himself down and appeared to have a wry smile on his face.

"I was lucky, Garrett. He wasn't after me. He was either chasing that girl or fleeing the police. I tried to stop him—"

"You disarmed the man!"

"I was lucky," Balcombe said. Now the smile looked smug, and Garrett hated him even more. The plan hadn't worked. He'd failed to make Balcombe draw a knife, but it didn't change his conviction. Balcombe could still meet the profile.

He'd have to come up with a better plan.

Chapter Thirty

Laura Quincy's body had been found under the Peak tram rails near the top. She'd died from a blow to the head, where she'd fallen and struck a rail. That's what the report said. There had only been a superficial autopsy. Her death had been classed as misadventure. Her bloods showed a high degree of intoxication and drugs. She'd been so drunk she'd been barely conscious, Munro suspected.

She'd been seventeen.

The file included a short statement from her father. He said she liked to party. He confessed to knowing about the drinking but denied knowledge of drugs. She frequently went out on a Saturday night with friends and didn't return until after he'd gone to bed. However she was always home in the morning—that is until that fatal night in July 1953.

The father couldn't name any specific friends that she partied with, and no one came forward with any sighting of her that evening.

"Why wasn't a full autopsy done?" Munro asked Fai Yeung. He knew the case had been five months before his friend had been appointed to the Island pathology team.

Yeung shook his head sadly. "You know what it's like, Babyface. Too much work. Too much pressure. A job comes in with 'simple autopsy' on it. Who are we to ask?"

"So, it won't have been your department's choice?"

"No, but we see a thousand cases like this a year. It looks like an accident. The police determine it was an accident. No way are we going to say anything different."

Munro understood. It was the same for him and his team. Too many crimes and not enough resource.

The other thing he regretted was the investigating officer. Munro had been in the team, the senior sergeant under DI "Old" Bill Teags. But Teags hadn't assigned it to him, and Munro only vaguely recalled the case.

The signature on the report was that of DC John S. Reece. Munro didn't know what the S stood for, but everyone called the boy "Sunfish" Reece behind his back. It was unlikely to be his real name. Sunfish seemed appropriate because of the boy's blotchy white skin and thick lower lip. He also had the brains of a fish.

So why had Teags given the kid the job? Old Bill was in a nursing home now after a breakdown and, more recently, a stroke. He wouldn't be able to answer the question. But Munro had his own answer. Reece got the job because of his connections. He was a young Englishman whose father worked for the government. The man was also a member of the Hong Kong Club.

Irrespective of his ability, "Sunfish" Reece was being groomed for a senior role.

"What are you going to do?" Yeung asked.

"Dig a bit deeper," Munro said. "It may be nothing, but it's my only solid lead. I'm going to speak to the parents and visit where she died."

* * *

Philip Slater was a driver for the Peak Tram Company. Munro had met him before. He was a young, thin man whose company uniform looked a size too large.

"Good morning, Mr. Slater."

Slater had just come out of the office. He froze mid step, his skin paled. "I can't say it's good to see you, Inspector."

Munro smiled. "Oh, and why's that?"

Slater's eyes narrowed. He didn't reply, but Munro knew. He didn't like Slater and the feeling was no doubt mutual.

"Laura Quincy," Munro said. "Let's go into the waiting room and talk."

Slater's face was hard. "I want a white officer present."

Munro sighed and shook his head. "You aren't a suspect, sir. I just want to talk about the girl who died here a year ago."

Slater said nothing for a minute, and Munro expected an excuse. He thought Slater would say he was about to drive a tram down the hill and any meeting would have to wait.

But he didn't. "You can have a few minutes." Slater wagged a finger. "And if there's any suspicion that you're stitching me up… Then the meeting ends, and we make it more formal."

With a quick backward glance as if to check whether anyone in the office was watching, Slater led the way to the station's waiting-room.

It was a cooler day than yesterday, but the inside still smelled hot. Metal and varnish, Munro thought. There were people queuing for tickets and a couple waiting on a bench.

Munro indicated the corner where they'd previously had a meeting.

Slater still looked nervous, and so Munro pointed to another bench. He wanted Slater at ease, not worrying about how the police might twist his words.

Once seated, Munro said, "I'm not investigating Laura's death. I working on a different case and her name came up." He tried a reassuring smile, which probably looked fake. "In your own words, just talk me through finding her."

"July seventh," Slater said, looking up as though visualizing. "I wasn't a driver back then. I arrived early and was checking the rails."

"You did that every day?"

"Once a week. Occasionally there's damage, but it's more about checking everything's tight. No loose nails. No problems with the struts, that sort of thing."

"And on the seventh?"

"I'd only gone thirty yards when I spotted something on the ground."

"So, it was on the elevated section?"

"Yes, just beyond the end of the platform."

"What did you see?"

"A white leg and a bit of pale blue. The blue was her dress."

None of this detail had been in the brief statement taken by Reece. The investigating detective had focused on *where* rather than *what* Slater had observed.

Slater seemed more relaxed now. He added: "So it was lucky I was checking the rails that day. If I hadn't spotted her, she could have been there for days unnoticed."

"You didn't go down to investigate?"

"No, I reported it and the police came within twenty minutes... I don't remember precisely."

"That's OK."

"But I do remember thinking it was odd. I mentioned it to the detective, but he wasn't interested."

"What was odd?"

"I don't know, just... Well, the papers said she'd been walking on the rails, and I couldn't picture it."

"Would you show me?"

Slater inhaled. "If you're going to stop the tram... You know the boss won't like the disruption."

Munro did know. He'd had the trams stopped before and needed to get approval. "Is there any way you can show me without us stopping them?"

Slater grinned. "How's your head for heights?"

Two minutes later, Munro was at the end of the concrete platform with the Peak tram employee. A red sign warned of danger.

Only one tram at a time came into the station. On the left were parallel sheet-metal runners for the wheels. Munro estimated the width of each to be a little over a foot. After five yards, the left-hand runner ended and became a rail. The one on the right continued. Between them was a moving cable.

"You walked on that?" Munro said, pointing to the right-hand runner.

"Yes. Come on."

Slater stepped easily across to the second runner and started walking. Munro was more cautious. With a bad knee, his sense of balance wasn't what it used to be.

He moved cautiously on the strip of metal little more than a foot wide. Slater was pulling ahead. He went past where the left-hand one ended and kept going.

"How far?" Munro called to him.

"Not very."

Munro kept going. There were rectangular concrete supports every ten yards. In between, there were cross beams and a lattice supporting frame. On the right were sloping white rocks. On the left was the drop, down to the town and harbour beyond. Munro might have enjoyed the view if he hadn't felt sick.

"Here," Slater said, a few yards in front of him. He pointed to the bushes and undergrowth. "Like I said, lucky I saw her."

Munro looked where Slater was pointing. It was a little beyond the left-hand rail.

"See what I mean about odd?" Slater said.

Munro shook his head. His brain wasn't functioning. All he could think of was getting back to the platform.

"If you fell here," Slater explained, "you'd either fall on top or through. And if you went through, you'd be down there." He pointed directly down. "So the only way she could get where I saw her was by walking the left-hand rail. And you can see that's just a rail. You'd be crazy to walk this runner. You'd be double crazy to try and walk along the rail." He looked at the vibration in the cables. "Better hurry back. Betty's due any minute."

Betty was the B-tram.

Munro scuttled the thirty yards back to safety. Slater jumped to the left-hand runner so that he could overtake and made it to the platform first. As Munro scrambled beside him, the tram rumbled up.

"That was exciting," Slater said. "Guess I just paid you back for how you treated me last time."

I guess you did, thought Munro.

Chapter Thirty-One

Georgina Swift packed away her things and gave Gookey, the leprechaun, an affectionate tap on the head. After Charles Balcombe's description of him being a goblin, it made her question her own interpretation. Whatever he was, he was a good-luck charm that had been with her for over ten years.

In their sessions, she'd questioned Balcombe's relationships. Deep-rooted mental problems nearly always came down to upbringing and familial issues. The fact that he had no parental role model for his interactions with the opposite sex explained a lot. He thought he was satisfied by his trysts, but it was unlikely.

Balcombe appeared shallow. Initially. But after their second session, when he'd really opened up, she saw him as much more complex. She had spent a lot of her free time, and quite a bit of working time, thinking about him.

And as she said goodnight to her ugly statuette, she realized there was more than a professional interest in her patient. Charles Balcombe was a bad boy and exceptionally good looking. He had alluring eyes and a mischievous smile.

She shut the office door and descended the stairs. "It's been too long, Georgina!" she chided herself. It had been almost two years since her last abortive relationship: a failed engagement to Giles Le Saux. "Now you're fancying men you shouldn't!"

She stepped onto Gage Street and locked her door. Mr. Robinson from the piano store waved to her through the window.

He was close to sixty, and she could see right through his lecherous smile.

"Doctor Swift?" A call made her swing around. When she saw who it was, she almost lost her footing.

Charles Balcombe was immediately at her side and holding an elbow.

"Are you all right?"

"You gave me a shock," she said and laughed. Then regretted the laugh because it made her sound foolish.

"I was just passing," he said. "I was hoping to bump into you."

She straightened her back and composed herself. "I don't run sessions out of the office, Charles, if that's what you're after?"

"No." He smiled, and she felt her heart flutter.

Come on, Doctor, you're better than this! she told herself and in the back of her mind registered that she sounded like her father. *After all these years, he's still telling me what I can and can't do.*

She started walking and realized she was going in the opposite direction of the hospital.

Balcombe said, "You told me to think about my relationships."

"I did."

"I have."

They took a few paces, and she resisted the urge to ask a question.

He said, "You are right. My sexual liaisons—"

She looked around, hoping no one had heard him speak so openly to her in the street. "Can we save this for the privacy of my office on Monday, Charles?"

He continued. "I'm ending them all."

"Ending not ended?"

"I've ended two and I've two more to go. I'm not just saying that. You were right, they were meaningless. Worse than that, they were devoid of emotion."

"Love," she said.

"You're right. I should have said devoid of love."

She turned a corner, still going the wrong way, but saw it as an opportunity to end the conversation and her confused feelings.

"I'm very pleased, Charles. Let's continue on Monday."

"I'd like to continue tonight," he said.

She stopped and looked at him, hard. "I hope you're not suggesting—"

He looked genuinely mortified. "No! No! I meant we could have dinner. I'd like you to have dinner with me."

She smiled with relief, then covered her embarrassment with a hand.

"I'm afraid—"

"You have other plans? Of course."

She said, "I'm afraid I don't date my patients."

"I could end our sessions."

"It would be too soon, Charles. You're making progress. I would be very unhappy if you stopped them just because of… well, I'm sure you see that by ending too soon, you could be avoiding the root causes. We've only had four sessions and" —she stopped and gave him her best serious expression, hoping he'd accept it— "we're only scratching the surface. You see that?"

"I do."

He has such deep, expression-filled eyes. Is this feeling real or am I projecting? Could there be a future between us?

He was smiling at her and she felt herself falling towards him, but only for a second. She clenched her fist and steeled herself.

"Once I'm happy that you no longer need analysis, then I'll let you take me to dinner."

"I'll hold you to that, Georgina."

I hope you do.

He took her hand lightly. She expected a farewell shake, but he just held it.

"They're filming at the Peak tomorrow morning. I'm"—he looked uncomfortable—"acting." She was curious, and he laughed lightly. "Nothing too impressive. They just want to film me climbing as though I'm getting away from the bad guys. Don't ask me about the plot."

"It sounds like fun," she said. And before she could properly think about it, she was agreeing to check it out.

Chapter Thirty-Two

Artland Co. was on Lockhart Road. As far as Munro was aware, it was just an art supplies shop. Now, as he entered, he saw that it had become double-fronted with one section for supplies and the other an art gallery.

"You sell artwork now?" Munro said as he met the proprietor. He immediately regretted the question because the answer was right before his eyes. He smiled and started again. "Mr. Quincy, I assume?"

"That's me and yes, I do." He appraised Munro quickly. "Are you with the police?"

"DI Munro, sir."

"Not here to view or perhaps purchase then?"

Munro had seen the price tags. "Not today, Mr. Quincy. Maybe after the big annual bonus."

He wasn't being serious, but Quincy didn't seem to recognize the humour.

"So how may I help you today, Inspector?"

There were three other people in the shop, two in the supplies section and one browsing the paintings.

"Is there somewhere we can speak privately?"

Quincy frowned, looked dubious and then called: "Mai?"

A Chinese woman, about fifteen years younger than Quincy, appeared at the rear.

Quincy said, "Take over while I talk to this gentleman."

Mai nodded with her eyes on Munro. He sensed she didn't like him for some reason. Perhaps she guessed what he represented. The police had a bad reputation. On occasion, especially concerning the Chinese community, that reputation was justified.

"My wife," Quincy said once they were in a living area behind the shop.

"Second wife?" Munro figured because Laura Quincy's skin showed no sign of mixed race.

"Three years ago. Mrs. Quincy number one, ran off with a sailor." He snorted. "Not very imaginative, I know. Anyway, she did me a favour. Know what I mean?" He winked, man-to-man. "So, how may I help you this afternoon?"

"I don't want to be insensitive, but I wonder if you could tell me about your daughter?"

"Grace is fifteen and at school in Switzerland. Is everything—?"

"I meant Laura."

Quincy's expression changed. One second, he looked concerned that something had happened to his younger daughter in Europe. The next, his face was full of confusion.

"What about... Laura? You know..."

"Yes, I'm sorry, sir," Munro said. "I don't wish to be insensitive about your loss."

He was going to say more, but Quincy interjected. "I told everything to that other inspector."

"A year ago." Munro nodded. Although it hadn't been DI Bill Teags. Sunfish Reece had done the interview. "An accident, I understand."

"Yes."

"What can you tell me about it?"

"Isn't it in your reports?" Quincy frowned and shook his head. He turned and started to make a cup of tea for himself.

"Mr. Quincy, could I just hear it in your own words?"

Quincy turned sharply away from the counter with its kettle and cup. "Why?"

"Because her name has come up."

"Come up? Who by? Who brought up Laura's name?"

Munro noticed that the man's left hand was shaking. *Is it with anger or distress?* Munro wondered.

"Sir, at this time, I can't tell you more. It's part of an ongoing investigation."

Quincy half nodded and turned back to making tea.

"She died from a fall. Banged her head on a tram rail."

Munro waited a beat. "Her blood showed she'd had a cocktail of alcohol and drugs."

"Drugs?" Quincy said, sounding surprised. He didn't turn around. He breathed, then added: "Don't they all?"

"Do they, sir?"

He saw the man's shoulders shrug. "Who knows what the kids get up to these days? Too many parties. A privileged life. Debauchery. That's why I've sent Gracie to Europe." He turned around, his eyes narrow and tense. "Anything else, Inspector?"

"What was Laura doing on the tram rails?"

Quincy sucked in air, swelling his already large chest.

"Shouldn't there be a white officer present?"

Munro blinked with surprise. "Only when taking a formal statement. Usually when questioning a suspect."

"Am I a suspect?"

"No, sir. Why—?"

"You mentioned another case. An *ongoing investigation*, you said. We all know what the police can do. I've not done anything wrong, and I know of no crime."

Munro shook his head. This meeting had taken a hairpin turn that he hadn't expected.

"Sir, I just want to talk about Laura."

Quincy shook his head. "I don't appreciate being ambushed like this."

"It's not an am—"

"Next time you want an interview, you warn me in advance, and you're accompanied by a white officer."

Chapter Thirty-Three

Twelve days gone

Balcombe had expected to climb the crag a couple of times. But he didn't know the film industry. He didn't know that they needed the perfect light. They played with alternative scenarios. They required multiple shots of the same thing, just in case something was slightly different. It was also clear that the director hadn't a fixed impression of the scene.

There were no movie stars at the Peak that morning. As had already been explained to Balcombe, the director shot everything without them first. He used stand-ins and kept the filming of the big stars to the end. That way, it saved them time and money.

"Mr. Gable won't stand around all morning while we get the scene right," a director's assistant explained.

They also explained that Balcombe couldn't climb in his usual gear. He had to wear a suit, because that's what Mr. Gable would be wearing.

Balcombe knew nothing about the character except what he'd been told by Thelwell the casting director. Clarke Gable was a modern-day pirate, which meant that he didn't have a pegleg, hook or eye-patch. Climbing with those would have been a challenge too far, even for Balcombe.

Instead of pirate duds, Gable would wear a crisp light-grey suit and Brogues.

Balcombe had been measured for the clothes and Costume had brought six sets.

The clothes were too big. Balcombe shook his head and asked for a belt as the trousers were loose around his waist. He added: "Which tailor produced these?"

The Costume guy chortled. "The clothes fit Mr. Gable. We measured you for these." He then produced a padded vest and waist band.

"And why six pairs?"

"Just in case," said the Costume guy.

Balcombe soon discovered what that meant. The first pair of trousers split at the crotch on his second ascent. He could imagine the hoots of derision in the cinemas around the world, if that had made the final cut.

The director also made him change the jacket three times because of unacceptable creasing.

"You've got to look like you're in peril," the director's assistant explained for the tenth time, "but don't look like you've been dragged backwards through a hedge."

They shot the moves from below. They added other men—the bad guys pursuing—the assistant explained. Balcombe could look down and away but not back or down towards the camera.

That was easier said than done because, in the awkward clothes, he was more focused on the effort of climbing than remembering where the cameras were.

They moved to filming from above and the director screamed at him. "Stop looking up!"

The second time from this viewpoint, Balcombe slipped. His footing went, and he was left dangling by one hand.

When he got to the top, the director was beside himself with excitement. "That was fantastic! Do it again."

So, Balcombe repeated it although the second, third and fourth times were all staged and no longer perilous.

After almost four hours of filming, they were done. One of the "bad men" had complained that all the filming could be reduced to less than five minutes in the movie. Another warned that scenes could be cut altogether. They may never appear.

Balcombe didn't mind. His face wasn't in it, and it had just been for fun—although after so much repetition the enjoyment had worn thin.

There was a small crowd on the Peak path watching the activity but kept back by the crew. Balcombe guessed that a shot capturing an audience might ruin the illusion.

He kept an eye out for Georgina Swift but hadn't spotted her in the onlookers. So it was a pleasant surprise when he saw her on the Peak path as he was leaving.

She waved a flashed her gorgeous smile as he approached.

"Did I miss anything?"

His face fell. "You've only just arrived?"

She laughed. "I'm kidding, Charles. I've been here for over an hour. You were amazing."

Balcombe noticed a Chinese man dressed in servant-whites loitering close by with a basket. His eyes were averted, but Balcombe could tell he was attentive.

"Is he with you?"

"I thought you might be hungry," Georgina said. "I've brought you lunch—a picnic." And it was impressive. They found a flat section of grass and her Chinese servant spread a blanket and opened the basket and then retreated a respectable distance. Inside the picnic hamper was a bottle of wine and two glasses.

There was roast chicken and sandwiches, canapés and crudités, and bowls of sliced fruit.

Georgina asked Balcombe to pour them wine. They sat and she chinked glasses with him.

While climbing. Balcombe didn't admire the view; he only watched out for rain. He didn't climb in the wet. Now, sitting on the blanket looking out across the island and the diamond-sparkled sea beyond, he realized it was a perfect afternoon. Not a cloud in the sky, a cool light breeze and a beautiful companion to enjoy it with.

She said, "I used to picnic up her with my mother before the war. This takes me back to being a kid. Carefree and footloose... before the war, of course."

She told him that her mother had been a botanist by training. She'd enjoyed walking and studying the flora inland. It sounded like she could have been something, had a career, but Georgina's father's career as a pathologist came first.

"What happened to her?" Balcombe asked, drawing the conclusion that Georgina's mother had passed away.

"Cancer," she said matter-of-factly. "She was only thirty-nine. Father brought me up."

"Interned at Stanley?" Balcombe asked, knowing where the Japanese had imprisoned the whites during the war.

"Philippines," she said. "I'd just come back after my training but instead of working as a psychologist, during the war, I assisted in the hospitals—mostly nursing, but back then anyone with any training could do anything. I acted as a midwife and surgeon on the same day."

"But you returned to psychology when you came home?"

"It's all I ever wanted to do."

He said, "I wish I'd had the similar motivation. I flip-flopped and reading history isn't a vocation."

"So, what did you do after college?"

Such was the relaxed atmosphere and comfortable companionship; he almost told her the truth. Instead, he cut the conversation short by saying that he'd worked for the British government.

If she picked up on his lie, she didn't show it. "But you have a passion," she said after a sip of wine. "Even if it is dangerous."

She said she'd seen him dangling from one hand and that he'd seemed to slip a few times.

He didn't deny it. "I've never climbed in a suit and hard shoes before," he said. "It really was dangerous."

She breathed, or maybe it was a sigh. "I don't understand why you risk your life, Charles. Unnecessarily, I mean."

"Have you ever tried it?"

"Climbing? No!"

He leapt up and took her hand. The next moment, he was pulling her towards an outcrop that was only ten feet tall.

"I can't do it," she protested.

"Kick off your shoes," he said, leading her to the foot of the rock. She complied after a hesitation. He showed her where to place her first foot, then her hand. "Use the legs more than the arms," he said.

Taking her weight, but holding Georgina around the waist, he helped her rise off the ground. She made two more moves and then fell back into his arms.

She laughed. "I'm terrible!"

"Your first time and in bare feet. With rubber—"

"I'm terrible." She was still laughing. Her cheeks were flushed. "Thank you for catching me, but you can take your hands off me now."

He flashed a smile and raised an eyebrow. "I hoped you—"

She straightened herself, brushing imaginary dust from her blouse. "I'm sure you did, Mr. Balcombe!"

They returned to the picnic blanket.

"You're cross with me?"

Now it was her turn to smile, although hers was perhaps winsome. "Cross with myself for letting you lead me on."

"I'm being genuine."

"Honestly?"

"Honestly!"

"This wasn't a date."

"I understand that. You said before that you don't date clients. But afterward… afterward you will let me buy you dinner."

"Let's complete your sessions, Charles, and then we'll see."

Her words gave the impression that she wasn't sure, but the sparkle in her eyes told him everything he needed to know.

He said, "Best case, how many more sessions, do you think?"

"I wouldn't like to—"

"Best case."

"As I told you yesterday, you've made good progress." She thought seemed to shake the thought away and then smiled. "Two," she said.

"Put something in your diary." He flashed a winning smile. "Wednesday evening. Dinner with me."

She laughed. "It'll just be dinner."

"Of course!"

After dropping her off at Donell Street, Balcombe virtually danced back home.

Chapter Thirty-Four

It was Saturday night. There were always several parties to choose from, and Balcombe usually attended the best. However tonight was different. Roy Faulls knew which event Georgina Swift would be attending and so Balcombe picked that one.

There was a secondary benefit since Julia Wendsley wouldn't be there. Balcombe wanted to let time pass and emotions fade before he bumped into her again.

As they approached, the sound of Swing music carried on the air. The rear garden had been converted into a large dance area with flaming torches casting moving shadows that made the bushes dance the Jitterbug along with the crowd.

Balcombe figured there were nigh on a hundred revellers, half of whom were on the dance floor. The others milled around and swelled in and out of the house. Three sets of French doors were open wide, with a bar in one and food in another broad room.

A waiter offered champagne which Balcombe and Faulls accepted.

They'd been discussing the horses and that day's races. Balcombe hadn't placed a bet on Van Ness's horse but pointed it out to Faulls who had been happy with his win.

A THIRD IS DARKNESS

After an hour at the party, Balcombe said, "Are you sure Georgina's coming?"

Faulls nodded without conviction and changed the subject. "Do you know the Cartwrights?"

Balcombe didn't.

"Over in the corner. Middle-aged. The prim and proper looking woman in the grey and white?"

"I see her. Her husband's suit looks a thousand dollars."

"Bridge," Faulls said under his breath.

"I'm sorry?"

"If she or her husband ask you to join them for Bridge, it means something else."

"Like what?"

"Partner swap. That's what I've heard. There's a whole group of them, and the Cartwrights are the organizers. Sounds like they're setting up a card game, but it's all about naughty shenanigans."

Balcombe shook his head. The couple had now moved on to another group and didn't look the sort to be into sex, let alone wife-swapping."

Faulls shook his head. "You don't believe me."

"You're right."

"Fine, let's go over and ask them for a game."

Balcombe was about to point out that two men hardly provided the opportunity for a wife-swapping event when he felt a hand on his backside. He turned and caught the eye of the woman who had just passed.

"Wasn't that Marjorie?" Faulls said as the woman melted into the crowd.

Marjorie Grebe was another of Balcombe's women. She was on the arm of her elderly husband and when she reappeared, she touched her tongue to her lips suggestively.

Balcombe smiled politely and looked away.

"Let's get some air."

They collected more drinks as they moved outside and then strolled around the edge of the dance floor. Balcombe scanned the dancers and then watchers until he spotted Georgina Swift.

She was standing out of the torch glow and seemed to be in earnest discussion with a man. Her dress was body hugging, a spangly silver number that showed off her assets. The man was more formally attired, and his build made her look slight in comparison.

Faulls started talking to a young lady and encouraged her onto the dance floor. Balcombe found himself edging towards the doctor and her partner.

Something seemed off. The conversation wasn't cordial, the man's body language aggressive. Balcombe started towards them just as the man gave her a shove, turned and marched away.

"Georgina?" called Balcombe, closing in fast. "Are you all right? I saw—"

"Oh… Oh… Charles. I didn't realize you were coming." Her voice cracked with emotion and she blinked at tears.

"What the hell?" he said.

"I'm all right. Honestly, I'm all right. Could you get me a drink?"

He guided her inside and ordered a dirty martini. She knocked it back, ate the olive, and asked for another.

"I hate him," she said after a swallow.

"The man you came here with?"

"He's not… Giles… Giles Le Saux is my ex-fiancé. He's here with his new girl."

"Then he's an idiot," Balcombe said. "And, by the way, you look stunning tonight."

She forced a smile. "Thank you. He called me some terrible names." She was looking outside toward the dance floor and took a ragged breath. "I think I should go home. I can't enjoy myself with him here."

Balcombe followed her gaze and saw Giles moving awkwardly with his partner. "One minute," he said. "Excuse me."

With that, he left her by the bar and made a beeline for the ex.

"May I cut in?" he said to the dancing couple.

The girl beamed, assuming Balcombe wanted to be her partner.

"She's not available," said Le Saux. Close up, Balcombe realized the man had a couple of inches on him and was built like a rugby player.

The man looked half amused, half disbelieving, as Balcombe placed a hand on his arm.

"It's you I want. A word please."

Le Saux grunted at his young lady and left the dance area. They squeezed through until they were beyond the throng.

"All right, who are you and what do you want?" asked Le Saux, turning quickly ensuring the gap between them was only a foot. An intimidation tactic, Balcombe thought. Most men would probably step back. Balcombe remained close.

He said, "You upset Georgina."

"So? What's it to you?"

"Pushing a woman, making her cry isn't big." Balcombe pulled a smile. "I'd like you to leave."

Giles Le Saux snorted. "What?" Then he shook his head. "Listen, fella, she's a loon and a pest. I'm sure you believe you're doing the chivalrous thing, but it's misguided."

"Leave."

Le Saux snorted again and puffed up his chest. "Look, little man—oof!"

Balcombe jabbed a knife-hand below the man's ribs, quick and deep. The bigger man creased at the middle then straightened. As he was about to throw a punch, Balcombe jabbed him again, only this time it was an upward strike between the legs.

Le Saux yelped, causing heads to turn their way. Balcombe caught the other man as he doubled forward and pressed a thumb between his ear and jaw.

He felt the fight go out of the other man. Acceptance of defeat.

"It's all right," Balcombe said to those nearby. "He's not feeling well." And to Le Saux he said, "Next time I'll embarrass you and make a scene."

He released the big man. Le Saux took two staggering paces back, his eyes full of bewilderment.

Balcombe said, "You going?"

Giles Le Saux nodded, turned and walked away with as much dignity as he could muster.

Balcombe couldn't find Georgina afterward and accepted that she'd left anyway. He returned to the bar, got a drink, and circulated. He danced a little and chatted and avoided Marjorie Grebe. But then saw his opportunity and had a word with her.

Although disappointed, she accepted the end of their relationship and pecked him on the cheek.

"Come back if you ever change your mind, Charles."

"Thank you," he said.

An hour later, he was between conversations and looking for Faulls when Georgina appeared at his side.

"How are you getting along?" she asked, her voice huskier and loosened by alcohol.

He wondered what she meant.

"I've seen you flirting with the pretty ones."

"Just having a good time," he said, feeling judged. "And you'll be pleased to know I've finished with another girlfriend. Just one to go."

"Is the last one here?" Georgina scanned the crowd. "Let me see her."

"She's not. I'll have spoken to her before Wednesday though. Before our dinner."

They stood side by side watching the dancefloor. He offered to refill her glass and when he returned, she was no longer there.

Thirty minutes later, Faulls found him and said he was off to another party. Balcombe said he'd stay. He'd just seen Georgina on the dance floor. She switched partners, took another drink and then headed for him.

Her voice was more slurred by drink when she said, "Dance with me, Charles."

"Of course." He took her arm and joined the jiving couples.

In the lull between tunes, she said, "Do you find me attractive?"

"You're the best-looking girl at the party," he said honestly.

They started dancing again. After a few moves, she was close again. "Really?"

"Absolutely! Giles is an ass to have let you go."

The tune ended, and she pulled away. "Second door after the staircase," she said over her shoulder and skipped away.

Intrigued, two minutes later, he was opening the door to a drawing room.

There were candles burning on a hearth, creating a warm glow. The room smelled of wood polish with a hint of musk. Georgina was there. She pressed herself against him, pushing him back to the door until he could go no further. Her hands were on him. He felt her lithe body through the tight-fitting dress.

"You're gorgeous," he said.

"Shut up and kiss me."

Their mouths met, first tentatively but soon desperate. They became one, his back against the door, her body moving with his rhythm. Faster, absorbed by the passion.

The grandfather clock struck sonorously.

He broke away, shuddering.

"What's up?" she panted.

The clock continued chiming the twelfth hour.

He said, "This isn't right. You've had too much to drink. We have to stop. You're not thinking straight."

"Maybe I'm thinking straighter than usual." She pressed her body against him again.

"No, Georgina," he said. "Not like this."

"It's because I'm not dangerous enough for you, isn't it?"

"It's not—"

"I could make it risky. We could—"

"Stop!"

"Why?"

"Because, Georgina, you don't do it with clients. After is all right, you said so. We haven't finished."

The clock struck a final time and the silence seemed to rush in. Even the music outside quietened.

She looked at him pleadingly.

"Georgina, believe me, I want you so badly."

"Then have me." She closed the gap between them, but he held her away by her shoulders.

"You'd wake up tomorrow and regret it."

"Maybe, but for now—"

"No, you're better than this." He kissed her cheek lightly. "You're worth it and I can wait. Dinner on Wednesday, remember?"

Chapter Thirty-Five

Fourteen days gone

On Monday morning, Munro was waiting for Balcombe at the upper Peak tram station.

"Enjoy your... what do you call it, climbing session?" he asked as Balcombe approached.

"Yes, thanks," Balcombe lied. He hadn't had his usual adrenaline rush. It was probably the filming on Saturday that had killed the thrill. All that repetition and fake danger. Or it could be the analysis sessions with Georgina. Was it maturity? He'd lost the urge to have meaningless flings with married women and now he was losing the thrill from free climbing. Perhaps that was right. Perhaps that was the price of controlling BlackJack.

"Have you got time?" Munro asked.

Balcombe nodded.

"Do you know about Garrett's little trick?"

Munro shook his head, frowning, and Balcombe told him about the attempted set-up on Friday.

"He tried to make me use a knife," Balcombe finished.

"You're sure?"

"He was on the scene too quickly. It was clear he'd been watching."

Munro shook his head. "The man is dangerous. You have to watch yourself."

"I am. Don't worry."

Munro sighed. "I came to give you an update."

"Here? At the Peak?"

"It's relevant. There's still no sign of Patricia. Tanner senior said that his son was affected after someone died a year ago. She was called Laura Quincy. Same age and same school as Patricia Albright, although I found out they weren't in the same school year. Laura was one of the youngest in the year above Patricia. And the accident was twelve months ago."

"Were they friends?" Balcombe asked, knowing Patricia's father hadn't mentioned anyone called Quincy.

Munro said, "I've made enquiries and it doesn't appear so. None of Patricia's friends knew her although they did know about the accident. They'd had a service at school, and everyone warned about the dangers of the trams."

Munro then told him about what had happened in July last year.

"Why walk the tram rails at night?" Balcombe asked when the detective had finished. "If she missed the last tram, wouldn't she take the Old Peak Road?"

"Could have been a dare," Munro said. "Or maybe too drunk to think properly."

"Where did she live?"

Munro pointed straight down the hill. "The Quincy home is on Robinson. But I had another thought." He paused and pointed down the track at the rocks and trees before the tram line curved. "The Albright home is down there on Barker Road. A drunk girl walking the quickest way to Barker Road stop and then on to the Albrights."

"You're telling me that Patricia Albright was here that night?"

"I don't know."

"But?"

"Tanner was affected by the death of Quincy. So much so that he seemed to have changed his life, changed his bad ways." Munro held up a hand. "I know it's a stretch, but what if Patricia is connected. She sought out Tanner because she also felt guilty?"

"Guilty?"

"Affected at least. Two people with a common secret."

"It sounds tenuous."

"Except for one thing. I went to see Laura's father. He knows something, I'm sure. He was fine until I mentioned Laura. Then he got defensive. He wanted to know who had brought up her name. I tried to placate him by explaining I wasn't investigating her death, but had another ongoing investigation."

"What did he say about Patricia?"

"I didn't get that far. He shut me down and refused to talk unless it was official. Perhaps you'd have more success?"

★ ★ ★

In under an hour, washed and changed, Balcombe was entering Artland Co. on Lockhart Road.

There was an attractive Chinese lady at a desk in the gallery section. Balcombe browsed the paintings for a minute before the woman appeared by his side.

"See anything you like?"

Balcombe smiled. "May I speak with the proprietor?"

Her smile implied she thought he wanted to deal with a fellow white man. Which implied a sale.

"Terry?" she called.

A man appeared from a door in the back, behind the desk. The way he exchanged glances with the woman, made Balcombe suspect she was wife number two. It made sense. Most small shops were run by the owners.

Balcombe introduced himself. "Nice little gallery you have here."

"Thank you. It's in its infancy but growing. Is there a piece I can interest you in, Mr. Balcombe?"

"I'm afraid I've misled you, Mr. Quincy, I'm following up an investigation. You met DI Munro on Saturday."

Quincy's eyes narrowed. "And I told—"

Balcombe interrupted. "The inspector told you he was working on another case."

Mrs. Quincy had sat at her desk. The way she held her hands beneath the counter made Balcombe suspect she had a weapon under there, probably a shotgun.

Balcombe continued: "We're looking for a missing girl." He held out the photograph of Patricia.

Quincy didn't do more than flick a glance at the photo, and shook his head immediately.

"She's about the same age as your daughter. Might they have been friends?"

"No. I've never seen the girl before."

Balcombe said, "She might have been with your daughter when she died."

Quincy shook his head again. "You know what happened? She got herself drunk and fell off the tram rails. God only knows…"

A customer came into the art supplies side of the shop and after a glance at her husband, who nodded, Mrs. Quincy went over to serve the lady.

Quincy must have noticed Balcombe look at his wife. She had a good figure and was much younger than her husband.

Quincy said, "I got my priorities wrong. You understand that, Mr. Balcombe? I'd not been married long. I thought my girls were doing all right. I knew Laura liked to party with her friends. I hadn't realized she had got in with a bad crowd. I knew she had the odd drink."

"You didn't know about the drugs?"

Quincy swallowed and shook his head. "I'm surprised. I didn't… I didn't see the signs. She went out that night in July and didn't come home." His voice quavered. He swallowed hard again. "I'll never forgive myself. I'll not make that mistake again. That's why I sent my youngest away to Europe. She'll be safe there."

Mrs. Quincy was back. She snuggled into her husband, and he put his arm around her.

Balcombe noticed her eyes move to the photograph and then swing away.

"Have you seen her before?" Balcombe asked her.

"No," she said too quickly.

"Her name is Patricia." He saw worry in the new wife's face. "Was she one of Laura's friends?"

Mr. Quincy said, "I told you—"

"She came in here last week." Mrs. Quincy looked up at her husband. "You were out at the pub."

"Mai—" Quincy's tone suggested he wanted her to stop.

Balcombe said, "What did she want, Mrs. Quincy?"

"She asked if I knew about Laura. I told her to go away. I said—"

"That's enough." Mr. Quincy stopped her. "My daughter is dead and I don't need people coming here and suggesting it was anything other than an accident."

"Is that what Patricia did? Did she say it wasn't an accident?"

Mr. Quincy spoke before his wife could respond. "I don't know, and I don't care, Mr. Balcombe. I'm sorry that you can't find Miss Albright"—he handed back the photograph—"but my daughter got drunk, walked on the tram rails and fell. There's nothing more to it. Good day, Mr. Balcombe."

Balcombe didn't move, his eyes locked on Quincy's.

"Please leave, Mr. Balcombe."

"I said she was called Patricia. I didn't tell you it was Patricia Albright."

Quincy's eyes flared with worry. Then: "I recognized her. She's got distinctive hair."

"Is that who it is?" Mrs. Quincy said. "I didn't realize—"

"Shut up, Mai!" Quincy barked and pushed her away. His wife scuttled off, her head down.

Balcombe said, "Tell me."

"I'm saying nothing. I just recognized the girl."

"Although you said you didn't."

Quincy glanced at the desk and Balcombe wondered if he was thinking about the gun.

"All right." Balcombe pulled out the photograph of Geoff Tanner. "Was Geoff Tanner a friend of Laura's?"

Quincy flicked his eyes from the desk to Balcombe. "I don't know."

"Would you take a look at his photograph, please? Perhaps it'll refresh your memory."

Quincy glanced at it, then shook his head. "No."

"It's important because this young man was murdered last week, and it seems he knew something about Laura's death."

Quincy's face paled.

Balcombe said, "Did you know him?"

"No!" Suddenly Quincy was enraged. "I told you I didn't recognize him. Now I'd like you to leave."

Balcombe said, "I want answers."

"Answers get you dead." Quincy strode toward the desk and Balcombe suspected the gun was about to come out.

Balcombe patted the air with his hands. "I'm going. No need for trouble."

Quincy stopped and turned.

"Don't come back, Mr. Balcombe. You're not welcome, causing trouble. Don't come back."

Balcombe stepped outside.

Quincy was soon at the gallery's door. He shut it and switched the *Open* sign to *Closed.*

Chapter Thirty-Six

Balcombe climbed Georgina's office stairs. He flet a frisson of concern. How would she be after what had happened on Saturday night at the party?

He knocked on her door and she called him in.

There was nothing but professionalism in her face and voice. "Chair or couch, Charles?"

He took the couch, looked at the ceiling and relaxed.

"Have you had the nightmare or hallucination since our last session?"

"No. But I had a new dream last night. I was climbing a rock face, dressed in inappropriate clothing and chased by bad men." He was referring to his acting on Saturday, but she took him seriously. At least, that's what he assumed from her response.

"Let's talk about *bad*. What does it mean to you?"

"Well, I'm a Catholic. We know a lot about right and wrong, about good versus evil. About sin. Catholicism is the religion of blame."

Again she didn't pick up on any humour and he decided to stop being flippant. He wanted the sessions to end so that he could buy her dinner. And find out where that led.

He said, "Evil is usually perceived as the antagonistic opposite of good. Good is that which should prevail and evil should be defeated."

"You want to defeat it?"

"Yes."

"In your nightmare... the monster... the spiders... do they represent evil?"

"I imagine so."

"But you can't defeat them."

"No."

"Tell me about *goodness*. What does that mean to you?"

"The opposite of evil," he said before thinking, then reconsidered. "I suppose it's happiness, charity, justice... and love." The idea of Chinese philosophy flashed in his mind: yin and yang. Two basic principles. Opposite but entwined. Were good and evil the same? Was it part of the whole?

He realized she'd asked a question when she repeated it.

She said, "You mentioned love. In our last session, I asked you to think about your relationships."

"There's been no love in them. I also thought more about my parents. I never saw them show love to one another."

"Did they show you affection?"

"Not that I recall. My father was more of a disciplinarian. Spare the rod and spoil the child. That mentality. There was a thick leather strap that hung on the back of the kitchen door. I was terrified of it. He'd snap it together on his way to give a hiding with it."

"He hit you?"

"With the strap. Possibly with his hands a few times. My memory is a bit blurry. The main thing I remember is being afraid of him."

"You told me you saw your sister on his knee. Did he ever read to you like that?"

"No. I vaguely remember him reading to me as a young child but never on his knee."

"How did you feel about his relationship with your sister?"

"Nothing. I never thought about it. She wasn't his favourite though. My eldest brother, John, was the apple of his eye. John could do no wrong."

"Was he ever proud of you?"

"When I was studying the medical texts. When he thought I'd have a career as a surgeon. That's when he was proud. He hasn't spoken to me since I left home."

"Your mother left home when you were a child. When was that?"

He studied a crack in the ceiling and thought. Why couldn't he remember?

"Between the baby being stillborn and my older brothers getting killed. No, wait, I remember my mother holding out my birthday cake when I was eleven. I was obsessed by knights in armour, and she made a cake. It was a fort. She put my soldiers on it. So I was at least eleven. And I was fifteen when my brothers died."

"She made you a special cake. She must have loved you."

"Yes."

"What's the last thing you remember? The last time you saw her?"

He stared at the ceiling. There was nothing. No memory, just a void, just darkness.

She asked some more probing questions about his relationships with his father and mother. Each time she returned to his mother's departure, he drew a blank.

Near the end of the session, she said, "I would like to try something, Charles."

"Anything."

"I want you to close your eyes and try summon the nightmare or the hallucination." He complied, and she asked him to talk through the nightmare.

At the end, she handed him the statue and he did the breathing and sensory description thing.

"Are you all right?" she said when he sat up.

"Yes, I..." He realized he felt a little woozy. "Did I pass out?"

"You were in the dream," she said. "You were there, Charles."

Chapter Thirty-Seven

Munro was in the meeting room at Government House. Albright had telephoned for him and looked uncomfortable when he came into the room.

"Ah, DI Munro, thank you for coming so promptly."

"I apologize for the lack of updates, sir." They hadn't spoken since last Wednesday.

Albright seemed distracted. He was looking at the painting of the transfer of Hong Kong to the British in 1841. Munro continued: "We're following a lead. Laura Quincy—"

Albright's attention snapped to Munro. "What?"

"A girl about Patricia's age, died last year."

Albright shook his head and blinked. "What are you talking about, man? Investigating some random death a year ago? Patricia has turned up. It's nothing to do with... what's her name?"

"Laura Quincy."

Albright sighed and returned his gaze to the painting. "I should have told you before. The reason she left was because of some silly squabble. Me and her. You know how girls can be, Inspector?"

Munro had no idea about teenage girls. He said nothing.

"Anyway," Albright continued, "Patricia came back yesterday. That's why I wanted to speak to you. You can stop looking."

"So, she's home with you?"

Albright didn't respond and Munro wondered if the Governor's aide-de-camp hadn't heard. He seemed to have a lot on his mind.

Munro said, "I just want to make sure. The young man she was seen with was murdered."

"Tanner?"

"Yes. I just—"

"Munro, she's fine," Albright said. "Although I confess that our disagreement isn't over. She came home on Saturday, collected some clean clothes then went off. She said she was staying with one of her girlfriends. And before you ask, I don't want you putting any hobnailed boots in by visiting her friends again and asking for her. I need her to come home in her own sweet time. She's fine."

"What time on Saturday?" Munro asked.

"What does that matter, man?"

"I'm just being thorough, sir."

"Right. Well, about three in the afternoon, I think it was."

Munro nodded. "Thank you."

Albright didn't shake his hand but ended the meeting with: "You've done a good job, Munro. Thank you. Now you can go back to proper policing."

★ ★ ★

Chief Carmichael grimaced. "What a bloody waste of time!"

"Yes, sir," Munro said, having just passed on Albright's message.

Carmichael shook his head. "At least it wasn't all you were doing. Looking for some higher-up's daughter? What did he say? Staying with her friends? Some of these people... they think we're at their beck and call."

We are, Munro thought.

"What's the progress on the burglary?"

It was one of Munro's other cases and he gave an update. The Chief asked some questions and looked like he was about to dismiss Munro, so he said what was troubling him.

"Sir, what about her friend?"

"Pardon. Her friend?"

"Patricia Albright's friend. Geoff Tanner, the one found murdered. Isn't it—"

"You're off the case, Munro. We've just talked about that."

"Yes, but Tanner—"

"The connection was tenuous." He waved a dismissive hand. "I spoke to the Commissioner... Not linked. The Albright girl is with friends. Tanner's murder isn't related. It's being handled by Kowloon." The Chief nodded as though making sure Munro got the message. Loud and clear. "Now, back to the proper job, Munro."

Munro returned to his desk, busied himself with his caseload, and took updates from his team. But his conversation with Carmichael troubled him. On the one hand, he reacted like Munro was giving him news about being off the case. On the other, he'd clearly already spoken to the police commissioner about it and Tanner's death.

He knew.

When the Chief's out, Munro decided, he'd call Kowloon and ask how the Tanner investigation was going.

That decision helped him focus for the rest of the afternoon but before the end of the day, it was lost again. A card arrived. It was a note from the Japanese soldier, Kaito Hashimoto.

It said he was sorry and would like to make peace. He was staying in Hong Kong for two more days. He provided the name of his hotel and also an address in Japan.

Munro's mind flashed back nine years. His beautiful Yan was on the floor being thrashed mercilessly by the soldiers. She had a good soul. She would have forgiven them, but Munro never could. Tears blurred his eyes.

He flung the card into his desk and slammed the drawer shut.

Chapter Thirty-Eight

Balcombe came out of the King's Building where he'd had dinner. It was a cool night and he decided to stroll along the quay before turning for home. Straight after his session with Georgina Swift, he'd made contact with his last remaining girlfriend. Again, the parting had been amicable, and it felt right. It seemed to be part of the healing process. He was sure that BlackJack hadn't killed anyone since the incident on Cosmopolitan Dock. Five nights and no murders. The nightmares were fading too.

A black Austin 8 pulled up beside him. At first, he thought it might be police, but when he saw the man in the back, he suspected Jardines militia.

The man in the back opened the door from the inside.

"Get in, Mr. Balcombe." His accent was heavy South African with something else.

Balcombe looked at him. The man was huge—hunched in the seat—possibly more than six-five. His heavy features appeared more Slavic or Russian than South African.

"I have better plans," Balcombe said with a dismissive nod.

"Captain Van Ness would like to speak to you." Pause. "It's in your interest."

Balcombe put his left hand beneath his jacket and slid a knife up his sleeve. He got in.

The giant waited until Balcombe pulled the door shut. Then he drew a gun. It looked small in the man's beefy fist.

"No need for that," Balcombe said. The gun was in the right hand, so their weapons were far from one another. Balcombe thought he could switch hands quickly, but would it be quick enough?

He sat back. The car drove off. "Where are we going?"

"To see the captain."

The car turned around and went east, across Statue Square, past the Royal Naval Docks and onto Gloucester Road. Within a mile, they were at the wharf with warehouses that took fruit, vegetables, and meat. There were junks and cargo boats along the quay, but it was dark and closed for the night.

Except it wasn't all closed. They were almost at the cargo handling basin when the car slowed.

Balcombe saw activity ahead. Men carrying boxes came from a boat with no lights. They went into a warehouse and returned empty-handed.

The car entered the building and stopped.

Inside, there was dim lighting. Balcombe could see the men stacking the boxes. There was a mezzanine level with a figure watching. No one spoke, and the whole operation moved in eerie silence.

The giant signalled for Balcombe to get out of the car. Then he directed Balcombe to a metal ladder. Their feet clanged loudly as they climbed. Balcombe glanced down and noted that the big guy still had the gun in his fist. He was also keeping his distance. Smart. Probably cautious in case Balcombe kicked out.

At the top, Balcombe stepped towards the figure on the platform. The man had his hands on the railing, watching the activity below. He didn't turn.

"No need for the gun, Andrej."

The big man slid his gun away.

The man at the railing continued: "Mr. Balcombe, thank you for coming."

"Good evening, Captain."

Balcombe stood beside Van Ness and looked down.

"I saw Scarlet Pimpernel race on Saturday."

Van Ness said, "Did you bet on her?"

"Not this time."

"You should have."

"The odds weren't favourable enough for me."

The Jardines' captain said nothing for a minute. There was just the sound of shuffling feet and the thud of boxes.

"How is your investigation going?" asked Van Ness.

"Not much progress."

"I've asked you here because I have some advice."

Balcombe waited.

One of the men dropped a box and received a whack to the legs for his trouble. He didn't cry out. Only the sound of the stick hitting flesh rose up to the balcony.

Van Ness said, "You were warned about Bai Long."

"Did they torture and kill Geoff Tanner?"

"Bai Long has effective ways of dealing with problems and things they don't like."

"And they didn't like Tanner?"

"You need to take care, Mr. Balcombe. You need to stop your investigation." Van Ness turned and looked into Balcombe's face. "I like you. So I'm letting you know. If they think you're a problem, they won't hesitate to deal with you. You are working unofficially with the police but they can't help you. Bai Long isn't afraid of the Law."

Chapter Thirty-Nine

Fifteen days gone

"They threatened you?" Munro said in the morning when he met with Balcombe in the secret office and Balcombe started to talk about his meeting with Jardines last night.

"I didn't say that. I said it was a warning. Van Ness said that Bai Long wanted me to stop investigating. I only felt threatened at first. On the way there, a big chap had a gun on me. His name was André. Another South African."

"His name's actually Andrej with a j. Lieutenant Andrej Vladar. He's from Yugoslavia originally, or his parents are. Although I think he's from South Africa. Came with Van Ness as one of his men before Jardines. You don't want to get on the wrong side of him."

"I don't intend to."

"What were they doing in the warehouse?"

"I don't know," Balcombe lied. There was no point in directing the police at Jardines. He didn't know for sure they had drugs in the boxes being stowed and the whole thing could have been a test. If the police turned up at the warehouse the next day, Van Ness would be sure

Balcombe had reported it. Then he was bound to be on the wrong side of the giant.

Munro said, "Van Ness didn't say why he was warning you?"

"No, but it's interesting that this happened after my visit to Quincy. It could imply you were right about a connection. Tanner knew something about Laura Quincy's death. Patricia appears to be in hiding after running away with Geoff Tanner."

"That's what I wanted to meet with you about," said Munro. "I saw Ernest Albright yesterday. He asked to see me."

Balcombe waited as Munro paused.

"He told me that Patricia had come home."

"So, she's no longer missing? That's a relief."

"Well, here's the thing. He said that she'd been home and got fresh clothes, then left again. Early Saturday afternoon. He said it was all a misunderstanding. They'd had a squabble and it was no longer a concern." He paused. "I'm to stop looking for her. She'll be staying with another friend."

"Did he mention Tanner?"

"No." He paused and shook his head at a thought. "But my boss did. He said it wasn't my case. The cases aren't linked."

Balcombe snorted with derision. "You're—"

"Deadly serious. And what's more, I rang the investigating officer in Kowloon before I came here."

"At least it's being investigated."

"Barely. He's been told it's a bottom of the pile case. It's been classed as a drug-related gang killing. It's been tied in with the Cosmopolitan Docks' deaths."

"It's being buried."

Munro nodded.

"So, *you've* been asked to stop and *I've* been warned off. Do you believe in coincidences, Munro?"

"I'm a detective. There are rarely genuine coincidences in our line of work."

"Agreed. So, we carry on."

Munro removed his glasses and cleaned them. "I can't. It would be career suicide. If Albright says stop and the whole thing was a favour, the Chief won't approve."

"What about Geoff Tanner? Burying his case suggests—"

"Don't read between the lines, Balcombe. There are targets and politics. Getting a case off the books doesn't mean anything for the chief of police or commissioner except for keeping the statistics clean."

Balcombe nodded and paced. He understood bureaucracy. The Army was built on bureaucracy and bullshit orders. "All right, Munro. You can't investigate, but I can. Then I continue alone. I'll keep you updated."

Munro replaced his glasses and smiled wanly. "Although we have no leads except your warning. And since you've been warned, you're taking a big risk."

"I don't shy away from risk. You know that." Balcombe smiled. "I'll talk to Mrs. Albright. This story about—"

"You'll do no such thing!" Munro snapped, suddenly animated. "I'm lucky your previous visit didn't come back to bite me. Neither will you approach any of the other names on that list. Patricia's friends are now officially out of bounds."

Balcombe stared out through the grimy window. He had nowhere to look except perhaps revisit Tanner senior and Quincy. Neither of those seemed likely leads.

"Something will turn up," he said eventually.

Munro nodded. "If there's a problem, then you're right, something will turn up."

He held out his hand and Balcombe was surprised. Normally, the relationship was tense. A marriage of convenience, but Munro seemed genuinely friendly for once. He accepted the handshake.

"Thank you, Charles," Munro said.

Balcombe nodded. They walked to the door.

Munro said, "I hear your sessions with Doctor Swift are going fairly well."

"They are."

"But you haven't mentioned the blackouts."

"I will. I want to be cured." Concerned that Munro might challenge him on what that meant, he quickly added: "There's another incentive. I like her a lot."

"Georgina's a nice girl," Munro said on the stairs. He stopped and turned to show Balcombe a serious face. "She's got a good heart, Charles. Don't break it."

As Balcombe took a walk along the front and then an early lunch at Jazzles. The whole time, he pondered on the problem. He couldn't approach Mrs. Albright. He couldn't approach Patricia's friends without the risk that they'd report back to her father. Laura Quincy's friends might provide a lead, but that would mean persuading Mr. Quincy. Why was Quincy so worried? If he couldn't get Mr. Quincy to talk, could he persuade wife number two? Alternatively, he realized, he might get a list of Laura's classmates from her old school. Perhaps one of them might know something.

He was wondering how to approach the school when he entered the lobby of his building. Bruce, the concierge, signalled to him, waving a piece of paper.

It was no longer about finding Patricia, it was about her mystery. What was she doing with Tanner, and why was he killed? Balcombe and Munro needed a breakthrough. In investigations like this, it could take time. As he read the piece of paper, he knew it wouldn't take much time at all.

Chapter Forty

The note was from Munro. His news must have been waiting for him at the office and he'd telephoned it straight through to Balcombe. Geoff Tanner's furniture store employer had telephoned. He wanted to meet Munro urgently.

Balcombe had an appointment with Georgina Swift today at two. He was unlikely to be back in time.

On Queen's Road, he told Albert that he was going to Kowloon.

"I'll come too."

"No," he said. "Firstly, the furniture shop is on Cameron Road, so not far from the ferry. Secondly, I have a job for you. I'd like you to check with Doctor Swift whether she can move my appointment to... let's say after 4pm."

Albert nodded. "I'll wait for you at Star Ferry pier."

Balcombe sent her off and within an hour was walking into J.L. George, the furniture store.

He was greeted by a beanpole of a man, tall and thin, wearing a double-breasted suit that highlighted his narrow body.

Balcombe offered his hand and received a cool, sinewy shake.

"Mr. Cooke? I'm Charles Balcombe representing the police."

Cooke cleared his throat and seemed suddenly uncomfortable. "I didn't call you."

"You left a message for Detective Inspector Munro."

Cooke swallowed. "No offence intended, Mr. Balcombe, but I don't know you. I'd rather speak to DI Munro."

"I understand." Balcombe flashed his old credentials which showed he'd been a military police investigator. Cooke still didn't look convinced.

Balcombe decided to be honest. He explained that he was supporting Munro who had been taken off the case. He added: "Geoff Tanner was murdered, and he was seen with Patricia Albright, who was missing." Balcombe didn't explain the complexity of them being told not to investigate anymore. He didn't get that far because Cooke had gone pale. He sat down and gulped air.

"Are you all right, sir?" Balcombe asked.

Cooke took a breath. "This whole thing... It's a lot... it's a worry. Poor Geoff."

"Can I get you a drink of water?"

Cooke shook his head. He scrutinized Balcombe. "How do I know you are who you say you are?"

Good question, Balcombe thought.

"I'm genuine," he said. "I want to get to the bottom of this and neither Munro nor I are happy about being told to stop asking questions." He thought for a moment. "You have a telephone. Call DI Munro again and check with him."

It took five minutes for Cooke to compose himself and finish the call. Balcombe could hear one side of the conversation and it sounded like Munro hadn't been available.

Cooke came back. "He wasn't there."

Balcombe grimaced with frustration.

Cooke said, "But I've made a decision. You do seem genuine and the fact you knew I'd made the initial call and were happy for me to check… well, I'm going to trust you."

"Thank you."

"I've an apology to make. Please let DI Munro know that I'm sorry I lied to him when he asked about Geoff."

Balcombe's relief at being trusted turned to disappointment. It was just an apology.

Cooke continued. "I knew where Geoff was. In fact, I knew where Patricia was too."

Balcombe's eyes widened. "You did? Where?"

Cooke pointed to the ceiling. "They were staying upstairs. I was a bit uncomfortable at first. You know… unmarried couple."

"They were together—a couple?"

"That's the point," Cooke said. "They weren't. Geoff's a good"—he choked—"*was* a good lad. He was protecting Patricia. They were in hiding."

"Do you know where she is now?"

"No."

Balcombe asked to be shown where they were staying, and Cooke took him to the rear of the shop and up a staircase. Above was a storage room with more furniture and packing cases. Balcombe noticed a back door and saw a fire escape led down to an alley.

"That's how they came and went," Cooke explained. He led the way to the far end of the room. "And they were sleeping here."

There were two single beds with mattresses. Both had sheets and cushions as pillows. They were unmade. There were clothes and bags on the floor. There was also evidence they'd eaten here; scraps of paper were piled in a corner with flies buzzing around.

The furthest bed was screened from the other by packing cases. Cooke pointed to it. "That's where Patricia slept. They weren't a couple."

Balcombe picked up a knapsack and tipped it onto the bed. There were a few dirty clothes inside and a toiletry bag. There was also a bottle of pills called aminophylline tablets. A piece of paper had also fallen out.

"I gave her that," Cooke said. "She wanted to know the name of a newspaper reporter. Someone she could trust." He paused. "She didn't want to go to the police. She said they couldn't trust the police."

The writing on the paper read: *H Hawkins, The HK Telegraph.*

"Did she say why she didn't trust the police?"

"No. She said she didn't know who to trust except for Geoff and by then he'd been... been murdered."

Balcombe carried on searching through her belongings.

"When did you last see Patricia?"

"On Saturday morning."

Three days ago. According to her father, she'd gone home for fresh clothes on Saturday afternoon.

Balcombe felt around inside a pocket of the knapsack. Caught in the lining was another piece of paper. It was a ferry ticket to Macao dated Saturday. It had been punched.

She'd gone to Macao on Saturday.

"Did you know about this?" Balcombe asked, showing Cooke the ticket.

"No, but I knew she was excited. That's why she wanted the reporter's details. Patricia said she was sure she was going to get what she needed."

"And you haven't seen her since Saturday morning?"

Cooke shook his head.

"But she's been back," Balcombe said. "Because of the ticket. She came back and left her knapsack."

"Yes," Cooke said.

"You knew?"

"I'm sorry, I'm nervous. I said I wouldn't tell anyone." Cooke sat on the bed. "I don't know what to do. Geoff was murdered and Patricia thought someone would kill her. I want to do the right thing, but now I'm worried about her."

"When was the last time you saw her?"

Cooke swallowed hard. "Monday morning. She came back from Macao on Sunday and, as I said, she was very excited but anxious at the same time. She said she couldn't tell me in case… well, in case I got murdered too. I called DI Munro today because she didn't come back last night."

"Where did she go?"

Cooke rubbed his face with a shaking hand. "I don't know. Poor girl…"

"It could be nothing," said Balcombe, trying to reassure. "Perhaps she's staying with a friend."

Cooke swallowed again. "I don't think so."

"Why's that."

Cooke reached over and picked up the bottle of pills. He said, "Patricia was asthmatic. She wouldn't stay away and not take her pills. I found it this morning. That's when I decided to telephone DI Munro."

"You did the right thing."

"Thank you." Cooke levered his lanky body up and stood.

"She'd come back from Macao excited. And you don't know why?" Balcombe asked because he now knew Cooke had a problem with the straight truth.

"I don't know."

"Could she have gone to the reporter?"

"It's possible."

"Apart from calling Victoria Police Station, have you made any other recent telephone calls?"

"Before this morning… let's see. I made a call to the supplier on Thursday."

Balcombe led the way quickly back to the ground floor. "Call the operator. Ask if there was a call from your number on Monday morning."

It took a matter of seconds to get an answer.

"Not Monday, but there was a call on Sunday night." Cooke nodded. "She called the Telegraph."

Chapter Forty-One

Munro met Georgina Swift outside her therapy room.

"Want to come inside?" she asked, her tone flat, giving nothing away.

He smiled. "And have you look into my head?"

"Sometimes it helps to talk."

Georgina knew about his wife, her easy death at the hands of Japanese soldiers. She undoubtedly knew he hadn't moved on. He still saw her reflection in windows and still talked to her every day. Was that wrong? Wasn't that normal after a loving relationship when one person died? Surely it was healthy.

However, she was right. It was good to talk about bereavement. The only problem he had was the other stuff. His secret. His relationship with BlackJack the killer.

Is that what this is all about? Did I refer Balcombe because of my own issues?

She was looking at him expectantly now.

"All right," he said. He had to do this. After his conversation with Balcombe about the sessions, he'd been worried about her. Balcombe was a charming man. Would she sort out his head or fall for him? She needed to know the truth.

Georgina sat at her desk. He sat opposite. Her eyes were on him the whole time and he had the sense she was assessing, processing his every move. It's what she did, and she was good at it. What he didn't like was being on the receiving end of her scrutiny.

His eyes fell on the silver statue.

"My lucky leprechaun," she said with a smile. "It also helps as a prop and icebreaker at times."

He nodded. "All right, I'll get to why I'm here. I'd like an update on Charles Balcombe."

"He's making progress."

Munro said, "Has he mentioned the blackouts?"

She frowned and looked thoughtful. After a couple of beats, she inclined her head and spoke slowly. "It was you, wasn't it? You referred him to me."

"Yes."

"He thinks it was his friend Roy, but it was you." Pause. "Why the subterfuge?"

Munro felt a rush of annoyance. "Doctor—"

She held up a hand and smiled kindly. "I've known you a long time. I'm just trying to understand, trying to piece together a puzzle that doesn't fit."

His irritation subsided. "What do you mean?"

"We met through your work. Every case you've referred to me has been for professional reasons. You've needed the psychoanalysis of a criminal. Balcombe is different."

Munro said nothing.

She said, "He's your friend."

"Yes."

She looked deep into his eyes then shook her head. "But he's not really, is he?"

Munro glanced at the door, and she seemed to read his thoughts.

"How did you meet? What do you have in common?" She paused as he met her gaze. "Why do you care about him?"

"I can't tell you."

She waited, letting the weight of silence build.

"Sometimes, people just care," he said, hoping it sounded like a genuine answer. Then he elaborated: "Most people don't analyse why they care about someone. And in my job—"

"As a detective." Georgina Swift raised an eyebrow.

"As a civil servant." He shrugged and breathed. "You want to analyse me then, all right. I joined the Force because I care. I want to do the right thing. I want to help innocent people."

She was looking at him with soft eyes.

He said, "Yan was innocent."

"And she died at the hands of a murderer."

"Yes."

"But you were already a policeman. You have a strong sense of justice. Were you bullied as a child?"

"Yes."

She waited for more, but he shook his head. His lips were tight. He knew she'd managed to get to him and he felt like opening up, but he had to stop himself. This was about Balcombe. He didn't need his own psyche analysed with the potential damning conclusion that he was a criminal. That was his bond with Balcombe, and Munro knew that the judicial system would never understand or accept the legitimacy of his role in it.

"And that's it," she said quietly, breaking into his thoughts. "That's your motivation."

"I'm sorry?"

He started to rise.

"What is the point?"

He stood, facing her. "The point?"

"I come back to the initial question: Why? The real reason you referred him."

"He drinks too much."

She shook her head. "Come on, Munro. Most people drink too much." She looked away and back. "You're afraid he's destructive. Not self-harm... A danger to others."

The way she delivered this made him wonder whether she'd been waiting this whole time. It sounded like sudden inspiration, but she was smart. She wanted to get Munro talking before delivering this assessment.

"You're afraid he could have a criminal mind."

"Not really," he said, and then regretted the expression.

She'd picked up on it. "Everyone knows Sigmund Freud's three-component model of the psyche: The ID, ego and super-ego. But that model doesn't address criminal mentality and you know my specialism is the assessment and treatment of criminals."

Munro said nothing. Impulsively he wanted to sit in the chair again, but he also wanted to get away, escape this uncomfortable conversation.

"I can't get to it. I can't reach the *thing*. And I think you know what it is."

"The *thing*?"

"Yes."

Munro shot a glance at the door.

"I told him that a third of the mind is darkness," she said. "He likes that because it fits with his perception of good and evil, right and wrong." She paused and raised a finger. "Of course, we all know the problem with perceptions. They depend on the way our brains are wired. Most criminals justify their behaviour."

Munro's throat constricted. Was she talking about him again. Did she suspect?

She clenched her fists. "Are you afraid he's a murderer?"

He said nothing.

"My God, you are!" Until this point she'd been detached and professional. She unclenched and tightened her fists again, and he wondered if it was a control mechanism. She had feelings for Balcombe, he could read that, and she was forcing her professionalism to control her emotions.

"I didn't say—"

She unclenched and clenched her hands. She breathed. "You didn't need to. Your expression said it all."

"Where do we go from here?" he asked after clearing his throat. "Perhaps you should stop?"

"No. Now I know about the blackouts." She took a breath. "The trauma. He's reliving it. I want to understand him."

She stood, and he felt more comfortable now the pressure to sit and stay was gone.

Munro shook her hand.

"Thank you, Doctor."

She nodded. "I want to keep trying. I want to help him with his darkness."

Chapter Forty-Two

At the pier on the island, Albert said, "Doctor Swift said she can see you today at five."

"Excellent," Balcombe said. "Now let's go to Wellington Street."

"You're going for a drink, master?"

He heard the disapproval in her voice. She knew he liked the single malt whisky at the Wellington Inn.

"The *Hongkong Telegraph* building. As fast as you can and no more cheek, Albert."

"Yes, sir," she said.

When she stopped outside the tall, colonnaded white building, Balcombe told Albert to get a message to Munro.

"Let him know I'll meet at the usual place at six-thirty," he said, allowing thirty minutes past his therapy session with Georgina. "Also, let him know that Ernest Albright has lied."

Albert left her rickshaw and walked in the direction of the police station. Balcombe briefly watched her go and wondered what he'd do without her. Ever since they'd met—ever since he thought she would blackmail him—she'd been an asset.

Inside the building there a reception desk with two severe-looking ladies and no way past.

"I'm here to see Mr. Hawkins," Balcombe said to the first lady.

She looked at him suspiciously, he thought, although it was possibly her natural expression. "Do you have an appointment, sir?"

"No, but—"

The second lady piped up. "He's not here."

Balcombe switched his attention to the seemingly more amenable of the two ladies. "And where might I find him?"

"I don't know. He hasn't shown up today." She raised her eyes. "Some of these reporters…"

"Helen!" the first receptionist reproached her colleague.

Balcombe smiled disarmingly. "May I speak with someone he works with?"

"Without an appointment?" the first said, shaking her head. "You'll be lucky."

"I'd like to try my luck, if I may?" He maintained the winning smile.

The first lady shrugged and picked up a telephone as though it weighed ten pounds. She spoke to someone, then someone else. Then to Balcombe she said, "And you are?"

He gave his name. She repeated it into the mouthpiece, paused and listened. She looked like she was about to tell Balcombe no one could see him.

He said, "I'm working with the police on a murder investigation."

She spoke into the phone and listened again. The telephone receiver went back down with a heavy *thunk*.

"Someone will be down shortly."

Shortly turned out to be half an hour. A bespectacled, gray-haired man appeared at the bottom of the marble stairs to the left of the reception desk.

"Mr. Balcombe?"

"Yes. I'd like to talk about Mr. Hawkins."

The man nodded and Balcombe thought he probably appeared considerably older than his true years. His eyes looked tired with age, but his skin was tight and he moved like a thirty-year-old.

The man didn't introduce himself, just pointed to a bench against the wall on the other side of the lobby. They both sat.

"You say you're working on a murder investigation?"

"Geoff Tanner."

"All right." His old eyes narrowed with consideration.

"But specifically," Balcombe said, "I'm following up a lead regarding a young lady. She called Mr. Hawkins on Sunday evening."

The man's eyes registered recognition.

Balcombe continued: "She had a secret she needed to report."

"Interesting."

He knows something but is giving nothing away.

Balcombe said, "Her life may be in danger. She didn't know who to trust."

"Did she trust you?"

The truth was the best policy here. Balcombe said, "No, but she doesn't know me. Cooke, the manager at J.L. George, the furniture store, didn't know me either but he trusted me enough to let me know she called Mr. Hawkins."

The newspaper man leaned back and blew out air.

Balcombe said, "Her name is Patricia Albright. She's the daughter of the governor's aide-de-camp."

"I'm well aware of who Ernest Albright is, Mr. Balcombe."

Balcombe said nothing. He had nothing more to offer.

Then the newspaper man surprised him. He leaned forward and closer. "Howard did get a call from her on Sunday evening. It was about eleven o'clock as I recall."

"Did he tell you details?"

"No, but he was very animated. He said he'd arranged a meeting with her in Kowloon on Monday." The reporter raised a hand. "And before you ask, Howard didn't tell me anything else. I don't know where they met. He'd promised the girl, you see. She was worried and, you're right, she didn't know who to trust. If anyone."

"Thank you."

"She spoke to the right man, Mr. Balcombe. Howard is as trustworthy as the day is long and you can't say that about many in our line of work." He chuckled. "Even me."

They both stood and Balcombe shook the man's hand.

"Thank you, again. Do you know where I might find him?"

"He's not at home and he's not here. If he were sick, Howard would have called in, but he didn't. I'm hoping he's following up the girl's case."

The man's eyes looked very old again suddenly.

Balcombe said, "But?"

The newspaper man sighed. "There's always the other possibility. If her life was in danger, maybe his life is in danger now too."

Chapter Forty-Three

After Munro had gone, Georgina emptied her stomach until only bile came up. She'd fallen for a patient. Not only did Charles Balcombe have psychological issues, but Munro suspected he was a criminal—a murderer no less!

At the party she'd been drunk. Even so, she'd considered sleeping with him. What if she'd become involved? Not just emotionally, but physically. What if she'd given herself to him? The thoughts kept going round and round in her head. She'd been such a fool. Too much drink and bumping into Giles.

She retched again and splashed cold water on her face.

She cancelled her morning appointment and sat and fretted. What should she do? Should she cancel Balcombe's appointment? Could she go through with it?

An hour passed and she focused on her training. She was a strong woman. She would get through this. After all, nothing had happened. They'd only kissed, and she'd been intoxicated. She'd been clear that a relationship couldn't happen until he'd finished his sessions.

You can do this, she told herself. *And you have to do it today. Delay will only make it worse.*

Then Balcombe's effeminate Chinese boy came to the office and told her Balcombe would be delayed. Before

Georgina could think too much about it, she confirmed five o'clock. She'd keep herself busy until then.

Thirty minutes after Albert had left, Georgina felt better. A talented pianist was playing a soothing tune downstairs. It helped.

She took out her notes and read them dispassionately. Balcombe was just a client with a problem. She was his analyst.

She pulled out a book by Hervey M. Checkley. In it was a checklist for identifying a psychopath. Surely Balcombe wasn't a psychopathic killer.

But his personality met three of the key indicators: charm, boldness and impulsiveness. His impulsive nature was the most important, since many successful gentlemen could tick the other two boxes. He was impulsive and reckless. He didn't experience fear like other men. He thought nothing of death.

Then again, he wasn't manipulative and violent. Was he? How well did she know Charles Balcombe? Not well at all.

She read and re-read and took notes. Despite knowing her subject already, she found it hard to think, found it hard to remember.

She went to the hospital and paid a surprise visit to the mental asylum. She took some case files and occupied herself by reading and assessing those for a while, but the distraction didn't last long. Her mind kept flicking back to Charles Balcombe and her near miss with him.

And then the door opened, and her patient walked in.

"You're early," she said and heard the nerves in her voice.

"Are you all right, Georgina?"

She tasted bile. The bravado she'd constructed over the past hours evaporated fast. It had been an illusion.

"Not feeling so good today," she managed to say.

"Shall we rearrange?"

"No," she said more firmly.

He smiled, and she guessed he thought that this might be the last session. He was probably already undressing her in his mind.

She pointed to the couch and automatically asked him how he was.

He spoke about his dreams and said he thought he was getting better. "The focus, the goblin-statue idea, really helps."

She said, "We previously talked about your relationships."

"We did."

"How do you feel when discussing them?"

"Which ones?"

"Let's start with your parents."

He took a breath and thought. She recognized that he did this when it was genuine consideration. "I don't feel much, to be honest. I know that's interesting. I didn't feel love from them and in terms of my other relationships, they didn't show me how to be affectionate, empathetic... or love."

He's analysing himself now.

"All right, and the girlfriends." She felt her throat tighten as she said the word. Did he see her as a conquest? He just admitted he had no empathy.

"I've seen the error of my ways."

"That sounds a bit glib," she said, quicker than intended.

"They are over. All of them. I've fallen for someone who isn't married."

She said nothing. Her throat constricted again.

"Sorry," he said. "I'll keep it professional."

She nodded and took a breath.

"Have you been totally honest with me?"

He smiled. "I'm glad you asked. There was one thing... blackouts. I also have blackouts and they were becoming more frequent."

He's confessed to the blackouts! Had Munro told him to confess?

She took a breath and dismissed the thoughts rushing into her head. "You were saying: *were* becoming more frequent?"

"Sometimes daily. But since I've been seeing you... Well, I've not had a problem for a week."

"Have you ever killed anyone?" She said it quickly and his easy, straightforward response surprised her.

"Yes." He paused. "Most men have killed someone... wars do that to a man. It's kill or be killed."

But he said he'd worked for the government. Is he admitting he's a murderer?

He looked concerned, probably realising his mistake.

"I didn't tell you the full story before, Georgina." He sounded earnest. "I've been in the army. I killed people in the army."

She wanted to tell him to stop using her name, to call her Doctor Swift, but that would be too obvious. She had to handle this carefully. If he was a psychopath, who knows what he was capable of?

He added: "I don't enjoy talking about it, that's why I deflect by saying *the government.*"

After a beat, she said, "It's good that you feel you can talk about it now." Pause. "You've experienced extreme violence."

"Yes."

"Have you been violent at other times?"

"I've felt aggression," he said, and she knew he'd deflected.

She said, "To move forward you must confront what's holding you back." Pause. "You have to be completely honest with yourself and it'll help if you can be completely honest with me."

She let the words hang in the air for a minute before speaking again. "Charles, have you ever been aggressive?"

He took a breath. "I'm sure I have."

"Are you aware of ever manipulating anyone?"

"No."

"What about your lovers?"

"No." There was a smile in his voice that made her skin crawl.

Am I being unreasonable? Have I committed the sin of jumping to a conclusion and made the man fit the profile?

She snapped out of her thoughts because he was speaking again.

He said, "Maybe they would disagree. But I can honestly say I didn't intend to hurt them."

Normally, she wouldn't shy away from difficult questions. She decided to press ahead. This needed to be done. No point in skirting around it.

She focused on her checklist and asked directly: "Did you ever feel the need to degrade or humiliate them?"

"No, I did not."

"Would you describe your interpersonal relationships as unstable?"

"I hadn't thought of them like that. I suppose you would."

"Did you feel abandoned by your parents?"

He didn't answer immediately. "I wouldn't put it like that. Perhaps it was more like an emptiness."

She looked down at her notepad so that she didn't look at him. "Who is the monster in your dreams?"

"It's my darkness. I want to destroy it. The monster is me."

My God! He's admitted it.

He said, "I asked you about curing people."

"I said I provide tools."

"Like the goblin," he said.

She said, "Brains can be rewired. That's the point of therapy. And if that doesn't work, there are drugs and in severe scenarios there are more invasive treatments." She didn't need to specify operations and electric shocks.

"I prefer the therapy," he said and laughed although it covered his discomfort. "Tell me about the darkness again."

"What is dark?" she asked.

"The absence of light?"

"And how do we control the dark?"

"You want me to say *by switching the light on*?"

"Something like that. What is light?"

"I don't know. Energy?"

"The dark is nothing. Literally nothingness. Light is power. It is control over the dark."

He nodded.

She said, "The time's up. You've made excellent progress." *And there's a monster lurking just beneath your skin.*

"I think the therapy is working," he said. "Seriously."

She said nothing.

"You're good for me," he said and her skin crawled.

She forced herself to speak. "That's good." She winced at her poor expression.

"I have real feelings this time. And you're single."

She looked at him and figured he was thinking rather than feeling.

"What about the darkness?" she asked. "Can you stop killing?"

"Yes."

She took a long breath and felt her fingers tingle. She clenched her hands so that he didn't see them shake.

"Charles…"

"Yes?"

"There was trauma in your past. You need to face it." She paused and swallowed. "You need to face what happened to your mother."

Chapter Forty-Four

Before Balcombe had gone into Georgina's property, Albert had met him and said there was a problem. DI Munro wasn't at the police station and they didn't know when he would return.

When Balcombe reemerged on Gage Street, Albert said, "He's still not back."

Balcombe's head seemed all over the place. Georgina had been so formal this time. Of course that was her job, but after Monday's session she wasn't expecting many more. And of course, on Saturday, they'd become close. She'd watched the filming at the Peak. They'd picnicked afterward, and at the party she'd been willing. Admittedly, she'd been drunk, but he'd been honourable.

They'd become close. He was starting to feel something he never imagined. After his conversation with Munro, he'd decided to be open with her—as much as he could be. If the blackouts stopped, then maybe he could control BlackJack.

Maybe he could stop being BlackJack.

But it hadn't gone to plan. She seemed distant, anxious even.

While he was deep in thought, Albert took Balcombe to Victoria Police Station. Once there, the desk clerk told him why Munro hadn't returned. There had been a domestic incident near Stubbs Road. It was a classy neighbourhood. Nice properties overlooked Happy Valley Racecourse. The clerk added it looked like the wife had pushed her husband down the stairs. Munro had been there all afternoon.

Balcombe decided to wait. The news about Patricia being away at the weekend when she had allegedly returned home was big. That and her meeting with the Telegraph reporter was starting to look bad for Ernest Albright.

It was dusk and getting dark quickly when Munro's car drove into the police station car park.

The driver got out. Munro followed, then paused, with the door still ajar when he saw Balcombe jog over.

"What is it?" he asked, although raised a quieting hand until his driver was beyond earshot.

"Big developments," Balcombe said. "The furniture store chap was the lead we needed." Balcombe went on to update Munro about Patricia and Tanner having stayed above the store. After Tanner's death, Patricia had gone to Macao on Saturday—in the morning.

"On the Saturday she was collecting her things from her parent's house?" Munro shook his head. "What was she doing in Macao? Was she back by early afternoon?"

Balcombe shook his head. "Not possible. Albright must have lied. I don't know what she was doing, but she appears to have come back on Sunday having discovered whatever she was looking for."

"The secret?"

"Whatever that is." Balcombe saw movement out of the corner of his eye. Someone was coming their way. "Cooke called you because he's worried. She left on Monday morning and hasn't returned."

"Who hasn't returned?" The voice came from the figure who'd walked towards them. Inspector Garrett.

Balcombe ignored the question. "The person of interest made an appointment with a newspaper reporter," he said, so that Garrett didn't know about Patricia. "And *he's* not been seen since yesterday either."

Munro started to speak but Garrett spoke over him. "Listen ladies, it's good to talk, but important things are afoot."

The others looked at the bearded inspector.

Garrett said, "Munro, the Chief urgently wants an update. Your latest murder—"

"Possible murder."

"—and your other caseload. I think the Commissioner is pressing for a report, so you're needed." He paused. "Which is a shame because I've just heard we've a source who thinks our man"—he made a sweeping motion with his hand as though carrying a knife—"the one who attacked you, Mr. Balcombe, is over by the docks *and*, I'm told, he knows about Bai Long."

Balcombe and Munro exchanged glances.

Garrett continued: "Since you saw his face—the man with the knife, Mr. Balcombe—"

"He didn't attack me," Balcombe said.

Munro waved a hand. "Go with him."

Balcombe frowned. He didn't like Garrett or his methods. "You're sure?"

Munro was already walking away to report to his boss, "Yes," he said. "You've got pieces of this thing. Bai Long could be the glue that puts it together."

Garrett got into the driver's seat of the car Munro had vacated. Balcombe hesitated, then joined him.

They were soon driving west, onto Queen's Road, and past Balcombe's building. They kept going.

"Which docks?" Balcombe asked.

"The Chinese ones."

Since they were heading west, Balcombe guessed he meant the ones near West Point.

"Oh dear." Garrett pointed over his shoulder and Balcombe looked at the backseat. "Oh dear, Munro left his satchel."

"Let's hope he doesn't need his notes."

Garrett drove on. "I'm sorry I've given you a hard time," he said. "Before now."

Balcombe didn't comment. They crossed over onto Des Voeux Road, the road running parallel. It was well lit. The trams ran this way. To their right was the sea. Away from the streetlights, the roads and quay were inky black.

They came off Des Voeux. Garrett said, "You've a good working relationship with Munro. I hope to earn your respect and you'll also work with me."

Balcombe turned to look at Garrett. Was he being genuine? Was he playing games?

They passed the Chinese wharf and *godowns*. Garrett drove on. They passed West Point and then a large building called Williamson's. There was a jetty called People's Pier Number 5 and another wharf before Belcher Bay.

Garrett stopped and tucked the car between properties. "We'll approach on foot," he said.

They got out and Garrett drew his revolver.

"I'm not armed," Balcombe said, although he quickly moved a knife up his left sleeve.

Garrett shook his head. "We'll be fine. It's just a meeting. They'll expect money"—he patted his breast pocket—"which I'll give them for information about Bai Long, whoever or whatever they are. Your job is to recognize the man with the knife, from the street.

They walked a block, then switched to a parallel alleyway. "No," Garrett whispered. "I don't like it. Too dark."

They retraced their steps and went around. Their vision was poor. Anyone could have been hiding in shadows. They heard the scurry of rats and other things in the dark.

"Almost there," Garrett said, then turned a corner and abruptly stopped. In front of them were three men. Despite the poor light, Balcombe could see they were small, wiry and Chinese.

"The man who attacked you... Is he one of them?" Garrett asked.

"I can't see well enough."

The men took one pace forward and moved so that they were about six feet apart.

"I don't like this," Balcombe whispered.

Garrett spoke loud and confident. "Don't try anything, I'm armed."

"You have the money?" one of the men said.

"Tell me what you know first," Garrett said.

The men took another pace. Five more and they'd be face to face.

Garrett said, "Bai Long. Tell me what you know."

"It means White Dragon."

"And?"

"And now you hand over the money." They took another pace.

Balcombe let the knife slide into his hand.

Garrett raised his gun. "Come no closer. I'm armed."

"You have the money?"

"Yes." Garrett reached into his jacket and snagged a bundle of notes. He held it in his left, the gun aiming at the middle of the three Chinese men.

"Throw the money this way," one of them said.

Garrett said, "What is Bai Long?"

"A person."

"I want—" Garrett started to say, but before he could finish, he lurched forward. In the dim light, Balcombe saw someone behind him. An ambush.

The knife came out and by the time he'd slashed Garrett's assailant, Balcombe had become BlackJack.

Chapter Forty-Five

The man behind BlackJack gurgled and dropped the cosh he'd used on Garrett. His arterial spray caught BlackJack in the face. BlackJack wiped it away just in time to see one of the original three—the right-hand man—lunge forward. The other two were moving as well, but a fraction slower.

BlackJack sidestepped the attacker on the right and rammed his blade under the chin of the middle man. It was six inches of steel, half an inch wide and razor sharp on both sides. His weapon of choice when concealed. It slid up with no resistance from palate, tongue, roof of the mouth, behind the eye sockets. Devastating injuries but not intended to kill. Not immediately anyway.

BlackJack was strong. He could hold his man up by that blade and he now used his victim. He rotated and the man became a shield against the third man.

The middle guy caught a blade in the back from his witless friend. BlackJack kept his momentum going and, as he pulled his knife free of the middle man's jaw, he was spinning. The third man went with him, three men in a dance until the final attacker was in line. Lined up, he could take one at a time. Or like bowling pins.

BlackJack thrust along the line.

As he pushed, he jerked the blade from the middle man's skull. Blood gushed. A lot of blood. A lucky strike. One in a million. Not behind the eyes, but through a small aperture at the back of the mouth: the foramen ovale. The knife had gone through the pons at the top of the brainstem and no doubt deeper. The victim went down like a sodden-heavy towel.

The witless third man was unbalanced. Both him and the first man were still on their feet. They hadn't gone down like bowling pins, after all.

BlackJack danced away from the fallen middle man. Third was still between him and First. He jabbed Third. It wasn't for damage. He'd seen the technique used in a fight in Malaya and had visualized himself doing it. It worked a treat. The stumbling third man twisted away from the pain and unsettled his balance further.

Another dance and the man's vital organs were exposed. BlackJack thrust fast for the heart. In. Out.

The third man keeled sideways, dead, carried by his own unbalanced movements.

The first man was either smart or greedy. As BlackJack finished off Three, One had dived for Garrett's fallen gun.

He was quick despite the darkness, and he would have won the fight if he'd used the revolver straight off. But he didn't. He went for the bundle of notes too.

So maybe he was just greedy. Because he wasn't smart. He used his knife-holding hand to snatch the cash. The gun was pointing at BlackJack but the man wasn't completely focused.

BlackJack was on him before One's full attention snapped back. He kicked the gun-hand and followed up with a slash of his knife.

The man dodged and tossed the knife into his right. He was up and attentive.

An expert knife fighter, BlackJack realized as they circled one another. His opponent's footwork was light and deceptive, and his grip switched from overhand to underhand and back. One jabbed and feinted, trying to draw BlackJack, looking for an opening.

But BlackJack was equally practised. He was also taller, with an advantage of three inches' reach.

One lunged and followed with a leg sweep. BlackJack let the man catch him on the calf, made it look like he'd go with it, fall right, but swerved right. His thrust struck One in the side. A second later, he'd fooled the opponent by switching hands and catching him across the wrist.

One's knife dropped, and it was all over. BlackJack slashed and the Chinese man went down.

A worthy opponent, BlackJack thought as he moved for the death-strike. Instead, he held the man's throat until he no longer squirmed. But One wasn't dead.

BlackJack ripped the Chinese man's shirt. He didn't have his scalpel, but his knife sliced the man's chest open almost as smoothly.

He said, "You, my friend, will find out what it's like to have your heart squeezed."

But before he inserted his hand, he heard a police whistle and saw flashes. Or were the flashes in his head? They were images of Balcombe's mother. Images of a hand bashing down. Again and again.

The whistles.

BlackJack staggered to his feet. He rubbed a bloodied hand on his face.

Got to get away.

On weak legs, he went down to the water, glanced left and right. Something drew him right. A getaway car?

There was more noise behind him now—shouts and whistles. He went along the quay, ploughing through the darkness. To the left, water flickered enticingly.

He saw a floating pontoon. It called to him.
Come and lie down.
Breathe.
BlackJack stumbled onto the partially submerged jetty. He lay on his back and closed his eyes.

Chapter Forty-Six

Balcombe looked at his eyes in the car's rear-view mirror and knew he'd been BlackJack again. He could hear commotion and police sirens.

Memories came back in fragments. Garrett had brought him here. Munro's briefcase was in the back because he'd vacated the car at the police station and rushed away. Garrett had taken Munro's car.

They'd come to the back of the wharf near West Point. Garrett had set up a meeting to pay for information about Bai Long. But the Chinese men had ambushed them both.

For a second, he considered driving the car. The keys weren't hidden under the dash. No keys then. Hotwire it.

But what if Garrett is alive?

If he was and Balcombe ran, it would imply guilt. He had to find out what had happened to Garrett.

Slinking through the darkness between the rear of the *godowns*, Balcombe made his way back to where they'd been attacked. It was easy to find because the police were there. He saw cars and spotlights.

Then he saw Garrett sitting in the back of an ambulance van with a bandage on his head. Balcombe saw no blood. Which was one good thing. BlackJack had killed the attackers, not Garrett.

There were four of them. In the spotlights, Balcombe could see bloody bodies strewn on the ground.

Garrett would know it was him.

Or would he?

Balcombe quickly formed a plan. He'd seen a man in the Army do something similar to get out of an assignment. He exposed his torso, then gripped an inch of subcutaneous flesh. Without hesitation, he stuck his knife through and pulled it out. Twin holes gaped and oozed blood. A flesh wound that looked much worse than it was.

He ripped his shirt and jacket to give the impression of the blade passing through.

He already had bloodstains on his skin and clothes, not washed off by the water, but he wanted more. A cut to the scalp produced a cascade down the right side of his face.

As he was doing this, he slipped silently towards the water. He had to explain why he was so wet.

Once at the dockside, he moved as close to the activity as he dared, then sprawled in the darkness.

He called for help.

Within seconds, there were searchlights on him. Men came and lifted him onto a stretcher. He tried to speak. He let his eyes flutter and then pretended to pass out.

Chapter Forty-Seven

Sixteen days gone

"What the hell, Garrett?" Munro said at the hospital. Garrett was waiting outside the ward. Balcombe's side had been stitched up, and he was sleeping.

"What do you want?" Garrett growled. He had a hand to his head as though it hurt.

"To talk about the foolish stunt you pulled last night, not least about lying to me."

"What are you talking about, Munro?"

"You told me Carmichael wanted an urgent update. It wasn't urgent."

"I thought it was." Garrett shook his head. "And about the incident: don't piss on my head and tell me it's raining."

"What's that supposed to mean?"

"It means, I know it went wrong. I don't need you to point it out. I thought it was worth the risk for a breakthrough in the Squeezed-heart cases."

"Paying money for information on Bai Long?"

"I had backup. It went south faster than I expected, and they were too slow."

"And Balcombe? Why did you really drag him into it?"

Garrett pulled a smile. To see what happened and—ah, good he's awake."

Garrett pushed into the ward and Munro hurried behind him. He'd heard third hand what had happened. Garrett had been knocked out and fortunately missed the action. Four Chinese men had been murdered—"butchered" was the description by an officer at the scene—and Balcombe mysteriously injured and found at the water's edge.

Balcombe took a cup of water and knocked back a painkiller.

"How are y—?" asked Munro.

Garrett spoke over his last word. "What happened, Balcombe?"

"My side stings and my head hurts, but apart from that I'm not too bad, all things considering. Thanks for asking." He looked at Garrett as he spoke, as though it had been the bearded white detective who was concerned about him.

"I want it in your words, and we'll have a formal statement," said Garrett. "But for now, tell me what happened from the point I was hit?"

"I didn't see what happened to you. At the same time you went down, the four Chinese men in front—"

"There were three in front of us," Garrett said, explaining to Munro.

"Four," Balcombe said. "Three and then one further back. He was the one who stabbed me."

Garrett blinked and shook his head. "Four?"

Balcombe said, "They fought the man who hit you."

Garrett eyes narrowed. He rubbed his head, presumably where he'd been him. "A fifth man?"

"The attacker. And he wasn't Chinese. He was white."

"White? You're certain?"

Munro said, "Anything else you can tell us about him?"

Balcombe shook his head and breathed, and Munro guessed it was an act, but a good one. "Wait, yes. He was big. I remember seeing him look big compared to you Garrett." He raised his hand as though working out height. "A giant. Perhaps six-five or six-six?"

"Go on," Munro said. "Explain again what happened."

"It was mayhem. The big man was there. Garrett was on the floor. The Chinese men were going crazy. They had knives. I think the big man had a knife. I ran, but I ran into the path of the man at the back. He stabbed me and I remember thinking I've just got to get away, so I kept going. I thought if I could get to the quay, I could hide."

"It was dark. Did you know the wharf?"

"No. I've never been there before."

Munro thought Balcombe sounded convincing although he knew BlackJack had struck close to there just over a week ago.

Balcombe continued: "I got to the edge. It was brighter because of the water. I could see better but I slipped on something and went over. I think... well I must have blacked out. The next thing I remember is the sirens and then the searchlights."

Garrett was looking at him with flint in his eyes.

"You had a lot of blood on you, Balcombe."

"Did I?"

"How do you explain it?"

Balcombe shook his head. "I can't. I'm sure you got blood on you. There was a lot of it flying. The giant was hacking at them like a maniac." Balcombe paused then looked from Garrett to Munro. "This... this giant isn't the man you're looking for, is he? Is he the one you thought was me, Garrett?"

Munro was quick. "There's only one giant I know of on the island." He looked at Garrett, confidential, one detective to another. "I'll give you a name. He could be our man."

Garrett said, "You'll come down to the station as soon as you're released from here, Balcombe. We'll have that statement and a better description of this shadowy giant." He then walked away and motioned for Munro to follow. In the corridor, he wanted the name.

"Lieutenant Vladar," Munro said and explained about Jardines militia.

"Right," Garrett said, "I'll speak to this Vladar chap and find out where he was last night."

"You think Bai Long is one man?"

"You might not have heard, but one of the victims was sliced across the chest last night." He drew a hand under his left rib.

"Squeezed-heart?"

"No, but he didn't have time. The police disturbed him. This could be our man, Munro. The White Dragon."

Chapter Forty-Eight

Balcombe was at the police station after an early lunch. Albert had picked him up from the hospital and taken him home so that he could freshen up and change.

"I failed you, master," she said.

He shook his head.

"I did," she continued. "I tried to follow the police car but lost you on Des Voeux Road. He was too fast, and I didn't know where…"

"Albert, how could you have known what he was up to? Garrett was setting a trap for me. There was no need for me to be there, and he thought he'd see me use my knife. I was lucky."

He'd been exceptionally lucky that Garrett had been knocked out. Lieutenant Vladar wouldn't like the finger pointed at him, but Balcombe's plan was to deny it. Providing Valdar wasn't covered in blood, found holding a knife and had an alibi for last night, then all would be well. Garrett would be off chasing the wrong person again and may even get in trouble for it.

Balcombe had another appointment with Georgina at two. He needed to make a statement at the police station, but would make it short.

"Shall I ask for a later time again, master?"

"No. Thanks, Albert. I'll make it."

He needed to see Georgina. He'd been BlackJack again, but it had been different. He hadn't gone looking for death. He'd defended himself. Despite no memory of anything his alter ego had done, he was sure progress was being made. It had to be.

The *bring back the reality* technique had helped him get out of the hallucinatory state.

And he'd had a flash of his mother. Had Georgina caused that? Was it a memory trying to resurface or was it imaginary?

★ ★ ★

Munro wasn't at the station. DC Tattersall took Balcombe's statement and explained that the inspector had dropped everything for an urgent visit to Kowloon.

"He missed Mrs. Quincy," Tattersall said. "You were helping with that weren't you?"

"Mai Quincy?" Balcombe asked.

"No. Sheila." Tattersall looked uncertain. "She said something about a second wife telling her about the boy who was murdered."

"Geoff Tanner."

"That's right."

So the second wife had spoken to the first Mrs. Quincy and she'd come to find Munro.

"Did she say anything?"

"I got an address—"

As soon as Balcombe got it, he raced out of the police station and told Albert to take him there.

"You'll be late for your appointment with the doctor," Albert said.

"Run as fast as you can, then."

And Albert did. Balcombe wanted to make contact and learn whether Sheila Quincy knew anything important. There was a good chance, he thought, that the case was already beyond anything she could help with.

But he was wrong. After the ex-Mrs. Quincy explained that she hadn't married her sailor-boy, she said she got on well with Mai Quincy. The new wife was worried Quincy hadn't told the police everything. Sheila Quincy knew Geoff Tanner.

"Was Geoff Laura's friend?"

"No, but she knew him. He seemed all suave and sophisticated, but he was a bad influence. A good-looking boy, I think he acted as a lure."

"A lure?"

"For someone else."

"Laura wouldn't say, but I have this theory that the Tanner boy was being used by someone else."

★ ★ ★

Balcombe apologized for needing to dash off and promised to return with Munro, if the information proved useful.

Albert was concerned about the time and arrived on Gage Street five minutes after his allotted appointment time.

The door beside the piano store wouldn't open. He went into the store and waved to the unassuming man running it.

"I've an appointment with Doctor Swift," Balcombe said. "Her front door appears jammed."

"Ah, yes," the man said wiping is brow. "I think it'll be locked. Appointment you say? I believe she's cancelled her appointments for the day. Not feeling well, I believe. Perhaps you missed the notification?"

"That'll be it," Balcombe said, although Bruce the concierge was efficient. He'd never failed to pass on a message or note before.

"Do you happen to know her home address?" Balcombe asked.

The piano man looked uncomfortable. He wiped his brow again. "I don't think..." Then he seemed to compose himself. "It's right that the doctor keeps her work and private life separate. It wouldn't be appropriate for me to disclose her home address."

"Of course."

Balcombe went back onto Gage Street where Albert was waiting.

"I have a job for you," Balcombe said to her. "Find out where Georgina Swift lives. I asked the man in the piano shop, but he's too cautious."

"One of her patients. He probably thinks you're a crazy person."

Balcombe laughed.

She said, "I'm sure I can get it. Where will you be, master?"

"At the Cheero Club although I'll go via what was the Hart Hotel. I'll walk. You go and do your stuff."

★ ★ ★

Phil "Powerhouse" Ellis was behind the bar. The place was packed, and he had two barmen helping him. The place sparkled like a new penny and smelled of paint rather than old tobacco and alcohol.

Ellis caught his eye.

"The film star!"

The people around the bar heard and turned to look who'd come in.

Balcombe shook his head. "Only from the rear, I'm afraid. They didn't film my face and I won't be in the credits."

Disappointed people turned away. Balcombe reached the bar and Ellis pointed to the far end where it was quieter.

"So, you're still here, Powerhouse?" Balcombe said.

Ellis waggled a finger at the packed room. "I'm Tweedie now, aren't I lads?"

A chorus of cheers went up and Ellis turned his attention back to Balcombe. "As you can see, the lick of paint and infamy has done business a world of good. I hope you're not here for poker, because the cards room is now for diners."

"Diners?" Balcombe laughed. "So, you're staying, not selling up?"

Ellis poured a shot for himself and Balcombe. "It's a good job. I should have checked the small print. That sneaky producer, or his legal guy, or whoever."

"What?"

"They told me they'd buy the business afterward, but it wasn't in writing and… well at least they covered the cost of the improvements and I'm not complaining about all this." He waved his hand at the crowded room. "I just hope it lasts."

Ellis went to pour another shot, but Balcombe shook his head.

"I'm sure it will," he said. "And I'll make sure people know you've gone upmarket, serving food."

Ellis chuckled, "Steady on, don't oversell it!"

Balcombe turned to leave.

"Do you play backgammon?"

"No."

"It's a betting game." Ellis grinned. "Gamble fifty dollars and I'll throw in the good stuff."

Two minutes later, they were sitting in the kitchen with two glasses of Glen Grant and a backgammon board.

Forty minutes later, Balcombe had lost his fifty but enjoyed the game and company.

Ellis said, "We should do this again. And if you get too much into debt, you can teach me to climb. I could do with a bit of excitement." He patted his belly. "This lifestyle hasn't been kind to the fighting-fitness."

Balcombe pumped his hand and agreed he'd return.

Outside, he was surprised to see Albert waiting. He checked his watch. An hour had passed since he sent her off to get Georgina's home address.

"Got it already?" he asked.

"I'm highly talented, as you know." She smiled and bowed. "Actually, I confess it was easy."

"Because?"

"She lives upstairs above her office."

Balcombe recalled the door with nothing on it. There were three floors. No doubt that door led to a staircase and her private rooms.

Albert continued: "And there's a backdoor. She uses that one to get in and go upstairs to her private rooms."

"Well done," Balcombe said. "Instead of Cheero, I'd like you to take me to Gloucester Arcade and the flower shop there."

The Clover Flower Shop was reputedly the best on the island. Balcombe ordered a pretty bouquet of cream roses which included delicate white flowers for variety.

On the card, he wrote: *Thinking of you. Charles.*

Albert took him home afterward.

Munro was waiting for him there. He had a haunted look in his eyes.

Chapter Forty-Nine

"What is it?" Balcombe asked Munro when they were in the building's meeting room off the foyer.

"She's dead. Patricia Albright is dead." He took a breath and shook his head. "I've just got back from the scene. In an insurance office in Kowloon. The office manager found the bodies late this the morning. It would have been earlier, but the room wasn't in use."

"You said bodies?"

"Patricia and Howard Hawkins. Murder-suicide," he said. "She was in a chair, shot in the forehead. He was on the floor having bitten a bullet. An old Webley service revolver was next to his hand."

Balcombe shook his head. "She went to him with the evidence or answers—what she'd been looking for."

"Something about Laura Quincy's death."

"Something sensitive. Something she found in Macao. Something she couldn't entrust to the police. She delivers it to Hawkins who then kills her. And then he takes his own life?" Disbelief edged the end of his sentence.

"That's what the scene tells us."

"Then the scene's lying, Munro."

Munro nodded. "You and I know it, but the Chief is already accepting it as a straightforward case. I've been told to write it up as such. Case closed."

"No question of motive?"

"No discussion."

Munro paced, pensive.

Balcombe said, "What do you want to do about it?"

"I want to talk to Mr. Albright."

Balcombe stood. "Let's go."

"It's my case, Charles."

"I'm as involved as you, Munro. Neither of us are comfortable about this. I bet Albright knew what Patricia was investigating. I reckon that's what they argued about. He knows something."

Munro met Balcombe's eyes, held his gaze.

Balcombe said, "We already know he lied about seeing her on Saturday."

"But why involve me in the first place?"

"Only one way to find out."

Munro eventually nodded. "All right, let's go."

★ ★ ★

A member of staff opened the door to them. The maid wore a black armband and had puffy, red eyes.

Munro stepped forward. "Mr. Albright, please."

The maid looked at them as though he was speaking a foreign language.

Munro showed his warrant card. "DI Munro. I'd like to speak to Mr. Albright."

She blinked and thought. Her voice trembled with frailty. "I'm sorry, sir... You know what's happened... Mr. Albright... I'm afraid he's not here."

She was about to close the door.

"Mrs. Albright?"

"Sir?" The woman swallowed. "You do understand. Poor Mrs. Albright is in no state to take visitors. She's resting."

Munro stepped forward again, and the lady accepted him into the hall. Balcombe followed.

The maid tried again. "She's taken a sedative. I don't think—"

"Take me to her, please," Munro said firmly.

After a hesitation, she led them upstairs to a closed door. She knocked, entered and closed the door after herself.

Munro and Balcombe waited. After a couple of minutes, the door opened.

"She'll receive you now."

Mrs. Albright was sitting up in bed, a night shawl over her shoulders. Her face was set, stoical. She'd applied makeup, but she still looked like she'd aged a hundred years since Balcombe had seen her last.

Munro bowed his head. "Please excuse the intrusion." His voice was soft and deferential.

Balcombe said, "I'm so sorry for your loss, Mrs. Albright. You must be devastated."

Elizabeth Albright's features collapsed. Tears flowed freely and her chest heaved.

"We should go," Munro said. "My sincere apologies."

They backed out and were about to close the door when she called them back.

"I can do this," she said, clenching her teeth. She paused for breath, then started again. "You were trying to find her. You were trying to help."

Balcombe said, "What did Patricia and your husband argue about?"

"Did she suffer, Mr. Balcombe? Did Patricia suffer in the end?"

"It will have been instantaneous. No, she won't have suffered."

Mrs. Albright switched her watery eyes to Munro. "Why did he do it? A newspaper man, they said. Why, Inspector. Why kill my little girl?"

"That's what we'd like to know, Mrs. Albright."

Balcombe said, "Patricia was looking for evidence. She argued with your husband."

"Yes."

"What was she investigating, Mrs. Albright? What did your husband not approve of?"

"Geoff Tanner, he said. Ernest told me he didn't like the boy." She looked across the room towards a dressing table, or perhaps the drawn curtains. There was a wedding photograph on the table. Maybe she was thinking about happier days.

Balcombe said, "It wasn't just about the Tanner boy, was it? There was something else."

Her eyes flicked back to him. "Secrets," she said. "Guilty secrets."

"Guilty secrets?" prompted Munro.

She took a ragged breath. "Always the Governor before family." Her voice trailed off, then came back. "It's always about Morris. Family should come first." Another ragged breath, then: "The war taught us that. Family."

She closed her eyes.

Balcombe leaned in. "What was his secret, Elizabeth?"

"The Governor." Her eyes flickered open briefly. "Family."

"Where is your husband, Mrs. Albright?" Munro asked, but she was no longer with them.

They waited a minute in case she came back and then left the room.

Downstairs, the maid showed them to the door. She looked even more distressed, and Balcombe wondered whether she'd been listening from outside the bedroom.

"I'm sorry we disturbed you," Balcombe said.

She nodded, her eyes betraying many unsaid thoughts.

Balcombe wanted to double check something. He said, "Were you working last Saturday?"

She blinked. "Yes, sir."

"Mr. Albright said that Patricia came home on Saturday. Did you see her?"

"No, sir."

"Thank you." He turned to leave.

"But I saw her on Friday night."

"Friday? Last Friday?"

"Yes, sir. She didn't come in, though. I saw her outside. She was going through the gardens."

"The gardens?"

"The back way. There's a path to the Governor's mansion."

★ ★ ★

"Of course!" Balcombe said. "That's why Mrs. Albright kept looking towards the bedroom curtains. It wasn't the dressing table. She was thinking of the Governor." If he'd opened the curtains, he would have been able to see the Governor's residence. "Governor Morris always comes first, she said."

"You think Albright is up there?"

"Whether or not he is, Albright has a guilty secret of some kind. We need to speak to the Governor."

They got into the car, but Munro didn't turn the key straight away. He stared down the road and breathed.

Balcombe was on the verge of walking up there on his own when Munro finally said, "Right," and started the engine.

He drove less than a hundred yards to the Governor's gates. Balcombe had never noticed them before. He hadn't noticed a small, one-man gatehouse, either. It made sense. The Governor was the most important man on the island. He had a mansion with grounds and a fence.

The drive curved through immaculate lawns. The sun was getting low and was still casting long shadows on the lower slopes and across Victoria to the Naval Dockyard. Across the water, golden light reflected off windows. But the garden was in the Peak's shadow. Balcombe guessed the governor preferred the view rather than worried about the last rays of sunlight.

The double gates were locked. There was a bell-pull.

Munro got out. Balcombe got out.

A gatekeeper opened the hut's door.

Of course there'd be a gatekeeper. That made sense. What didn't make sense was who the man was.

Lieutenant Vladar looked menacing through the bars of the gates.

Chapter Fifty

The Jardines' lieutenant didn't let them in. He said the governor had security concerns and there would be no visitors.

Vladar wasn't the least bit interested in Munro's status.

"No one," he said with a reptilian smile. "I don't care who you are."

"Governor Morris will want to see us," Balcombe said confidently.

"Why?"

"Because we have information about—"

Vladar interrupted. "The Captain seems to think you're an intelligent man, Balcombe. But standing here, asking questions about the governor"—he placed a hand on his holstered gun—"doesn't seem so smart to me. And as for you." His cold eyes flicked to Munro. "I hear you're a good detective inspector. Like your predecessor. And we know what happened to him." Again he pulled the reptilian smile.

Munro motioned for Balcombe to get into the car.

Vladar watched them turn and drive away.

Munro looked pensive.

"What was that about your predecessor?" Balcombe asked.

Munro didn't answer straight away. "Don't do anything stupid, promise me," he said at length. "Don't go up against them."

"You didn't answer my question."

"DI Bill Teags," Munro said. "He's in a hospice now. Had a breakdown during his last case. And retired due to *diminished responsibility for psychiatric reasons,* they said."

Balcombe said nothing. He could see Munro's mind working on more than the road as he drove down the hill.

"Now I'm thinking," Munro said. "Teags crashed his car into a wall, heading for the sea at East Point. We assumed it was attempted suicide. But… he was looking into another case and suspected the Jardines militia were involved. Nothing came of it. The case was quashed. I don't know what happened to his car. Now I'm wondering whether he intended to hit the wall. Was it deliberate? What if his brakes had been tampered with?"

Balcombe knew Jardines were involved in money lending and drugs, probably more. "They're above the law," he said.

"They protect the establishment, and the establishment protects them." He paused, then: "Did you notice Lieutenant Vladar didn't mention the incident at West Point last night? You gave his description to Garrett. And I provided his name."

Balcombe nodded. He'd been waiting for Vladar to accuse him and had intended to act innocent. He was going to say he hadn't said anything of the sort. But Vladar had been strangely silent on the subject. Either he was a good actor, or he knew nothing about being named.

They'd come down on Magazine Gap Road and were passing the hospital. Balcombe wondered if Georgina was feeling better. Was she working in there tonight?

They'd hoped today's session would be his last and they could have a meal together. He'd hoped they could begin the sort of relationship he'd never experienced before.

Perhaps tomorrow, he thought.

Munro was speaking. "I said, what should we do?"

Balcombe tore his eyes from the hospital.

"Jardines are acting as security for the Governor. We've been distracted. We don't need the Governor. It's Albright we're after."

"So, we wait?"

"Absolutely," Balcombe said. However he had no intention of waiting. After he left Munro at the police station, he walked to Tweedies.

Powerhouse Ellis waved to him when Balcombe entered. It was after seven in the evening and the place was packed.

"Another drink, or are you here to win your money back?" Ellis asked. Instead of replying, Balcombe signalled that they should talk in private.

"What is it?" Ellis asked once they were alone at the end of the bar.

"You said you wanted some excitement," Balcombe said. "If you're up for it, I have a plan." And five minutes later, after a shot of the good stuff, Ellis said he would do it.

Chapter Fifty-One

The night washed ink over the landscape. Balcombe could see lights on in the governor's mansion. There were also lights on the broad front gates. He'd been to the Albrights' house first and met the maid again. She confirmed that Mr. Albright hadn't returned.

Balcombe pulled on the bell.

The gatehouse door opened, flooding light across the drive. The giant came out. He didn't need a torch, but he shone one at Balcombe anyway.

Vladar shook his head. "You *are* stupid."

"I prefer foolhardy," Balcombe said.

"You're not coming in."

"I have a letter that the Governor will want to read."

"Let me see." Vladar came up to the gates.

"No. It's private. For the Governor." He paused. "I came back without the detective. It's too sensitive to share with him. And the police can't be trusted."

"This is bull."

Balcombe stuck the paper in his pocket. Time for another approach. "You're a big man. But your brain is the size of a pea."

Vladar said nothing.

Balcombe said, "On Monday night, when you had the gun on me in the car, you must have felt brave."

Vladar said nothing.

"Brave man with a gun." Balcombe paused. "You're big, but you're no fighter."

The torch flicked over Balcombe's body, presumably checking whether it looked like he was armed.

"Lift your jacket," Vladar said. Balcombe complied and turned around, showing an empty waistband.

The Jardines man put a key in the lock, turned, and cracked open a gate.

"Step inside," he said.

Balcombe walked through and stood just out of arm's reach.

Balcombe said, "I beat you, then I walk down the drive to see the Governor. You beat me and I walk away."

"There won't be any walking when I'm finished with you."

"No gun."

Vladar snorted. "I won't need a gun."

Balcombe glanced behind him, checking the amount of room. He fingered the knife in his pocket but withdrew his hand, empty. He needed his wits about him. He needed his memory. The last thing he needed was BlackJack to take over.

"Give me more space," he said and indicated where he wanted to stand. They moved back. Vladar was on the edge of the gatehouse's light. He smiled, full of confidence.

They squared off.

"The count of three," Balcombe said.

Vladar snorted again. "What is this?"

"One."

Balcombe drew up his hands into a classic boxing pose.

Vladar snorted and flexed his chest.

"Two," Balcombe said.

At the same time, there was a scuffling noise behind the giant. Instinctively, the man glanced.

His head turned first one way and then shot back. A large fist followed it and, as the Jardines man dropped like a felled tree, Powerhouse Ellis stepped into the light.

"That felt good," he said.

"Perfect."

"Shame it wasn't fair. One-on-one in a ring would have been more satisfying."

"He had a gun," Balcombe said, "and is at least five inches taller than you."

"I could have had him."

"Next time."

"There'll be a next time?"

"I hope not."

Ellis helped Balcombe tie up the Jardines giant and then they shook hands. Balcombe had said this was all he required. He'd known there was a back route to the mansion since Albright used it. He could have gone that way himself, but he wanted the guard immobilised. No point in breaking into the governor's mansion to then get shot as an intruder.

"How will you get back?" said Ellis, since they'd come in his car.

"Don't worry about me. I'll find a way."

"And after, when the big guy wakes up? He didn't see me, but he'll come after you, that's for sure."

"That," said Balcombe, "is a bridge I'll cross when it comes."

"Brave man," he said.

"A brave man without a gun."

Chapter Fifty-Two

Balcombe took the lieutenant's gun and stuck it in his waistband after removing the bullets. So far, his plan had worked. Using Ellis and keeping his hand off his knife had kept BlackJack at bay. But the gun wasn't to stop BlackJack coming out and using his knife. Balcombe planned to use it as a prop.

From a distance, he'd thought there were more lights on in the grand house. Inside, he found a lamp in the reception hall and dim lighting beyond. Balcombe worked methodically through the rooms downstairs looking for the governor.

He checked from room to room and found no one. But when he entered the west wing, he heard distant music. He followed the sound and quickly realized it was opera. Loud and mournful.

He opened the door to a room at the back of the house. The stench of alcohol carried on warm air.

There were lights, but not enough to make it bright.

Ernest Albright lounged in a chair beside a record player. There was an empty bottle of whisky on the floor. He had a bottle of brandy, held in mid-pour.

Albright looked up.

There was no surprise in his eyes. Perhaps because he was drunk.

Balcombe strode over and removed the player's arm.

Albright said, "You know the story? Verdi. *V'ho ingannato*. Rigoletto."

The words came out slurred and punctuated.

Balcombe said, "Where is he?"

"Rigoletto has a bag. He thinks his… his nemesis. Nemesis is inside." He gulped air then knocked back a shot of brandy before pouring another. "It's his daughter. Stabbed. Dying."

How appropriate.

"Where's the Governor?"

Albright peered through blurred eyes and shook his head exaggeratedly. "Not here. His Excell… His Excellency's not here."

"Where is Morris?"

"Abroad. Travelling."

"What's the secret?"

Albright swallowed another glass of brandy. "He's not here."

Balcombe closed in and took the glass from Albright's hand. "Patricia came to see Morris on Friday. What did he say to her?"

There was a long pause before Albright spoke with slurred aggression. "He told Patricia… he told her the truth!"

"What did he say?"

The aggression dissipated as fast as it had arrived. "He said Simon killed the Quincy girl."

"What?" Balcombe's brain fired with a hundred questions, but only "What?" came out.

Albright's eyes swept from the bottle of brandy in his hand to searching for a glass.

Balcombe said, "Who is Simon?"

"You didn't know. Of course you didn't know." Albright peered closer at him. "Why are you here? Why did you stop the music?"

"Who is Simon?"

Albright blinked. "The governor's son, of course."

"What happened? Was Simon on the tram rails with Laura?"

"What? Oh, the tram rails," he laughed although it came out as a sad splutter. He gave an exaggerated blink then looked like he'd fall asleep.

Balcombe kicked open the French doors and felt cooler air rush in. Then he pulled the drunken man to his feet and walked him to the opening.

Balcombe slapped Albright's face. "I want answers."

The governor's aide-de-camp's eyes were wide and scared.

"Answers! What did Simon do?"

Albright clenched his teeth. "He liked to party. He liked young girls." Albright gulped the fresh air and shook his head, probably to keep himself awake. Then he continued: "Girls. Not too young. You know what I mean?"

Balcombe nodded, uncertain, but he wanted Albright talking without interruption.

"Not too young," Albright said again, making sure Balcombe understood. "But he would... Drink and drugs. He got them with... then take advantage."

"He'd rape them?"

"No! Not rape. Not really. But they didn't... they didn't complain." He shrugged and stared into the garden. "Usually."

"Laura complained?"

Albright brought his gaze to Balcombe's face and thought. Then: "Can I sit down now?"

Balcombe let the man flop back into his chair. "Keep talking."

"Hmm. They fought. She banged her head."

"Laura and Simon? On the tram rails?"

Albright shook his head and pulled a face like Balcombe was an idiot. "It was just an accident."

"How did Patricia find out?"

"Patricia… she's dead." He reached for the bottle and Albright took a swig before Balcombe could stop him. "I killed her. Like Rigoletto." He wailed and Balcombe waited until the man took a shuddering breath and seemed calmer.

Balcombe said, "You were about to tell me how Patricia knew."

Albright shook his head. "The Governor told her."

"But how did she know to ask?"

"One of the boys. A boy at the party. Where Laura…"

"Was it Geoff Tanner?"

"Morris thought that telling her… telling her the secret would keep her quiet." He laughed sadly. "It should have been me. I should have told her. I should have warned her."

"Was the boy Geoff Tanner?"

"What? Yes."

So, Tanner had told Patricia to speak to the governor who had confessed.

"Where's the governor's son, now? Where's Simon Morris?"

"He's dead too."

The governor's son was dead? Balcombe had been on the island for nine months. He'd never heard anything about the governor's son's death. Had the news had been withheld? Probably.

"How did he die? When?"

At first it made no sense but eventually Balcombe got the explanation. Tanner wasn't the only one who knew what had happed to Laura Quincy. A gang member did too. She'd fallen during a fight with the governor's son and died from a bang to the head. To prevent scandal, the body had been moved from the mansion.

It took a few attempts to make sense of drunken Albright's words, but finally Balcombe understood. The gang had moved the body. They had put Laura Quincy's body below the tracks to make it look like an accident there.

But that wasn't the end of it. The gang started blackmailing the governor. Simon was sent away. Albright didn't know where, but the boy had guilt issues and hadn't stayed away. Albright said that Simon was going to confess and say the gang helped by getting rid of the body.

"Who is the gang?"

"They killed him," said Albright. "I never saw him. Somehow the gang found out and intercepted him."

It still didn't make much sense to Balcombe.

Albright had said he'd killed his daughter, but he meant indirectly. He hadn't protected her.

Balcombe said, "The gang killed Patricia because she was exposing it all?"

"Yes."

"They killed Patricia and the reporter?"

"Yes."

"Who is the gang?"

"I don't know."

"Guess."

"I've heard the name Bai Long."

Balcombe nodded. "Why are Jardines acting as security?"

"To protect the Governor… protect him from the gang." Albright shook his head as though it was an obvious statement. "He might confess. Then where's their blackmail money? They could still try and blackmail him but he's also a threat."

Balcombe said, "This has all come from the Governor?"

"Yes. He confessed to me."

"And then went away?"

"Yes. It was too dangerous. After Patricia said she wouldn't keep quiet." Albright suddenly started sobbing. "Patricia, I failed her!"

Balcombe walked out of the room and shut the door. The mournful opera immediately started playing.

Balcombe thought about the jumbled story that he'd eked out of Albright. It was a good story, but it didn't hold water. Not all of it.

Only one way to test it.

He'd seen a telephone in a room off the entrance hall. There was a number on the table beside it with the initials JM. Balcombe dialled the number.

"Captain Van Ness," the voice answered. JM: Jardine Matheson or possibly Jardines Militia.

Balcombe took a breath and altered his voice, tried to sound younger. "Mr. Van Ness, it's Simon Morris."

There was a long silence on the line except for the sound of the electrical hum of wires. Did Van Ness know Simon's voice? Could he hear the fake?

Eventually, in a flat tone, the Jardines' man said, "Simon, you're back."

"Yes, Mr. Van Ness."

"Where are you?"

"At my father's place."

"One of my men is there. At the gatehouse. Did you see him?"

"A Jardines' man? No, sir. There's no one here from Jardines, Mr. Van Ness."

"Your father's away."

"Yes."

"Are you all right? You sound… different."

"I've had enough," Balcombe said adding distress to his tone. "Too many people have died, Mr. Van Ness. I need to tell the police."

"That would be inadvisable, Simon."

"I can't take it anymore. The secrecy…" He faked choking, as though he was too emotional to finish.

"Stay there, Simon. I'm on my way."

Chapter Fifty-Three

Van Ness came through the front door. Two men flanked him, and Balcombe was relieved that neither one was Vladar. They'd not seen the giant trussed up behind the gatehouse.

If Van Ness was surprised by Balcombe's presence, he masked it well.

He signalled to his men, who then frisked Balcombe, removing the gun.

"Where's Simon Morris?" Van Ness asked tersely.

"That was me on the phone. Simon Morris is dead."

Van Ness's eyes showed amusement.

Balcombe said, "But he's not dead, is he? Of course not, otherwise my little ruse wouldn't have fooled you. You came here expecting Simon. We both know he's alive. The Governor sent him away, he's in hiding."

"What do you think you know, Mr. Balcombe?"

"I know what I've been told. That a gang, possibly Bai Long, covered up a crime—"

"It was an accident."

"It wasn't an accident. Simon and Laura Quincy fought. She banged her head. Maybe she was defending herself against a rapist."

Van Ness's face showed nothing. "All right, go on."

"The gang arranged the body to be moved. Then they blackmailed the Governor. And your role…"

"To protect the Governor from the Bai Long."

Balcombe shook his head. "That's just it. You see, it doesn't make any sense. I guessed because they wouldn't have killed Simon. That would have been killing the goose that laid the golden egg." He paused, watched Van Ness's eyes. "Jardines weren't needed for protection."

"What were we needed for then?"

"For the blackmail. And when I called pretending to be Simon, you accepted it immediately. As I said before, you never thought Simon Morris was dead. Even Albright thinks he's dead, but you know he isn't."

Van Ness clapped his hands. "Very well done! I always suspected you'd impress me one day. I should have offered you a job."

Balcombe said nothing. He saw the guard on the right place a hand on his sidearm.

"What's your plan now, Mr. Balcombe? You must have a plan. Blackmail me?" He chortled. "Unfortunately, you no longer have a gun."

Balcombe said, "I want to understand. Why keep it up?"

"To protect the Governor, of course. He's the one with the power in Hong Kong. And the man behind the king is the true king."

"So, you influence who he releases from prison?" Balcombe had seen hardened criminals pardoned in the New Year. "And turn a blind eye to your activities?"

Van Ness nodded. "I heard you were acting in the Soldier of Fortune film. You know what, Mr. Balcombe? I am Clarke Gable. I am the pirate." He waved his arms expansively. "I can do what I please."

"You're above the law."

Van Ness inclined his head. "Or you could say that I am the law."

Balcombe said, "And in return, the Governor and his son get silence."

Van Ness said, "You aren't thinking big enough, Mr. Balcombe. It's much bigger. The whole of Hong Kong gets my protection. Imagine what such a scandal would do to the banks! Would do to trade. This isn't just the Governor's secret, it's Hong Kong's secret."

Van Ness nodded to the man on the right and the gun came out and pointed at Balcombe.

Balcombe said, "You killed Patricia Albright."

Van Ness pouted. "Tsk tsk. It was the newspaper reporter who killed her before taking his own life. Although he did need some encouragement."

"And now you're going to shoot me."

"Only if I have to." Van Ness smiled. It appeared more genuine than his lieutenant's reptilian smile, but it was fake none the less.

Balcombe knew he didn't have a chance. Van Ness didn't mean that. He meant he'd only shoot him in the governor's mansion if he had to. Because then they'd have to clean up the mess. Much easier to kill him away from the mansion. Not a murder. Maybe an accident on the Peak tram rails.

Balcombe said, "Before you do anything you regret, just tell me one thing. You killed Laura and Geoff Tanner as well."

Van Ness smiled again. "Isn't that two things?"

"You wanted the police to think Tanner was a drug dealer. He was never at Cosmopolitan Docks buying drugs. You told the police he'd be there so you could set it up. They'd see a white boy buying drugs and jump to the conclusion it was him. But it wasn't. So when he died they'd assume it was a drug deal gone wrong."

"It was you who gave me the idea. I wasn't even aware of the Tanner boy until you came to see me." The man on his left took a step forward. Van Ness continued: "Now, if that's all the questions, let's go for a walk."

Balcombe waited until the man on the left was close enough. Then he picked up the knife he'd secreted on a table beside him.

They'd made two common mistakes. He'd carried the gun expecting them to disarm him. Having found it, they'd thought *gun* rather than *knife*. They'd searched him and hadn't found another weapon.

The second mistake was to assume he was right-handed. The knife had been lying on the table by his left hand. Balcombe was ambidextrous, and by the time they realized what was happening it was already too late.

He slashed the man on the left, slicing his throat before pulling him around as a shield.

* * *

That was the last thing Balcombe remembered. He'd known BlackJack would take over as soon as the fighting started.

Two hours later, he heard gunshots. He saw a stabbing, slashing knife. It was in his hand, but he wasn't trying to kill the monster. No. He was the monster. They knew it and were afraid of him. The blood flew. The knife flashed. More gunshots. Broken, dying men.

This happened. I'm not dreaming, I'm remembering.

He was awake now, but the hallucination started. Or was he still in the dream? The hand was trying to blot out the light, smoother his face, strike him. He couldn't get away, couldn't stop it.

Focus, breathe. Georgina Swift.

He got flashes of her office. He saw her face. Was she there?

"Georgina?"

Focus on reality. Grab something real.

The goblin. Hold the goblin. Feel its contours. It is real, the hallucination is not.

The room stopped being blurred. The psychedelic hands evaporated. He wasn't in Georgina's office. He was outside, lying on grass under a tree. It wasn't in bloom anymore, but he recognized it: the ornamental cherry in the cathedral gardens. The Gothic building loomed ghost-like in the darkness.

Then he focused on himself. His hands were slick with blood. But that wasn't what alarmed him. In his left hand was the goblin from Georgina Swift's office.

Chapter Fifty-Four

"When's the first steamer to Macao?" Balcombe asked Albert. It was early, the sun not quite on the horizon, although the hustle and bustle on the streets had already begun. They were mostly Chinese on their way to work or setting up shop.

"Nine o'clock." Albert looked at him through narrowed eyes as though reading his soul. Did she know what he'd done? If she did, she didn't say anything about last night. Instead, she simply asked, "Why do you want to go to Macao?"

He ignored the question. "Take me to Gage Street." Once in the back of the rickshaw he said, "Last night—"

"You gave me the night off," she sounded defensive as though he'd expected something. "Remember? You went off with Inspector Munro."

Balcombe leaned back and wondered. What had happened? He expected three bodies at the governor's mansion. Were the police there now, wondering whether Bai Long had struck again?

And then what happened? Where did he go after the fight with the Jardines men? How did he get Georgina's statue? His stomach knotted. He knew the only rational explanation but couldn't admit it.

When they neared the piano store, his stomach churned, and bile pushed into his throat.

There was a police car was on the street, a crowd of onlookers and a cordon. A police officer guarded Georgina's black office door.

On weak legs, he walked into the piano store. The man he'd spoken to before was standing close to the window. His face was pale, his eyes empty.

"What's happened?" Balcombe asked.

And then his worst fears were realized.

"Doctor Swift… She… There's been a break in. Doctor Swift has been murdered."

★ ★ ★

Munro came down the stairs from the top floor. He'd seen a lot of deaths, but he wasn't desensitized by them. Each one affected him and this one more than most. Georgina Swift had been a beautiful young woman, full of life with a glittering career ahead of her. He had no doubt about that.

And now she was dead. She'd been bludgeoned to death. That was clear. She was lying on the floor of her bedroom wearing nightclothes. There was also blood. A knife wound to the chest.

Munro guessed it had been quick. The killer had broken in through the front door on Gage Street. He'd found Georgina in her bedroom.

She'd probably been disturbed by a noise but by the time she was out of bed it was already too late. No lengthy confrontation, just a stab and series of blows to her head. She was barely recognizable. Yeung would confirm the number of blows on the mortuary slab, but Munro guessed more than ten. A frenzied attack.

He'd also know which came first. From Munro's experience, the lack of blood suggested the stabbing came after. Was that to finish off the dying woman?

Munro went downstairs to the working floor. DC Tattersall was in the doctor's office.

"This door has been forced, sir," he said as Munro looked around. "It doesn't look disturbed though."

Munro nodded numbly. This was a deliberate, targeted murder. The killer came into the building with one intention: obliterating the life of Georgina Swift. But he'd also been in the office. Why? Did he think he'd find the doctor here during the night?

"Get it all dusted for prints," Munro said.

Why come in here?

There would be a reason. Munro's eyes swept the room until they settled on the desk. He remembered it from when he was here before. His chest constricted, a cold hand on his heart.

"There was a statue," he said after a breath. "On the desk."

Tattersall glanced around. "Not here now, sir."

Munro swallowed. "Look for it. That could be our murder weapon." His eyes fell on an open book. Moving around the desk, he could see it was an appointment's diary.

The left-hand page was for two days ago. She had two appointments, one of which was for Balcombe. The right-hand page had a block of time for work at the hospital. There was a cancelled 2 pm appointment, again for Balcombe. And it the evening there was another cancelled appointment. Only this wasn't work.

In her own hand, she'd written: keep free for dinner with CB.

Chapter Fifty-Five

Balcombe couldn't stay outside Georgina's place. He wanted to go in. He wanted to see her, but he forced himself away.

"Take me home, Albert."

Focus on the job, his inner voice told him. *Deal with this later.*

Bruce, the concierge, had an odd expression on his face when Balcombe went through the lobby. Fifteen minutes later, Bruce looked relieved to see Balcombe reappear.

"I found a photograph for you. Just didn't expect you back so soon, sir." Bruce handed over a newspaper clipping with a photograph of Simon Morris posing beside a new Mercedes. An arrogant, privileged young man. A young man who thought he ruled the world. A young man who thought he could have anything he wanted. Including Laura Quincy.

Balcombe tipped the concierge and noticed beads of sweat on the man's forehead.

"Everything all right, Bruce?"

"Yes, sir," the concierge said, but Balcombe sensed something was off. "Out again so soon?"

Focus on the job.

Balcombe had too much on his mind to worry about a doorman having a bad day. He found Albert waiting outside.

"I'd like you to take this to the Radio Communications Service," he said, "and get this message wired to the port at Macao."

He handed her a piece of paper. She didn't look at it, but he knew she would. What would she think? Would it make any sense to her? Probably not.

She said, "So you're not going to Macao?"

He started walking towards the quay. "I am."

She kept up with him, having left the rickshaw in the street. "Why?"

One question laced with a thousand other questions. She'd asked earlier but this time he decided to answer.

"To meet someone."

She looked like she expected more, but he wasn't willing to share.

"I should come too."

He forced a smile and shook his head. "Not this time, Albert."

"But—"

"But nothing, Albert." He knew he'd snapped at her but he didn't need this on top of everything else. He stopped and pulled out a bundle of cash. "Payment in advance—a week's wages, since I don't know how long I'll be away."

After a hesitation, she took the money silently. Her eyes were still full of questions.

In the Star Ferry queue, he looked back and saw she was standing still, watching him.

The ferry took him to Kowloon harbour, where he queued at the Canton Steamer ticket office for the Macao boat. There was a man at the front of the short First-Class queue, complaining. When Balcombe took his place, he found out why. There were no First-Class tickets available.

"I'm terribly sorry, sir," the ticket man said, his face creased, a testament to his genuine concern. "The American film crew—"

"The film crew?"

"The production company has taken the First-Class deck, sir. There's only Second-Class available on the Tak Shing or—"

"Second-Class will have to do," Balcombe said.

"—Or you could get the next boat. SS Fat Shan leaves in three hours."

Balcombe already had his wallet out. First-Class would have been eighteen dollars. Balcombe's ticket cost less than a third of that.

There was a mixed atmosphere on the second deck. Roughly a third of the passengers were angry at not being on the top deck. The rest seemed excited at what was taking place above them. The film stars were there: Clarke Gable, Susan Heyward and names Balcombe hadn't heard of before. Passengers strained on the side rails, leaning out so that they might catch a glimpse.

Balcombe, on the other hand, avoided the crush and enjoyed a seat. The service wasn't what it would have been above, but the tea was acceptable.

He could hear the director and others shouting instructions and was reminded of his experience being filmed, over and over again, as he climbed the Peak's crags.

A passenger tried to spark up a conversation. The man was travelling to Macao. For a gambling holiday, he said. He called Macao the Las Vegas of the East. Maybe it was, but Balcombe was going for a different reason. And he didn't want to make idle conversation. He wasn't in the mood. The gentleman gambler soon got the message and left Balcombe to watch the rugged coastline on his own.

Balcombe saw other people drinking, and he wanted a whisky. But he knew that one glass would lead to many. He resisted the strong urge. To distract himself, he wrote a note. He detailed everything he'd learned and worked out about the death of Laura Quincy and Patricia Albright's investigation. Tanner had told Patricia about his guilt. He introduced girls to Simon Morris and his private parties. Morris abused them but Laura Quincy had fought back. Maybe her death had been an accident, but Van Ness's men disposed of the body. Tanner had been complicit in Laura's death. Patricia had asked her father and rowed with him. Finally, the governor had confessed to her. He'd said that Simon had died but she hadn't believed it. Patricia had travelled to Macao and uncovered the lie. The big secret. Simon Morris was alive and well. That had been Balcombe's assumption and Van Ness had confirmed it.

Then she'd gone to the newspaper reporter to expose the crime. But she'd been murdered along with the reporter. Again by Van Ness and his crew. Before he'd killed Van Ness last night, the Jardines man had admitted their role in the cover up and blackmail and elimination of witnesses. Except for Simon Morris. They needed him alive. They needed continued leverage against the governor.

When he finished, he sat back, breathed out and returned to looking out of the window. The waves and the bobbing became monotonous. He lost focus. The land blurred into the water.

His mind turned to the case. He thought about Simon Morris. Balcombe wasn't travelling to Macao to prove he was alive. The young man was undoubtedly continuing his lifestyle, continuing his abuse of young girls. He needed to be stopped.

One second, Balcombe was thinking about punishing Simon Morris and the next he was on Gage Street, Georgina Swift's door before him. Everything was dark and closed for the night. The black door was almost lost in the darkness. It wasn't locked. He reached for the handle, but the door was already ajar. He had a flash of climbing the stairs and then he was in her office. He wanted the goblin. He wanted to feel its reality. That's why he had come. He wanted to end the nightmare that was BlackJack. Was Georgina there?

He awoke with a jolt, remembering the dream but nothing about Georgina. What had happened next? All he knew was that he'd awoken under the cherry tree with the statuette.

"Are you all right?"

A middle-aged woman was standing next to his table.

"You look a little peaky," she said. "Are you all right?"

He realized he'd noticed her earlier, moving from table to table. Settling and talking and then moving off, like a nervous butterfly.

He took a sip of cold tea.

"Just confused. Just woken up," he explained.

"Ah," she said then: "Mind if I join you?"

Before he could think of a response, she was sitting opposite and talking.

She said she was an uneasy traveller and went pale each time the boat swayed. "I wondered if you were the same."

"It's safe," Balcombe reassured her.

"I keep thinking we'll sink," she said, gripping the arms of the chair. "I can't swim and there's never enough space on the lifeboats."

"We won't sink," Balcombe said.

A waiter offered tea or alcohol, but she took only water, sipping it anxiously. Balcombe accepted a replacement for his cold tea.

Once settled, she told him her name was Madalen Cannon. She spelled out her name and explained the origin, saying her parents made a mistake with the spelling of her first name. Then she went on to summarize her life story ending with a move to Hong Kong three years ago. She was looking for her husband who'd travelled to Macao for the casinos. Normally he would be gone for less than a week, but this time he'd been gone for three and she was worried.

Balcombe let her talk since it clearly helped her nerves. His lack of reciprocation didn't trouble her although she got a false name out of him.

When she stopped telling her stories, he asked, "You've heard nothing from your husband for three weeks?"

"Paul likes to gamble," she said, stating the obvious.

"I'm sure he's fine," Balcombe said, although he thought differently. Maybe Mr. Cannon couldn't return after a week. Maybe he had delayed his return to recoup losses. If Mr. Cannon had run out of money, he may have borrowed it. Which may have led to being unable to repay his debts.

She showed Balcombe a photograph. The man looked sixty, with a bulbous nose and lecherous eyes.

"Easily recognizable," Balcombe said.

"Please let me know if you see him," she said. "I'll be staying at the Palace Hotel."

Once he'd agreed, Madalen Cannon took her leave and tottered on nervous sea-legs to the next table. No doubt she'd regale them with the same stories and request for help.

The schedule said the crossing would take three hours and fifty minutes. Balcombe heard from another passenger that the film company had influence over the three-decked steamer. They expected delays. Balcombe knew all about multiple takes. But when the SS Tak Shing pulled around the headland and Barra Point, and into Porto Interior, it was only five minutes behind schedule. However, after docking, the passengers had to wait. The director wanted arrival and disembarkation shots, so the film crew got off, the steamer pushed away and then docked for a second time. Then there were shots of the stars disembarking, and another half an hour passed before Balcombe found his feet on the quayside.

Ignoring all the fuss of the filming and stars, Balcombe's first job was to locate the port's Radio Communications Service office. It was a little shed set beside a taxi-rank of rickshaws.

He went inside and was greeted by a little European clerk with round glasses and a pinched nose.

"Good afternoon," said Balcombe. "I believe you have a message for me." He gave his name and waited while the little man fished out a telegram and passed it over. The message Balcombe had sent to Macao was allegedly signed by Simon Morris. If the clerk wondered why Mr. Morris would send a message from Hong Kong to Macao about a meeting in Macao, it didn't register on his face.

"Ah," said Balcombe, sounding perplexed. "Mr. Morris requests that we meet at three this afternoon but has neglected to give me his address." He shook his head. "He assumes I know it. But I don't, I'm afraid. Perhaps you could—"

It was a minor gamble. Would the clerk know Simon Morris's address? The Hong Kong governor's son. A playboy. An important person, surely. He'd get lots of telegrams. So the clerk might know. But if he did, would he disclose it?

"You could ask at the general post office, sir."

Balcombe smiled and removed his wallet.

"You'd save me a lot of effort—and I could miss an important meeting."

The clerk's eyes glistened. "Not a problem, sir. As I said, you could ask at the post office and I'm certain they will say—"

Balcombe peeled off twenty dollars.

"—that you may find Mr. Morris in Salazar House."

Balcombe handed over the cash. "Of course! How foolish of me. I did know after all."

Rickshaws were lined up in the shade behind the next building and Balcombe asked a boy to take him to Salazar House. He hadn't asked the clerk for the street, but, as suspected, the rickshaw boy didn't need it.

The elegant Portuguese building was in the centre of the town on Salazar Square. When he arrived, Balcombe didn't get out.

He wanted a base for preparation, and if necessary, overnight accommodation.

On the boat, he'd obtained a street map. It had hotels marked, and he'd selected an unimposing one away from Central and the main nightlife.

Ten minutes later, he was checking in. He also handed over a letter and asked for it to be posted to Hong Kong. He wore a fedora and pretended he needed a handkerchief. The reception clerk saw very little of his face.

Twenty minutes later, wearing a different hat and clothes, and having shaved off his moustache, Balcombe was travelling back to Salazar House.

Up his sleeve was a knife.

Chapter Fifty-Six

Garrett went into Balcombe's residence off Queen's Road with two detectives. The doorman smiled nervously.

"You reported a problem in number six?" said Garrett in a voice that implied both parties were in on the ruse.

The doorman breathed. "I did, sir."

"What's the matter?" Garrett said, reading worry on the man's face.

"The man... you know... he came and went."

"So, to be clear, *he* isn't home?"

"Correct. You just missed him."

Idiot, Garrett thought. *A simple script all you had to do was stick to it.* Bruce, the doorman, had been passing all of Balcombe's communications to Garrett for the past three days. Garrett read and returned them. He'd hoped to gain proof of or a clue to Balcombe's undoubted nefarious activities. He hadn't got anything. Not even a secret message he suspected Munro was sending.

It had cost him fifteen dollars so far. This had better be worth it.

He gestured to his men, and they took the stairs.

They hesitated on the second floor.

"Room six is this way," one constable said.

Garrett smiled. "Up another flight."

When they reached the room at the end, Garrett said, "Watch and learn."

He took out a screwdriver and undid the number's top screw. Then he flicked the number over.

"Ah," said the men.

Garrett pointed and one man shouldered the door open. He could have used a key, but the door jamb splintered satisfyingly. If nothing else, Garrett would enjoy pissing Balcombe off by busting his door.

"Gloves on. Start searching," he instructed, and they worked meticulously from room to room.

Garrett's heart leapt when he saw the medical books. Was it just an interest? Garrett thought not. These academic texts suggested training. And they'd always expected the Squeezed-heart murderer was a surgeon. Could Balcombe have been a doctor once? He didn't seem old enough. But then again, his past was obscured. He claimed to work for the British government. He implied he was a secret agent. He lived like a gentleman of leisure, but he involved himself with private investigations. It was all very suspicious.

Garrett opened a well-thumbed book called Gray's Anatomy. On impulse, he set it down and let it open at a natural page.

"Oh my God!"

"Sir?"

He hadn't realized he'd said that out loud. The book had fallen open at a diagram of a heart.

"Right, men. You need to redouble your efforts. Check everywhere. We're looking for knives."

* * *

Munro hesitated outside of Balcombe's door. It had been broken open. Then he spotted the number had come unscrewed. The nine looked like a six.

What the hell?

Munro drew his gun and stepped inside. Then he understood. Garrett and two constables were tearing the place apart.

He was about to reprimand Garrett for his childish trick when one of the men gave an excited shout.

"Sir! Here!" He was on a chair, pushing through a hole in the ceiling. A hatch.

He climbed down with a tan-leather roll in his hands.

Garrett swung around, saw Munro, and grinned.

They both crowded the constable, who was unrolling the leather.

Munro held his breath as he saw the glint of steel.

"Got him!" Garrett shouted breathlessly.

Munro stared, hoping he looked surprised, but no one was paying him any attention.

"Scalpels, medical knives." The constable stated the obvious. The second leather roll contained the same.

Garrett was on the chair feeling in the space above them. He withdrew a cloth. Only it wasn't just a cloth. Garrett flicked it open. Inside was a stiletto blade.

Excitedly he said, "There's more!"

"My God," said Munro, hoping he sounded enthusiastic. "It must be him."

He turned. He felt dizzy. He should have planned for this moment.

His eyes were momentarily unfocused, and then he blinked and blinked again.

Beside Balcombe's favourite chair was a statue.

The leprechaun from Georgina Swift's office.

Chapter Fifty-Seven

"Where's your master?" Munro asked Albert.

"I don't know, sir."

Albert was totally loyal to Balcombe. Munro was sure the effeminate boy knew Balcombe's secret. The two of them were close. Albert was often on hand when BlackJack operated. Maybe the boy even knew about Georgina Swift.

Munro quickly snatched Albert's arm.

"I could arrest you."

Albert squired. "What for? I've done nothing wrong, sir."

Munro led the boy into a quiet doorway. "I know his secret."

Albert said nothing. Munro released his grip, but the boy didn't run away.

"I'm not trying to trick you, Albert. Your master and I have been working together. Not just police investigations. I know the things he's done. And you should know that some of the time"—Munro dropped his voice to a whisper—"he did it with my blessing."

Albert's eyes narrowed, suggesting he was considering the truth of Munro's admission.

Munro whispered something only Balcombe as BlackJack would know. The arranged murder of the prisoner released on New Year's Day. The body had never been found. The disappearance was a mystery.

But Munro knew the truth, and so did Albert.

The rickshaw boy nodded, then asked, "Why do you want him?"

"He's in trouble." Munro paused. "BlackJack's out of control, Albert. He's killed the doctor."

"The doctor?"

"Georgina Swift."

Albert's eyes bulged with shock.

"He needs help." Munro paused again. "Where is he?"

"Gone."

"Gone?"

"Macao. He's gone to Macao."

★ ★ ★

Munro and Garrett travelled to Kowloon and immediately went to the harbour ticket office. Garrett had picked up a photo of a younger Balcombe from his home. He showed this to the ticket clerk and confirmed Balcombe had bought a ticket for Macao.

"Second-Class?" asked Munro, wondering whether the ticket and telegram were an elaborate trick. Had Balcombe pretended to go to Macao?

The clerk explained the situation. First-Class hadn't been available. When questioned further, the clerk said he was sure he'd seen Balcombe board the steamer.

"Out of a hundred passengers?" Garrett challenged.

"Oh, more than a hundred, sir," the clerk said. "But there were two things. First, I thought he was one of the film stars and the other reason was he had a rucksack. All the other passengers hoping to travel First, had cases.

Munro and Garrett found the next boat, the SS Fat Shan, would be docking soon. However it wasn't scheduled to depart for another couple of hours.

Garrett said, "Not just the delay, but I don't fancy travelling in something called a fat anything. Is the captain called Stan? Fat Stan?"

Munro was in no mood for humour. "It's a luxury steamer, Garrett. And *fatshan* is a prestigious Chinese word. The best translation is *proper*."

"Nevertheless, I'll get us a motor launch."

Ten minutes later, they were at sea in a Marine Police boat, the two of them and a pilot.

At first the launch seemed a good idea, but once they were in open water, beyond Lantau Island, Munro wished he'd forgone breakfast that morning.

Garrett also looked a little green but pretended to be fine. They'd fallen into silence shortly after boarding the motor launch. The noise made conversation difficult. Not that Munro wanted to talk to the other inspector.

Eventually, Garrett met Munro's gaze and shouted louder than was needed. "He's done a runner, hasn't he?"

Munro wiped sea-spray from his eyes. That was his best guess. Balcombe had murdered Georgina Swift. He'd finally killed an innocent person. And then he'd fled.

Guilt lay heavily on Munro's shoulders. He'd told Roy Faulls to introduce Balcombe to the psychoanalyst. It wasn't Munro's fault that the doctor had become besotted with Balcombe, but it was his fault that he told her about his issue.

Munro told himself that she had enough experience to recognize his schizophrenia—if that's what it was—but she hadn't. She hadn't recognized the criminal in her patient.

The argument went back and forth in his head and he knew it was pointless. Nothing was going to bring Georgina back. He might convince himself that it couldn't have been prevented, that it wasn't his intervention that caused it, but it didn't change the facts. Georgina Swift had been bludgeoned to death with her statuette.

BlackJack had killed her because… what? Because he'd also believed there could have been a relationship. He'd been seen with her at a party. She had a personal appointment in her diary for dinner with him. And she'd crossed it out. She'd cancelled plans when she'd realized her mistake, realized what he was.

He'd killed her because she'd spurned him. Or had BlackJack killed her to spite his alter ego?

Garrett shouted, "What are you thinking?"

Munro shook his head.

Garrett said, "Balcombe is Bai Long. He's the White Dragon. I knew it all along! You should have trusted me, Munro."

Munro said nothing.

"Knowing he's Bai Long, means you've cracked a lot of old cases too," Garrett added. "You should be happy about that."

Munro shook his head. He didn't bother pointing out that the name Bai Long had been a myth for years before Balcombe had arrived on the island.

They travelled without speaking again for almost an hour. The only sound was the crashing waves against the hull and the spray peppering them and the deck.

"Penny for them?" said Garrett in a moment of relative quiet.

"You don't need me. Why did you want me along?"

"You insisted."

"You didn't argue."

Garrett smiled behind his unkept beard.

Munro guessed the reason. Garrett didn't need another embarrassment. He'd made blunders on the Squeezed-heart case and was out of favour with the Chief. Having Munro along provided security. They'd either both succeed or both fail.

"I'm not after your job, Munro. I hope you see that?"

Munro knew it was a lie, but he didn't care. As far as he was concerned, this trip was about damage limitation.

Outing Charles Balcombe as BlackJack could lead to exposing Munro's involvement. However he knew their arrangement couldn't continue, and the killer of Georgina Swift had to be brought to justice.

BlackJack could no longer be controlled. It was over.

What would Balcombe say when they found him? Would he tell Garrett about the arrangement? By accompanying Garrett, at least he'd know what the other inspector learned.

"Of course," responded Munro. "We're both professionals. The result is more important than the reward."

Garrett held out a hand and Munro took it.

"No hard feelings, Munro."

Because of the spray, their hands were damp and wiping them before and after was instinctive. However to Munro's mind, it symbolized the removal of false friendship.

When Macao's lighthouse finally hove into view, Munro breathed with relief. He'd be travelling back by steamer, whether Garrett joined him or took the motor launch.

They passed the external port and rounded Barra Hill with its church on top. There were hordes of junks tied up ahead of the wharves. The Canton Steamers docked immediately after, and the marine police pilot pulled up to a floating dock.

Munro and Garrett agreed that the first thing to do was to check at the communications office. Balcombe had sent a strange telegram to himself. If he was on the island, he'd have collected his message.

Garrett and Munro showed their warrant cards.

"Hong Kong police?" the clerk said.

"We're looking for this man." Garrett held out the photograph.

The clerk peered over his glasses. "He looks older now. Different."

"Most of us do," Garrett snapped. "So, you recognize him?"

"Yes, sir. He arrived on the SS Tak Shing."

Munro said, "And he collected a message from a Mr. S. Morris?"

"Yes, sir. Which was odd because he then asked where Mr. Morris lives and I explained that there are almost two hundred thousand people on the island."

"Thank you," Munro said, suspecting the clerk enjoyed the sound of his own voice and was about to give them a verbal guided tour. "Do you know where Mr. Balcombe went?"

"I'm afraid not. He said he had a meeting at three." He checked his watch. "Assuming he found—"

"Where would he go?" Garrett interrupted.

"One of the hotels?" The clerk handed over a map with hotels and entertainment venues marked.

Garrett asked where they could find the police station. Taking a rickshaw apiece, they travelled to the central police station and notified the authorities of their mission.

They left with a car, a driver and the promise of armed support should it be required.

Then they started working the hotels, showing Balcombe's picture and asking if anyone had seen him.

Chapter Fifty-Eight

Simon Morris did not live in Salazar House. Balcombe cursed. The communications office clerk at the port had either been mistaken or lied. Most likely lied. Balcombe was tempted to return and demonstrate his displeasure. Maybe later, he decided.

The police or the post office would be his usual optons for finding an address. But they were out of the question now he was effectively on the run. The Macao authorities might not know about him yet, but it wouldn't take long. His notoriety as the killer, known as BlackJack and the Squeezed-heart murderer, would surely spread. Newspapers in the region would pick it up in a day.

His disguise would work for the casual observer, but as soon as his face was known to the public, he'd find his activities restricted.

He had to move fast. He had to locate Simon Morris.

The second hotel he tried was The Palace. He was just showing the receptionist Morris's photograph when a woman's voice attracted his attention.

"Mr. Smith?" It wasn't the name he'd checked into his hotel under. It was the name he'd given to the nervous lady on the boat.

"Mrs. Cannon," he said nodding. For a second, he forgot his changed appearance and then worried at her expression.

"You look different," she said. "The hat. The clothes. No wait, you've shaved and…"

He smiled politely. "I must be going. I hope you find your husband."

"Oh," she said excitedly, "I already have!"

At that moment, Balcombe recognized the older man approaching them from the photograph she'd shown him. Her husband looked sheepish and Balcombe guessed Mr. Cannon had been enjoying himself. He'd not expected his wife to come looking for him.

"I was telling Mr. Smith all about you on the boat, dear," she said to him. Then to Balcombe: "He's been a naughty boy, Mr. Smith, but I've found him, and all is well."

Mr. Cannon shrugged guiltily. "I lost track of the days. You know how it is, old chap?"

"I do," Balcombe said. He touched his brim. "I must be going."

"Did you meet your fellow?" Mrs. Cannon asked and Balcombe remembered that he'd mentioned in passing that he was travelling for a meeting.

"Not yet."

"You're not sure what he looks like? Is that why you were showing the receptionist a photograph?" she asked.

"On the island? Let me take a look," Mr. Cannon said, and Balcombe found himself compelled to show them the newspaper clipping with a picture of Simon Morris.

Cannon's chin tucked back, and his nose seemed to protrude even more. "I know him! From the club. What's his name? Young chap. Likes the ladies. Lots of money. Ah yes, Simon."

"Simon Morris," Balcombe said.

"No. That's not it. I'm not sure of his first name, but he's definitely called Mr. Simon."

Balcombe suspected Morris had done the classic switch. He was probably calling himself Morris Simon now.

Cannon said that Simon frequented the Lisbon Club. "Casino, dinner, dancing, g—"

Balcombe knew the man was about to say *girls* but had stopped himself. Fortunately for him, Mrs. Cannon didn't notice.

★ ★ ★

The dress code for the Lisbon Club was evening-dress. Most men wore black dinner jackets, but Simon Morris arrived in white. He was young, tall and cocksure. He also had two bodyguards. Balcombe figured they were Jardines' men. They were protecting their asset. While Simon Morris was alive and free, his father would keep paying.

Balcombe considered buying an appropriate suit because he wasn't getting into the club dressed as he was. But the gentlemen's clothes shops were now closed for the evening. If he wanted to get inside, he'd have to wait until tomorrow night.

"Don't move!"

Balcombe swivelled his attention away from the club's entrance and saw DI Munro standing twenty paces away, his gun aimed and ready.

Chapter Fifty-Nine

They'd asked at every hotel on the island. Garrett wanted to check at boarding houses. Munro said they should check the nightlife.

"He's a gambler," Munro said. "Even if he's checked into a boarding house, my bet is he's found a casino."

"Which makes you a gambler too," Garrett said with a smirk. "You know? You bet."

Munro said nothing.

Garrett shook his head dismissively. "All right, driver, take us to the best casino and we'll start from there."

That casino was the Lisbon Club and, as they approached, Munro spotted a figure lurking ahead in the shadows.

After parking on a side street, they split up. Munro went directly for the figure in the shadows.

He drew his sidearm. "Don't move!"

The partly hidden man flicked a glance towards him, enough for him to see the face, enough to know he was right.

"Give up, Balcombe!"

"Let's talk," the killer said.

"Lay down your weapons,"—Munro was sure Balcombe would have knives—"then we'll talk."

Balcombe didn't move.

He said, "You know Geoff Tanner was murdered. Patricia Albright was murdered. Well, it was all about Laura Quinn. You were right. They were investigating her death, because it wasn't an accident. Tanner was sure because he'd been there that night—he provided drugs and girls. Patricia was suspicious because of her father."

"What's Albright got to do with it?"

"Don't come any closer," Balcombe said, recognizing that Munro had inched forward.

Munro took half a pace back.

"Albright was covering for the Governor."

"The Governor—?"

"Hear me out, Munro. The governor's son killed Laura. It may have been ruled an accident, but she was forced to have sex and she fought with him. However there was no chance of considering whether it was murder or an accident because they got rid of the body."

Munro was struggling with all the new information. "Who got rid of the body?"

"Van Ness. Jardines militia. And they've been protecting the boy and the Governor ever since."

"How do you know this?"

"Van Ness confessed. Albright will be ready to confess."

"All right," Munro said. "So now we know, put down your weapons and come peacefully. You can help with the conviction."

"No."

A scuffling sound came from Balcombe's left. The man turned that way then moved. A gun fired, and in the flash, Munro saw Garrett. The other inspector had crept up in the darkness and may have lunged at Balcombe. A gun had discharged but Balcombe seemed unharmed and it was Garrett on the floor.

Munro started to bark instructions, but Balcombe was already moving away. Fast.

"Garrett—?"

"I'm all right. I may have winged him." Garrett was on his feet and also moving off, giving chase it appeared. With his bad leg, Munro knew he wouldn't be able to keep up.

He hurried back to the car.

"Just go!" he said to the police driver who started to justify why he'd stayed in the car. Munro spoke over him. "Where will he go?"

The driver looked uncertain.

"Come on, man," Munro snapped. "You're local. Where's he headed?"

"I... er... This way's to the Salazar Square."

"All right, just drive."

The man jolted the car from the curb and drove towards the square. They both checked left and right.

Garrett was already in the square when they arrived. He'd stopped for breath. "He's gone that way," he said, pointing.

"A lot of streets," the driver said.

"The church on the hill—what is it?" It was the closest high landmark. And Balcombe was religious.

"Penha Chapel."

"Head for it."

Garrett continued down the road where he'd last seen Balcombe.

Within two hundred yards, the driver stopped. "This is the best way up to the church."

They waited a moment before Munro decided Balcombe wouldn't necessarily know this was the best way. And to get here, he'd have to double back.

"No, I'm wrong," he said. "Drive on."

They followed the curve of the hill until Munro told the driver to stop at the next intersection. Balcombe appeared, slowed, looked directly at them. Then he started running again, going right.

"He's heading for the harbour.," the driver said. "Unless he comes back, there's only the avenue at the end of that street, then the harbour, docks and wharf."

Munro told his man to follow. When they got to where they'd seen the fugitive, Garrett met them, gasping. He opened Munro's door but didn't get in. With hands on the open door and roof and feet on the sill, he rode it like a running board.

"Where's he gone?" he shouted down at Munro.

"Back to the harbour."

The driver was already heading west. They came out onto a wide, tree-lined avenue. To the right, Munro saw where their marine police launch had docked. The wharves were beyond.

If he'd gone left, Balcombe could loop around the hill and go to the church. But he'd be exposed. Munro instructed the driver to turn left and, for a few yards, let the headlights sweep around.

His gut told him this was wrong. The driver reversed. Garrett jumped off and Munro got out. They walked towards the harbour, passing the last of the avenue's camphor trees and reaching the decking that ran the length of the quay. To the left were a hundred boats, tied together and creaking in the night waters. There was one small building, a hut of some kind. To the right was a hundred yards of open space before a customs house and the communications office plus a couple of others.

Balcombe was fit, but he'd run at least a thousand yards to get here. Maybe much more due to the indirect route he'd taken. Would he be tired? Would he have risked running another hundred yards without cover?

* * *

Balcombe had been hit. Garrett's wild shot had grazed his arm and, although he wasn't losing much blood, it was enough to affect him.

He crouched by the shelter. When he'd burst through onto the quay, he'd thought the little wooden building would offer decent cover. But now he was there, he knew it was little more than a shelter and temporary store.

As he crouched, he saw the police exit their car and come across to the quay. He'd made the right decision to hide here. He wouldn't have made it to the units to the right.

What would Munro do?

There was another man with them. He was sent towards where the steamer had docked. Munro turned towards where Balcombe was hiding. Garrett hesitated and then followed.

Both men had their guns ready.

Both men would see him within a minute.

Balcombe moved.

* * *

Munro saw something scuttle from the cover of the building opposite the junks.

"Balcombe!" he called. "Give yourself up. There's nowhere left to run."

However Balcombe had other ideas. He darted towards the boats and Munro now saw that there was a series of jetties stretching out into the water.

Garrett fired a shot. "Stop, Balcombe!"

Munro held up a hand. "We take him alive."

"Just a warning shot. He needs to know we'll shoot to kill if we have to."

"He already knows that from back at the casino," Munro snapped.

They reached the jetty. Balcombe was a silhouette against the glow from the silver-dark sea. He looked like he'd reached the end.

Munro and Garrett started down the floating pier.

"Far enough," Balcombe shouted when they'd traversed half.

"Give up," Munro called. "I'll get you help."

"We tried that, remember? And now Georgina's dead."

He sounded remorseful.

"What happened, Charles?"

"I don't know. I don't remember doing it."

Garrett scoffed and Munro had to remind himself that the other man didn't know the situation. He didn't know that Balcombe had an alter ego he struggled to control.

Garrett moved sideways and Munro realized he was clambering across a boat maybe heading for a parallel jetty. He was soon lost in the darkness.

Balcombe called, "I need to know you'll do what's right. I need to know you'll bring Simon Morris to justice."

"Of course," Munro said, although it came out too quickly.

"For Laura and Geoff and Patricia. Munro, you have to do it. There's been a cover up at the highest level and you need to expose it."

"I will."

Balcombe switched his attention left, and Munro guessed he'd heard Garrett getting closer.

Munro started walking forward.

"Give up, Charles. I'll get you help."

"Stop or I'll shoot!"

Munro realized Balcombe had a gun in his hand. He was pointing it towards the boats on the right.

"Drop it!" Garrett barked.

Munro closed in. "Drop it, Charles!"

Afterward, he didn't know who had fired first. Garrett claimed it had been Balcombe. All Munro could remember was that as soon as the gunshots started, he'd discharged his weapon at Balcombe. All six bullets.

Chapter Sixty

In the morning there was blood where Balcombe had been standing. There was a gnarled stick on the decking. In the dark it had looked like a gun.

Both Munro and Garrett had emptied their revolvers. Munro alone thought he'd struck Balcombe at least three times.

"So, where's his body?" asked Garrett.

"It'll turn up. There's a hundred little boats. It'll be stuck under one of them."

But Balcombe's body didn't turn up.

Munro would always wonder. He knew that a body, once out at sea, had a low chance of recovery. The fish would eat it before it washed ashore.

The following day, a letter arrived at the police station, from Balcombe. It provided the detail of what he'd said in Macao.

Before writing up what had happened, both Munro and Garrett went up to the governor's mansion. The guard on the gate was a different man. He told them Governor Morris was away. Like his predecessor, the guard refused entry without a warrant, but Ernest Albright appeared.

Munro thought the man looked a wreck, like he hadn't slept for days. But then his daughter had recently been murdered, so that could explain it.

"How can I help, gentlemen?" he asked.

Munro thought Albright would refuse, but he allowed them inside the governor's home. They walked around and saw no evidence of the melee that Balcombe had described in his note. There were no dead bodies and no signs of blood. No sign of any kind of disturbance.

Had Balcombe got it wrong?

Perturbed, the inspectors travelled to the Jardines headquarters on Caroline Hill.

"Captain Van Ness, please?" Munro said at the gate.

The guard shook his head. "You haven't heard?"

"Heard what?"

"The captain and two of our men were lost at sea yesterday. Their boat sank. Lieutenant Vladar has assumed command. If you'd like to speak to him…?"

Munro pulled a tight smile. "That won't be necessary."

Balcombe had written that there had been Van Ness and two other Jardines men at the mansion. BlackJack had killed them.

As they got in their car, Garrett said, "Coverup?"

"Got to be. Too big a coincidence."

They sat in silence all the way back to Victoria Police Station. When they got out, Garrett spoke first.

"We both need to write this up."

"We do." Munro stared down the hill and focused on the edge of the Supreme Court building, just visible behind the banks.

"We got the Squeezed-heart murderer," Garrett said. "That's something. A big something."

Munro nodded. *But not the scandal involving the governor. His son is guilty and three kids died because of him and the coverup.*

"Not coming in?" Garrett asked, as Munro turned away.

"Going for a walk to clear my head."

Munro went down to the front and walked along Victoria quay. He stopped outside the building where he used to meet Balcombe. The man had been evil. Their arrangement needed to end. If it hadn't ended like that, who knew how many more innocent people would have been killed by him?

And he couldn't forgive Balcombe for killing Georgina Swift. When he'd discharged his gun into Balcombe last night, that's what he kept telling himself. Balcombe wasn't human. He was a monster.

Munro kept walking and eventually came to his destination. Mr. Quincy's art supplies and gallery.

Quincy looked at him with nervous eyes when he walked down the gallery. Then the man turned and went into the back room. Munro followed.

"You lied to me," Munro said.

Quincy looked at him, his face full of uncertainty.

"You knew Laura had been killed."

Quincy opened his mouth, but no words came out at first. Then he said, "It was an accident."

"But you knew it wasn't on the tram rails. You knew she'd been moved."

Quincy shook his head. His eyes started to fill with tears. Then he forced out words that sounded lost. "I suspected."

Munro said, "They paid you off. That's how you could afford to expand—to set up a gallery. I thought you might be trading something illegal. How can an art supplies shopkeeper make enough to create a gallery, let alone send his daughter to be educated in Europe?"

Tears started to roll down Quincy's cheeks. He didn't bother to wipe at them.

Quincy took a shuddering breath. "What could I do? It had happened. It was too late. I couldn't go up against the Jardines militia. I couldn't go up against the governor!"

"What about his son, Simon?"

Quincy swallowed.

"What about Simon Morris?" Munro repeated.

Quincy took another shuddering breath to compose himself. "I thought about it. I wanted to get him. But... My wife... But then Simon had an accident and died anyway."

Quincy breathed and straightened his back. He nodded to himself and wiped away the tears.

Munro said nothing. Van Ness or the governor had created a story of Simon's death to appease Quincy. What he said next confirmed Munro's belief.

"It was better to accept the money and use it for Gracie," Quincy said. "I think Laura would have approved."

Munro shook his head.

"Let's hope you're right."

When Munro left, he'd imagined he'd feel better after exposing the truth about Quincy's bought silence. But he didn't.

Quincy hadn't been able to fight the establishment. BlackJack could have killed Simon Morris and got some kind of justice. But what could DI Munro do?

Nothing.

There was no evidence, and the people who knew the truth would never tell.

Chapter Sixty-One

Munro knew he was a good policeman. He'd been frustrated with the system. The British were too strict, the petty criminals were caught and imprisoned. The justice system was creaking, and the prisons packed beyond decency. Even the Japanese hadn't crammed so many in a cell.

And now he knew that it wasn't just a problem with the system. Even worse, the highest authorities were corrupt.

The governor's son was guilty. The governor and his assistant were guilty of a conspiracy of silence and accepting blackmail by Jardines. Did more people know? Did the police commissioner and chief of police?

His wife Yan, had lots of good phrases. He could imagine her voice now: *You can't chew a stone, Munro. If you try, it will stick in your throat.*

She would be right. He could do nothing.

In the office, Garrett had his head down, presumably writing up his report. No doubt he'd be the hero of the hour. He'd known it all along. He'd caught and brought down the Squeezed-heart murderer—albeit with support from Munro. He'd also say that Charles Balcombe was

Bai Long, the White Dragon. Balcombe would be blamed for the criminal activities of Jardines.

Garrett glanced up and nodded at Munro. Munro nodded back and immediately felt bad. It was like he was acknowledging they were co-conspirators. They weren't. Garrett might be able to sleep at night, knowing the truth. Promotion would outweigh any guilt he might feel.

"Sir?" DC Tattersall came to Munro's desk. He looked uncomfortable.

"Yes, James?"

The junior officer placed a file in Munro's hand. He swallowed. "You'll... You need to read this, sir."

The file was on Doctor Georgina Swift's murder. Tattersall had written it up. He'd taken the lead in Munro's absence and was probably nervous about the quality.

"I'm sure it's well-written, James," Munro said.

Tattersall continued to look uncomfortable.

Munro opened the file. There were the usual crime scene photographs. There was Yeung's pathology report and there was something else. Fingerprint analysis.

A statue of the Eiffel Tower had been found in Georgina's bedroom. It had blood and tissue. And it had fingerprints.

The murder weapon. Not the leprechaun statuette they'd found in Balcombe's rooms.

Munro felt his chest constrict. The fingerprints had been a match, but not for Charles Balcombe. They were a match to an ex-patient of hers. Five years ago, she'd diagnosed him as pathologically insane. He'd been in a mental asylum but escaped the night before he'd visited Georgina.

He'd killed her for revenge.

Tattersall was still standing at his desk. He took a breath. "He's in the gaol. When we picked him up, he still had the paperknife, that he'd stabbed her with, in his pocket."

Munro nodded numbly. *Not Balcombe.*

He rubbed his face. Tattersall was still talking, but Munro wasn't hearing him anymore.

He stood, took off his holstered gun, and placed it on the desk. He removed his warrant card and placed it carefully beside the gun.

"Sir?" Tattersall said.

Munro opened his desk drawer and found a card inside. He put it in his pocket, shook Tattersall's clammy hand then walked out of the office.

★ ★ ★

"Babyface!" Yeung said, as Munro found him at the hospital. "I hear congratulations are in order but—"

"I saw that it wasn't Balcombe who'd killed Georgina." Munro knew his voice was flat.

"But, my friend, that monster is out of your life!" He scrutinized Munro's face. "What is it? What's the matter?"

"I've quit. I've had enough of this system, of the bias and corruption. I've had enough."

Yeung froze, his eyes bulging with alarm. Munro guessed he was worried. Munro's old boss, Bill Teags had had a breakdown and tried to kill himself after the failure of a case. Yeung probably thought the same was happening to his friend.

"Don't worry, Fai. I'm just taking a break."

Yeung continued to look worried.

Munro gripped his friend's arm. "I'm going to put a ghost to rest." He swallowed. "I'm going to Japan. I'll visit the man who killed Yan."

"To kill him?"

"To accept his apology and maybe friendship."

"And then you'll come back?"

"Of course," Munro said before embracing his best friend. But he had no plans. He would pack his bags and say goodbye to the country he'd made his home. Maybe it was time for a new chapter in his life.

Because life was too short to dwell on the past and live with demons.

Chapter Sixty-Two

The night before

Balcombe wasn't having the usual hallucination. The demon wasn't there. A hand wasn't trying to smother or strike him. However he could see a vague figure like a mirage in the darkness. His old, best friend. The man's whose name he'd taken.

Charles? Is that you?
Yes.
It's good to see you.
Are you afraid, Joe?
His old climbing friend used Balcombe's real name.
Yes, I am.
But I told you, fear is God giving you the opportunity to be brave. It's what makes you alive, Joe.
I'm dying, Charles.
No, you're not!

Balcombe moved his hands. He could feel rough wood under his skin. And damp. That was water in the boat.

His hands slid to his sides and the damp became sticky. How many times had the bullets struck him?

This was no dream. There had been no blackout. He'd been shot by the police. In the end, he'd encouraged it. There was no way out. There was no escaping his demon, BlackJack.

He'd killed Georgina.

But why? Why had he killed her? Was BlackJack preventing him from having a proper relationship?

Balcombe had aimed his fake gun and wanted them to kill him. And the pain of the bullets, searing his skin, puncturing his body, had been welcome.

He'd gone over into the water. He remembered sinking and letting himself go. He remembered the swirling lights above, and assuming this was the end. He would drown and his soul—the good part—would transcend death.

But it hadn't been the end. He'd been pulled out and now he was lying in a boat, bleeding to death.

I'm dying, Charles. Let me go.

No response. Nothing. The darkness closed in. He lost sense of the boat. Charles wasn't there. He was alone and dying.

It wasn't your fault, Joe.

He heard another voice. Not Charles. A woman.

Mother?

Yes, Joe. I'm here now.

I'm sorry.

You didn't do anything wrong, Joe.

But I killed you.

No, you didn't. It was him. You saw him do it. You saw your father.

Balcombe had a flash of memory. His father striking her, again and again. He'd done it before, but this time, he'd gone too far.

Young Balcombe watched with disbelief as the mallet struck his mother's head again. Her eyes met his, pleading. But he was rooted to the spot. His brain couldn't comprehend the horror. It couldn't be real.

His father was calm. It was like he was tenderizing meat. Smack, smack, smack. Then he was on his knees, squeezing her neck.

Only then did he see his son in the hallway.

Balcombe remembered how the big man had approached him, all smiles and placid. He gave Balcombe a drink. "For your nerves," he said. And when Balcombe awoke, it had all been a bad dream. He couldn't remember. His brain had blocked the horror. Maybe the medication had something to do with it, but when his father had told everyone that his wife had left them, Balcombe went along with it.

But now the barriers had come down. Now he knew the truth.

His father was the monster. Not him.

You're a good boy. It wasn't you. It wasn't your fault.

But I've done bad things. You don't know. I'm as bad as him.

I know what you've done. You can come home now. I'm here waiting for you.

She'd always said they'd meet again in Heaven. She was here now, standing over him. Here to take him with her. To show him the way. He could see her outline. She reached out her hand. All he needed to do was take it and it would be over.

I'm ready.

Balcombe felt so cold. He tried but couldn't raise his arms. He couldn't take his mother's hand.

Mother!

"Don't leave."

Vaguely, Balcombe became aware of a different voice. It wasn't the ghost of his friend or his mother in the boat. It was someone else. A girl.

Balcombe smiled weakly.

"Albert, is that you?" He found his voice.

"Yes, master. I'm here."

"Albert."

"I followed the police. In a boat. I was waiting here." Her voice faded out. He couldn't concentrate. She was crying.

He wanted to reach up and touch her face.

Was she a dream as well?

He had no strength. His arms didn't move. He could no longer feel his legs. The cold was moving up and fast. He felt it in his chest.

"Don't leave," he heard her say. He imagined her tears on his face.

I have to go, Albert.

The cold was fading now. He imagined distant lights. He imagined a choir. He imagined his friend lifting his body.

And the last thing he heard was an angel's voice.

She said, "I love you, master."

Note and Acknowledgements

I'm grateful to Doctor Sara Hirst for reviewing the psychoanalysis chapters and Doctor Kerry Bailey-Jones for medical advice. Any errors in the interpretation are mine alone.
Thanks also to my team of early reviewers and bloggers plus my wife and Pete Tonkin who had to cope with an early version. Your feedback was, as ever, a considerable help.

The events in this story are fictitious. Although some details from the filming of Soldier of Fortune are accurate, there was no scene on the Peak's crags. However, the film is worth watching for the glimpses of Hong Kong in 1954, including shots of the Peak tram which features at the end.

Have you read the thrilling action mystery featuring Captain Ash Carter?

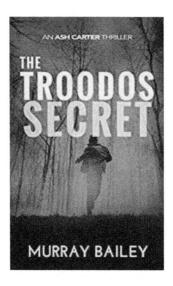

Ash Carter is called in to investigate the mysterious death of a commando in Cyprus. Working with Detective Sofia Mackenzie he finds that nothing is quite what it seems and no one is willing to tell the truth.

When another man dies, it appears that the truth lies in the mountains and the mines to be found there. Threatened and working against the clock, Carter and Mackenzie must solve the case or risk becoming the mountain's next victims.

Read on for the first four chapters:

ONE

I climbed out of the RMP Land Rover onto the yellow stone track. The strong scent of pine remained in the early morning air although the forest was thin in this area of the Troodos mountains.

My feet crunched on the stones as I walked past a black police van, a small car and a battered truck.

Four people were clustered beneath a particularly large pine tree. Sandy ground sloped beyond it as though just waiting for the tree to lose its grasp and slide away.

Detective Sofia Mackenzie looked up and waved and called to me.

"Captain Carter."

I could hear the tension in her voice. This was a new experience for her. A dead body.

Sofia was as tall as the men present, with her brown hair tied back in what I judged to be a professional if a little austere, style.

"What have we got here?" I asked.

There was a police photographer busily taking snaps of the body on the ground. I could see the arms and legs but the head and most of the body were covered by a twisted brown blanket. The photographer didn't move the blanket. He stopped and looked expectant.

There were two regular policemen plus another man.

THE TROODOS SECRET

This fourth man wore an old brown suit and carried a rifle over his shoulder. The suit looked heavy and unsuitable for warm weather. Then again, it was significantly cooler high in the mountains. On his arm was a tan-coloured brassard bearing the red-flame badge of a mountain fire ranger.

Sofia Mackenzie didn't reply to my question but looked at me long and hard before directing her gaze towards the body.

We'd been working together for almost a month, as a favour to my friend DI Charles Dickins. She'd returned from lengthy maternity leave and been assigned to the detective team. She was smart but with limited training and the CID team was woefully short-staffed.

I was a Special Investigations Branch officer awaiting my next orders and so the distraction had been an easy decision. She needed guidance. I had time on my hands.

Despite her British surname, she was a Greek Cypriot. Her English was near perfect and she could also speak Turkish in addition to her native Greek. The language skills could prove useful, should I ever need a translator.

Mackenzie and I closed in on the body and she signalled for one of the officers to raise the blanket.

I heard her breathe in and out.

The blanket went up and I clenched my teeth.

Not because of the body. I'd seen plenty of dead people before.

I'd expected a Cypriot. I'd expected to coach Mackenzie on handling a potential murder investigation.

But this was a white man. And from his age, physique and haircut, he was probably a soldier.

TWO

The photographer snapped more pictures of the exposed corpse.

The dead man's hair was mousey and matted with blood. There wasn't a great deal of blood. None around the body. Just clumps in the hair and trickles that darkened his shirt collar and brown leather jacket.

Mackenzie said, "Looks like he was out hiking."

She was right. He had appropriate walking boots and sturdy clothes.

"Any sign of a knapsack?" I asked.

She shook her head. "As you'd expect, I treated it as a crime scene straight away and minimized the disturbance. The footprints you see are all ours."

I nodded. "No prints from his boots?" I said, pointing to the body.

"No."

"Any sign of a murder weapon?"

"You're sure he was murdered?"

I said, "It's unlikely that he just banged his head. And I doubt he was killed here."

"Because?"

"There's no sign of a struggle, but, more importantly, blood on the ground. We're near the road, so I suspect he was transported here and dumped."

THE TROODOS SECRET

I pointed to unnatural striations in the dust.

"Your men didn't make these?"

"No."

"Then our perpetrator swept the ground to remove any footprints." I looked back up the slope and thought about the twisted blanket. "He probably rolled down but became exposed. The perpetrator had to come down and recover the body."

Sofia nodded. "He probably hoped the body would roll further."

The fire marshal looked Greek with a shock of hair that was turning grey. He had been watching me closely and I now stepped over to him.

"You found the body?"

Mackenzie translated into Greek for me and then back into English as the man answered. He told me he'd found the body two hours ago purely by chance. He'd been driving to his lookout station when he spotted the heap on the ground. He pointed north and gave the name of a hamlet just off the main road. The roads didn't have official names and the nearest one was referred to as MR1, or Mountain Road One. It was the first of the three original main roads that crossed the mountains. Though any driver soon learned that the standard definition of "main road" didn't apply here. The route went from east of Limassol to the town of Malounta on the other side before continuing to Nicosia. It went through the valleys and jinked around the hills as they rose.

The ranger said he drove up to the High Road and then turned towards the peak.

"I always check this tree," he said, tapping the big pine with his left hand. "One of these days it's going to slip down and do a bit of damage. I've asked for it to be cut before that happens."

"Did you touch the body?"

"Yes," he said in thickly accented English. "I checked he was dead before calling the police."

"You seem very calm," I said. "After all, you found a dead body."

"I fought in the war. Was in the 5th. Got injured"—he shrugged, and it was then that I noticed his left arm hung at an odd angle, as though the elbow joint went the wrong way—"and got captured, but I survived."

"All right," I said. "What did you do when you checked him?"

The man thought for a second. "I lifted the blanket and saw his face. The blood."

"Where did you touch him?"

"I… I didn't actually touch him. Just lifted the blanket. There wasn't any need, you see. I could tell he was dead."

We stood in silence for a minute. The birds chattered as though nothing was amiss, as though a dead body under the big tree was a natural occurrence.

Finally, Sofia said, "You checked his pockets." Her tone was challenging but assertive."

The man blinked a few times, possibly considering his answer.

She said, "From the look of the blanket… It had been wrapped but then disturbed."

She paused and we all followed her gaze. Then she looked at the fire ranger with piercing eyes. "Did you check his pockets for identity?"

"Yes I did," the man said. I heard relief in his voice, as though he was bottling up the truth, afraid to say it.

Sofia glanced at me with a slight smile on her lips. She'd guessed he'd done more than look and now she'd got him to admit it.

I nodded my approval.

"What did you find?" she asked the man.

"No money, if that's what you mean." He didn't blink, and I figured this was the truth. "Nothing. No identity. No money," he repeated.

So we had an unknown body. A soldier without some form of identity was unlikely. Which told me that someone had removed it.

"All right," I said, moving us on. "What about other vehicles? Did you see anything on the tracks this morning? Did you pass anyone?"

"I don't live far away and have to drive right over the peak to get to the lookout hut," he told me, repeating what he'd said earlier.

"Did you see anything suspicious even over that short distance?" I asked.

"Nothing up here."

That didn't surprise me. From the look of the soldier, he'd been dead a while. Not long enough to attract too many flies because it was early. But he'd been dead for more than a few hours, I guessed.

"Yesterday? Anything suspicious last night?"

"I didn't come this way last night."

"What about sounds?" Sofia asked.

He shook his head. "Nothing more than the usual."

She raised her eyebrows. "The usual?"

"Hunters. Going after the mouflon."

Mouflon were the large-horned goat-like animals that lived in the mountains. I'd heard gunshots before and knew poachers would occasionally hunt in the mountains.

The fire ranger continued, now looking at me: "You hear a few gunshots a day even though it's against the law."

Mackenzie said, "Anything else? Anything unusual happen?"

"No," he said with a chuckle. "Haven't even heard an explosion at one of the mines so far today. It's been quiet up here."

"What about yesterday?" I asked.

"Probably. I can't remember." He raised his hands in a shrug and again I spotted the awkwardness of his left arm. "You get used to it. Maybe they were blasting but I didn't notice. Then again it was Sunday, so maybe not."

Sofia took down his address and we let him go with the usual request to let us know if he remembered anything he hadn't told us. Then we signalled for the policemen to lift the body into the van and take it to the morgue.

Sofia was in the black car and I tailed along at the back. About halfway down the mountain we reached Upper Road and they filed west. I followed. It was a good flat road and I figured they'd either go all the way to Route Two or take a lesser road directly into Limassol.

As I drove back down the mountain, I thought about the blanket. I'd seen two thin coloured lines along one edge: pink and blue. I'd seen many blankets like it before; army blankets. However, they were also army surplus and could be picked up cheaply in most towns.

The convoy took the next left, and as it did so, I recognized the area. I'd parked here three weeks earlier. Hiking and following instructions to relax and enjoy my free time. And I had.

That is, until I ran into trouble.

THREE

Three weeks earlier

My usual pastime was physical exercise. I'd been an amateur boxer, and from the age of sixteen, I trained hard every morning. But Jim Dexter, CO at Dhekelia Garrison said I should try hiking. He said it was food for the soul and I needed balance in my life. He was an astute man and knew I was frustrated by the waiting game I'd been playing since starting my new role. My colleague Bill Wolfe and I hadn't shipped to the Canal Zone with the rest of the men when we'd left Mandatory Palestine. We'd been assigned special duties in the Near East. So far, for me, it had involved two stressful weeks in Israel, tracking down criminals. The rest of the time had been mundane, handling reports and sifting through alleged intelligence.

I'd killed some time by visiting DI Dickins in Nicosia and reviewing some of his caseload and then agreeing to coach Sofia Mackenzie. Wolfe was back in Israel and I'd been on my own for a month.

So I decided to give hiking a try.

I suspect Jim Dexter would have recommended a more leisurely stroll, appreciating the flora and fauna, but

THE TROODOS SECRET

it made a change from sitting in an office filling my time by reading dull reports.

I'd covered over ten miles and was considering turning around and heading back for my jeep when I heard a sound.

At first, I thought it had been an animal squeal or perhaps a strange bird, but when I heard it again it was unmistakable: a woman's scream.

Trees and hills don't make it easy to determine direction or distance, but I figured it came from ahead and slightly higher.

I started to run.

Moments later I heard a male voice shout, "Stop!"

It wasn't far ahead and I adjusted course slightly. Then I saw movement and ran faster towards it. The woman wasn't screaming anymore but I could hear pounding feet and suddenly she was there, in front of me.

I'd been wrong. It wasn't a woman. It was a slip of girl. For a second she froze, panic on her face.

She looked from me and then behind. I saw a figure moving fast through the trees after her. His proximity prompted her to move again, only she didn't run to me. She turned down the slope and scampered on.

The other person also changed direction, running faster on longer legs. I didn't think he'd seen me.

"Stop!" he yelled again.

"Hey!" I shouted. He was moving away too fast and I didn't know if he'd responded. Maybe he was making too much noise plunging through undergrowth to hear me.

I gave chase and saw the man burst through into a small clearing. By the time I reached it, he'd grabbed the girl. They were twenty yards ahead.

I didn't hesitate. I was running too fast to say anything that would make sense so I just roared. By the time I hit him, he was standing in shock with the girl at arm's length.

Her seeming acceptance of her fate—the apparent lack of an attempt to escape his grasp—registered in the back of my brain. But it made no difference.

My shoulder hit his pelvis and lifted him off the ground and I drove him for a few feet.

He recovered from the surprise quickly and stuck me with an elbow to my upper back.

"Never stay down!" Sammy, my Liverpudlian boxing coach, used to scream. "No matter how you feel, get back on your feet!" It wasn't about being in a ring necessarily. He'd had to take care of himself on the streets of Manchester and believed all his boys should have the same skills.

I rolled away and was immediately ready as my opponent scrambled up. He had an unusual appearance; a shaven head and thick black beard. And he was big. Bigger than my six two by another few inches. He looked solid too, with broad shoulders and thick arms and large calves beneath khaki shorts.

My back brain said: ogre. But to fear an opponent is to accept defeat. Another of Sammy's aphorisms.

I hit the big man in the solar plexus and ribs before he got off his first swing. I moved out of range.

"Who the fuck are you?" he grunted as he brought up his fists ready to throw another. I saw it coming, ducked it, stepped in and caught him with an uppercut.

The big man staggered back, his eyes rolled, and I thought he was going down. But somehow he stayed on his feet.

I should have finished him then, but as I moved, the girl's voice made me freeze.

"Stop! Stop it now!"

I swivelled to look at her. She was kneeling, tears streaming down her face. The big man didn't look like he was about to launch an attack so I moved well out of range, one eye on him, one eye on the girl.

THE TROODOS SECRET

"What's going on?" I said, my voice straining with the adrenaline coursing through me.

"You're being a bloody fool, that's what!" the big man said with venom. Now that the adrenaline was subsiding, I saw him more clearly. He wasn't an ogre, just big, ugly and heavy-set with a large belly, probably fuelled by beer.

I raised a placatory hand. "She was screaming. You were chasing her."

"Mind your own business." I saw him tensing up, looking ready to fight although I could see it was more bravado than real intent.

"I'm making it my business," I said.

"Stop it!" The girl was standing now, the tears had ceased. She walked between us.

I looked into her face. She wasn't afraid of this man, she was just sad. Now that I could see her close up I figured she was somewhere between twelve and fourteen. She had unkempt light-brown hair and had an odd combination of clothes: a cream-coloured dress but brown lace-up boots. Half dainty, half a tomboy, I thought.

"Are you all right?" I asked her.

The big man said, "You're butting into something you don't understand." There was less venom in his voice now.

"Enlighten me."

"I work for... for her dad," he said. Then he directed his comment to the girl. "You know he wouldn't want you out here." Back to me: "There are tunnels all over." Back to her: "They're dangerous, Annie. You're not allowed..."

Annie hung her head.

I bent and looked into her eyes. "Is it true? You know this man? He works for your father?"

"Fairfield Hodge," he said. "Mining."

I was still looking at her, reading her face, making sure it was true.

"Yes," she said.

The big guy held out a hand. "Come on, Annie, I'll take you home."

I took a step back.

"A misunderstanding," I said.

His eyes narrowed as he scrutinized me. I wasn't a threat anymore. I was contrite.

He said, "I should call the police."

I nodded. "If you must, but I'll tell them how it was. She's a young girl being chased by a big man. She screamed and I came to help."

"A bloody knight in shining…" he said as they started to walk up the hill, his hand on her shoulder. Then he stopped and turned. "Anyway what were you doing around here?"

"Hiking," I said.

He shook his head. "Not advisable. Apart from the holes in the ground, there are poachers out here. You're not careful you'll end up with lead shot in your arse."

"Thanks for the advice," I said, and watched the odd pair walk out of the clearing and into the woods.

FOUR

Coming down the mountain three weeks later, I wondered how the girl, Annie, was. Did she venture out on her own a lot? Was the big man, with a shaved head and bushy beard, charged with keeping a lookout for her? I didn't know and guessed I never would.

I was reminded of an incident when I was at school. On the way home, I'd seen an older boy pulling a girl's hair. I'd intervened and received a severe beating from the bigger boy. It was before I'd learned how to fight.

The worst part was that the girl never thanked me. She'd disappeared by the time I picked myself bruised and dirty off the floor.

I guess the big man was right. I tried to rescue damsels in distress. I had some kind of reckless, innate hero complex. Could I do anything about it? Would I learn not to intervene?

I doubted it.

It took half an hour to get down the mountain and into Limassol. I would have rather taken the body to BMH Nightingale at Dhekelia Garrison beyond Larnaca. But that was more than an hour away.

Once off the mountain, it was an unrelentingly hot day and I thought that the nearer morgue was a sensible option.

I'd not been inside the Limassol General Hospital before and followed the others. It was on Victoria Street, which went through the old town to the harbour. The police station was next door. They didn't have a CID unit here. That was in the police HQ in Nicosia.

"Wouldn't this place be more convenient for you?" I said to Sofia, nodding at the dirty grey-stone building as we went up the hospital steps.

"Yes," she said. "My life is here. I've done my time in Nicosia and hope the inspector makes this Limassol role permanent." She smiled and raised her eyebrows. "Have a word with him to make sure he does?"

She made it sound like a joke, but I could tell she meant it.

"I will," I said.

We followed the body inside and waited for it to be processed and taken into the morgue. Sofia had a word with a doctor and then suggested we find a café.

"Someone will fetch us when they've taken a preliminary look."

The shaded café was a police favourite it seemed, and the next hour was spent sipping our drinks and nibbling food, between Sofia getting up and greeting someone. Old colleagues had a soft spot for her, I judged.

Eventually, an orderly appeared in the doorway and beckoned us. We hurried back to the hospital.

"Ah," the doctor said as we approached. After a noticeable, awkward hesitation, he held out a hand. "Captain Carter?"

"Yes."

"Right. Sorry to keep you." His voice carried no hint of genuine remorse, nor did he introduce himself. I noticed that he only glanced at Sofia, and I sensed there was familiarity but not the open friendship I'd seen from her police colleagues. Many men in authority were male chauvinists. However I sensed there was more to it. A specific issue perhaps.

"What can you tell us?" I asked as he took us through double doors into the morgue. The lighting was dimmer, more yellow than most morgues I'd been in. I always find the usual harsh lighting adds to the chill of the place. Despite the smell of disinfectant and death, this softer lighting made it an easier experience.

In a formal voice, like he was reading a dull report, the doctor said, "A young man aged in his early twenties. Height, five ten. Weight, twelve stone ten pounds. He was fit and appeared to be in excellent health."

"Was he murdered?" I asked.

"Undoubtedly. Asphyxiation."

"Asphyxiation?" I said, surprised.

The doctor smiled, and for the first time, I felt patronized. "The blow to the head shattered his cranium, certainly, but it didn't kill him. You see the discolouration around the mouth and nose?"

I looked at the body on the nearby slab. All bar the head was covered with a light-brown sheet. It wasn't as dark but it reminded me of the brown blanket he'd been wrapped in. On one cheek I noticed slight marks—lines maybe. The nose was also darker than the rest of the skin.

The doctor placed a hand over his mouth while his thumb and index finger squeezed his nostrils.

"Like this," he mumbled through the hand. "Your young man was most probably unconscious and may have ultimately died from the concussion, but it was the suffocation that killed him."

"All right. What can you tell us about the time of death?"

"I can't be precise, of course. I understand he was found near the top of the mountain, so it will have been cold last night." He paused until I nodded. "But based on the latter stages of rigor, I'd say you're looking at late yesterday afternoon."

I said, "He was found on his back wrapped in a blanket."

The doctor raised an eyebrow. "The blood pooling suggests he'd been sitting, which suggests he was moved before rigor set in. I noticed his hands and the knees of his trousers were dirty."

"Can you determine the position he'd have been in when struck?"

"No. I was thinking you might want to look at the dirt."

Sofia Mackenzie spoke for the first time. "Why?"

The doctor looked at her and nodded as though properly acknowledging her. "It's not your typical dirt under his nails. It's not earth, so I don't think he'd been scrabbling in the woods, and… well, I'd just be speculating."

"Please do," I prompted.

"Well, the marks on his trousers look like they may have been wet."

Intriguing. There hadn't been any rain for more than a week. "Thoughts?" I asked.

"No," he said. "But you'll want your medical officer to investigate more thoroughly. This isn't really my jurisdiction."

"You know him?" I asked, wondering how the doctor recognized the dead man as being military.

"No," he said, "I'm not psychic but I recognize this."

He pulled back the sheet, exposing most of the body. I immediately saw the tattoo on the man's right forearm. A dagger with the word "Commando" written above the point.

"And based on his age—" the doctor said.

"He's too young to have been demobbed."

THE TROODOS SECRET

The doctor nodded then pointed to the other arm. We moved around the head of the table and saw another tattoo. This was smaller, on his left shoulder, and about the size of a two-shilling coin.
It was a skull with what looked like a dagger protruding from the top. Beneath it were the numbers: 5 9 47.

END OF EXTRACT

murraybaileybooks.com

IF YOU ENJOYED THIS BOOK

Feedback helps me understand what works, what doesn't and what readers want more of. It also brings a book to life.

Online reviews are also very important in encouraging others to try my books. I don't have the financial clout of a big publisher. I can't take out newspaper ads or run poster campaigns.

But what I do have is an enthusiastic and committed bunch of readers.

Honest reviews are a powerful tool. I'd be very grateful if you could spend a couple of minutes leaving a review, however short, on sites like Amazon and Goodreads.

If you would like to contact me, I'm always happy to receive direct feedback so please feel free to use the email address below.

Thank you
Murray

murray@murraybaileybooks.com

Printed in Great Britain
by Amazon

37169073R00185